The Dark Side of Midnight

Carol Hedges

USBORNE

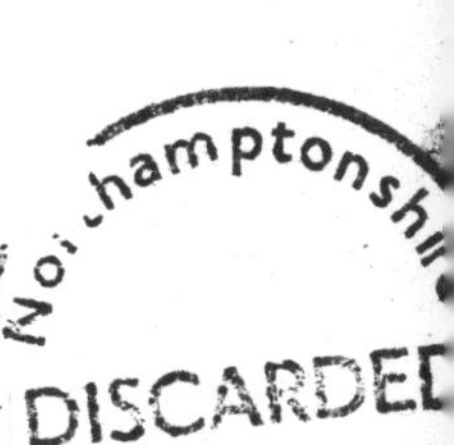

This book could not have been written without the help of some very special people. I would therefore like to take this opportunity to thank Joan Towle my teacher, my wonderful agent Caroline, together with Megan and all the team at Usborne.

Special thanks to my students for keeping me supplied with endless anecdotes. I also owe a big debt of gratitude to my friends in the Czech Republic and in Slovakia for sharing their beautiful countries with me. Thank you all.

First published in the UK in 2006 by Usborne Publishing Ltd., Usborne House, 83-85 Saffron Hill, London EC1N 8RT, England. www.usborne.com

Cover photograph supplied by Zoe Wray.

A CIP catalogue record for this book is available from the British Library.

JFMAM JASOND/06 ISBN 0 7460 6750 X Printed in Great Britain.

You will know the truth
and the truth will set you free.
John 8.v.32

DARK CLOUDS WERE MASSING ON THE HORIZON. THE RIDER GLANCED UP, AND SWORE UNDER HIS BREATH. HE KNEW EXACTLY WHAT IT MEANT: A STORM WAS COMING. NOT A GOOD OMEN. For this was Antarctica, the remotest place on earth, a white wilderness where temperatures could drop to below minus fifty-four degrees. The rider rechecked his coordinates, then jumped onto the Snokat. He had to hurry. There was not much time.

Deep in their snow hole, the two men waited, listening to the unending silence. Exhausted, huddled together for warmth, they had not moved, nor eaten, for days. Only a thin fragile thread of hope was keeping them alive. Nearby, a third man was curled in his sleeping bag. He looked contentedly asleep. But his two companions knew better: this was a sleep from which he would never awake. A few hours earlier, the man had finally succumbed to frostbite and the mind-numbing cold. Now he was dead. And over in the corner, a big, black body bag lay against the wall of the snow hole, its zip ominously pulled up.

The rider halted. He drew out his thermal imager, held it up and made a quick three-hundred-and-sixty degree scan of the horizon. Satisfied, he continued going forward, the Snokat skimming easily over the powdery white surface. He knew he was racing against time. And time was running out. Fast. The faint whine of the vehicle penetrated the icy prison walls of the snow hole. The two men sat up and exchanged disbelieving glances. Could it be? Or were exhaustion and cold making them hallucinate? The sound continued, got louder. Summoning up the very last of their carefully hoarded strength, they slowly and painfully began to tunnel their way out.

The rider waited. He watched the two men hatching from their frozen cocoon like a pair of grotesque insects. He saw them help each other to stand shakily upright, brushing snow from their purple, encrusted faces. He waited until they had both turned to face him, their snow-blinded eyes bright with joy and welcome. Then he drew out the sub-automatic, lifted it to his shoulder and fired two shots.

The Snokat bounced over the surface, leaping ice crevasses, racing ahead of the fast-approaching storm. Tied to its rear, the black body bag stood out sharply against the endless white of the polar landscape. The rider crouched low, pushing the machine to its limit.

Behind him, two bodies lay crumpled on the ground, their blood petalling the snow with crimson.

The first flakes began to fall.

JAZMIN DAWSON STOOD IN THE OFFICE DOORWAY, DOUBLE-CHECKING THE LUNCH ORDER ON HER FINGERS.

"A TUNA MELT ON RYE," SHE REPEATED, "TWO LEMON COKES, TWO Danish and a cream-cheese bagel."

"And whatever you want for yourself," Assia Dawson added, glancing up.

"Okay, I got all that," Jazmin said. "Catch you in ten." She spun round, her mass of dark curly hair whipping over her shoulders, and bounded energetically out of the room.

Assia smiled proudly after her daughter, then looked across the desk at her deputy and shook her head. "When did she grow up? And how come I missed it?" she asked disbelievingly.

"Hey, that's how it is nowadays," Hally Skinner consoled her. "I've got a niece just like it. Fourteen going on I don't know what. Turn your back and, suddenly, they're no longer kids. You better believe it! Uh-huh!"

"I guess you're right," Assia sighed reflectively. "Only somehow, my daughter just seems to have got there very quickly."

"Isn't that the truth," Hally agreed. "But at least you know you did a fine job."

Did I? Assia thought silently. Did I really? Her brow furrowed. Since her husband had died, when Jazmin was only six, Assia had been forced to work full-time to support them both. Over the years, this had resulted in so many broken promises, she thought regretfully. So many nights working back late. So many childminders. So little quality time. And now, seemingly overnight, her child had metamorphosed into a young woman. Right under her nose. A young woman whom she was beginning to realize that she barely knew.

Meanwhile, out in the hot, summertime city street, Jazmin waited in the lunch-line, clutching her purse and trying to pretend that she spent every midday queuing to buy her lunch, exactly like the adults around her. Her mind started drifting. She tried to imagine what it would be like to be just another faceless employee, like so many thousands of others working in the big city. Returning at night to her city penthouse, where her rich, handsome boyfriend would be waiting for her.

From this, it was only a short mental hop to her

favourite daydream: the one in which she starred as her alter ego Jaz Dawson, secret agent and crime fighter. Jaz Dawson was *hot*. She was everything her creator wasn't: tall, kick-ass gorgeous, with straight blonde hair and a peachy-clear complexion. She also looked good in skin-hugging Lycra and she didn't have a serious snack habit. Jazmin's left hand stole down to her imaginary utility belt, where her imaginary gun was clipped. She tightened her stance. She was poised, taut and ready to spring into action. She was coiled steel, invincible. She was...

"Hey, little girlie, you buying lunch or taking a nap?"

Jazmin came to with a start. Somehow, she'd reached the head of the line without realizing it. Oh pig! She must have mentally wandered off again. Stammering and fumbling her words, she blurted out the lunch order, embarrassed by the shop owner's pitying smile and his heightist comment, and also by the ripple of laughter behind her back. Feeling herself getting smaller and hotter, she collected her order, paid for it and stumbled out of the shop. Uh! Get a grip, she told herself severely. Or maybe next Take Your Daughter To Work Day, her mum'd choose to Leave Her At Home instead.

When Jazmin got back to the office, she discovered that her mum's desk was empty.

Hally nodded towards the far door. "She's taking a meeting with the boss," she said.

"Oh." Jazmin pulled a face. She placed the brown bag

and cans of drink on the desk. Her spirits sank. A meeting with the boss could only mean one thing. Her mum was probably going to be sent on another assignment. She slumped into her chair, shoulders sagging despondently.

"Hey, girl." Hally reached across for her lunch. "Don't look so down. Maybe it'll be good news – a pay rise. A long weekend. She could get lucky. Who knows?"

"Yeah, right."

"You want to hang out with me? I'm going to eat up on the roof terrace."

"Okay." Jazmin brightened. She got up and followed Hally out of the office.

It was peaceful on the roof terrace. The city lay stretched out below, a shimmering mirage in the heat of the midday sun, its sounds backgrounded to white noise. Jazmin leaned on the parapet and gazed across the familiar London skyline. The precinct where her mum worked was located in the main inner-city commercial area. She could see glass-topped malls and high-rise offices, their multi-faceted sides glittering like jewels in the bright sun. Dwarfed beneath them, she saw the London Eye slowly revolving, the white dome of St. Pauls. And in the distance the scribble of the river, a silver ribbon of movement touching the big city lightly on its way to a far-off sea.

This is my city, Jazmin thought. She'd been born here and had grown up in one of its many suburbs. She felt her heart swell with pride. Right now, in all the world, there was nowhere else she'd rather be.

"Nice view?" Hally said, as if she could read Jazmin's thoughts. She leaned her elbows on the wall and turned towards Jazmin, a serious expression on her face. "Hard to believe that people down there are getting beaten up, robbed and murdered even as we speak, isn't it?"

"Oh...I..." Jazmin stuttered.

"Sorry, didn't mean to upset you. I was only kidding, right?" Hally grinned. She put on a funny mock-official voice and intoned solemnly: "Crime figures are down fifteen per cent throughout the city. Murders and robberies: ten per cent. Street felony: two per cent. The number of carjacks has fallen by five per cent over the last six months." Hally paused, then whistled under her breath, her eyes widening in fake horror. "Hey girl, if we carry on being this good, the city could be crime-free in a couple of years and me and your mum'd be out of a job." She shot Jazmin a crafty look. "You couldn't see your way to doing a little littering on your way home, could you? Keep us fine upstanding crime officers in employment."

Jazmin smiled. Hally's sense of fun was infectious. But beneath the kidding, she also knew that there was more to the job Hally and her mum did than merely chasing kids for dropping litter. A lot more. The precinct where they worked was the London headquarters of GID – the Global Intelligence Department. Hally and her mum were members of ISA – the International Security Agency. It was their job to identify and then track down individuals, groups and organizations that were engaged in criminal activities that threatened global security.

It was a tough job, Jazmin knew that too. Dangerous even. And every time her mum had a meeting with her boss, it meant that something had come up, and her mum was being sent out on another assignment. Trouble was, lurking at the back of Jazmin's mind was always the terrible thought that, one day, her mum would be given an assignment from which she might not come back.

When Jazmin returned to the office, she found her mum seated at her workstation again. She was studying a document file, while absent-mindedly nibbling at her sandwich.

"Good lunch, hon?" she asked, without looking up.

"Uh-huh."

"Sorry I wasn't around. Listen, I thought you might like to back up some files for me this afternoon. You can use the machine in reception. How about it?"

Aha, Jazmin thought. Backing up files. Right. The old, familiar get-her-out-of-the-office-for-a-while task. It looked like her mum wanted to talk to Hally about something important. Assia handed Jazmin the access code. "Take as long as you like," she smiled, flipping the document cover over so that Jazmin couldn't read it.

Sure, Jazmin thought, pulling a wry face. You'd like

that, wouldn't you? She walked slowly out of the office, stood on the landing for a while, then doubled back and peeked in. Uh-huh. She was quite right. Her mum and Hally were sitting close together, heads bent over the file. They were talking in low voices. Their faces were serious and grave.

Jazmin took the elevator to the ground floor. Why couldn't her mother have a different job? she grumbled to herself. She sighed. Okay, she was incredibly proud of her mum – Jaz Dawson, her imaginary, crime-fighting secret agent alter ego was partly based upon her. But sometimes, Jazmin thought, she'd give anything for a mum who worked in an ordinary, boring, unadventurous, nine-to-five office job. Even if that meant the world was a little less safe as a consequence.

AT 6.30 P.M., ASSIA AND JAZMIN WALKED TO THE TRAIN STATION TOGETHER. THE PLATFORM WAS CROWDED WITH GREY-FACED, TIRED CITY WORKERS RETURNING HOME AFTER A HARD DAY. EVERYONE stood in silent rows, waiting for the superspeed silver bullet commuter express to pull in.

Assia eyed her daughter carefully.

"So, have you had a nice day?" she asked.

"Yeah, great. The best."

"Good. I'm really sorry I had to pass on lunch."

Jazmin shrugged. "Hey, I know how it is," she said

lightly, "when the big boss calls, you have to drop everything...don't you?" She cut her mum a lightning glance and waited to see if anything significant was about to be said.

"That's right," Assia smiled. She'd already started to work out what she had to say to Jazmin. She looked down at her daughter, at her stubborn chin and unruly dark curls, and sighed gently. Over the years, Agent Assia Dawson had diced with death and danger so often it was almost routine. So why was her heart sinking at the prospect of talking to her own daughter? It was plain crazy!

The silver train snaked into the platform, swooshing to a halt. The doors slid open and the tired crowd surged forward. Jazmin ducked under arms and wriggled around bodies until she managed to secure a precious seat.

"Swap you halfway," she said, grinning cheekily up at her mum.

Assia nodded absent-mindedly. She bent down and placed her laptop bag by Jazmin's feet.

"And how about a carryout for dinner?" Jazmin went on. "Save you cooking after your stressful day."

"Sure, whatever you want, hon," Assia agreed automatically, her brain still mindstacking their future conversation.

Jazmin smiled. This was easy.

"Sushi?" she asked innocently. They rarely ate sushi – her mum always said it was far too expensive.

"That'd be nice."

Jazmin stopped smiling. This was maybe too easy.

"Do you fancy some vintage champagne?" she suggested slyly, testing the water to see just how far she could push things.

"If you like."

"And we could hire a band to play to us while we eat?"

"Uh-huh."

Jazmin's expression changed, hardened. She frowned and glanced up quickly. Her mum was staring out of the window with a faraway expression on her face. Her body was swaying to the rocking rhythm of the train. Her lips were slightly parted. It was quite obvious that she was in another world. She hadn't been listening to a single word her daughter had said.

Jazmin pulled a face. She knew her mum. She recognized the signs. Whenever she went all preoccupied and distant on her like this, it always meant that something was going to happen. Something that her mum didn't want to tell her about. Which automatically meant that it was something that Jazmin wasn't going to like. She folded her arms and stared gloomily into space. All of a sudden, she was not looking forward to getting home.

LATER THAT EVENING, JAZMIN DAWSON SAT ALONE IN HER ROOM. SHE STARED OUT OF THE WINDOW, HER CHIN CUPPED IN HER HANDS, HER MOUTH SET IN A GRIM LINE. SO NOW SHE KNEW WHAT WAS going on, she thought to herself. And she was fed up. No, correction: she was Absolutely Fed Up. Her mum was going on another assignment. An assignment that was going to take her away from home and to a foreign country. After she'd promised faithfully that she would take some time out to be with her daughter.

That was the bad news. But this time, there was more. While her mum was away, Jazmin was going to be sent off to stay with her uncle and aunt – a decision that had been made without anyone asking her if she wanted to go. Without a single word of discussion having taken place. Was it any wonder she was feeling fed up, she thought angrily to herself?

Snatches of the conversation she'd had earlier with her mum replayed themselves in Jazmin's mind.

"I really think it's for the best," her mum said, after breaking the unwelcome news. As if she were doing Jazmin a big favour. She even tried putting an arm round her shoulders.

"As in: best for who?" Jazmin snapped back, wriggling free.

"Honestly hon, believe me. I haven't come to the decision lightly."

"But you've come to it without consulting me – right?"

"I'm consulting you now."

"No, you aren't. You're telling me. This isn't consulting, it's all been arranged."

Her mum sighed, ran her hands through her hair. "Look, you like Uncle Ian and Aunt Dee."

Jazmin's fists were bunched into tight angry balls. "He*llo* – I liked them when I was EIGHT, okay. I haven't seen them for years."

"Well, I don't expect even after six years of living in Hong Kong that they've changed much."

No, Jazmin thought to herself grimly, but I have. Totally. I'm not a kid any more. I don't like being pushed around and being excluded from decisions that affect me.

"And just think – it will be nice to see Ed and Clea again, won't it?" her mum coaxed.

Jazmin thought about her two cousins. Ed would be nineteen now – he'd probably be working. Too busy to spend time with her. And Clea? She'd be nearly sixteen. A better prospect. However, Jazmin only remembered her cousin Clea as a fat, spotty and silent nine year old. Her heart sank at the prospect of spending all summer in the company of somebody she barely knew and hadn't much liked.

"Can't I stay here?" she pleaded. "Please let me. I'm old enough to look after myself. I've done it enough times when you've been working late, haven't I? Granddad could pop in every now and again and check I haven't burned the place down. Hey, maybe he could move in, how about that? He's done it before when you've been away. He likes looking after me."

Her mum sighed again, shook her head. "I can't leave you alone indefinitely," she said. "And as for Granddad, he's getting too old and frail; it's not fair to burden him with the responsibility."

"It's not fair on *me*," Jazmin complained.

"I know," her mum agreed evenly. "I understand how you feel. But I don't want you home alone. I'm going to be out of the country for a while and I don't know when I'll be back. You know that's how it is in my job. I'm sorry."

"Not half so sorry as me," Jazmin muttered under her breath.

"You'll be fine. Try to see it as an adventure."

"Yeah – sure."

"Hopefully, it won't be for too long. Hey, look on the bright side – I bet you'll have a lovely time. You'll see – they'll probably spoil you rotten, you know how well-off they are." Her mum smiled encouragingly.

Jazmin cast about for something nasty to say. "You've always said money isn't everything," she sneered.

"Yes, I know."

"So?"

"So what?"

"So now you're saying money is the only thing that's important."

Jazmin saw her mum's mouth tighten. A bad sign, but she was powerless to stop herself now. Whenever they had a row – and they'd been having a lot of rows recently – she kept getting locked in a "so" loop. She knew it annoyed her mother. She knew it led nowhere, but she just couldn't stop herself. It was like a verbal tic.

"Look, hon, all I'm saying is that your uncle and aunt are really looking forward to seeing you and they'll give you a nice time," her mother responded wearily. "What's the problem with that?"

How long have we got here? Jazmin thought.

"So that's it, is it?" she said in a voice that could have performed surgery. "Bye Mum, bye Jazmin. See you sometime. End of story."

"I guess. If you choose to put it like that."

"Right." Jazmin stood up. "Thanks for telling me. Thanks a lot. I'm going to my room, okay. Stuff to do." And, turning her back on her mum, she stalked out of the kitchen, slamming the door behind her.

ASSIA DAWSON SAT AT THE KITCHEN TABLE, CRADLING A MUG OF TEA. RIGHT NOW, SHE KNEW JAZMIN WOULD BE STARING OUT OF THE WINDOW, HER CHIN IN HER HANDS. AND, IF IT HAD BEEN visible, there'd be a big black "unfair" cloud hovering just above her head. With flashes of lightning shooting out of it. Assia pulled a rueful face. She understood exactly how

Jazmin was feeling. She really did. The irony was that she hadn't even been asked to take this job on. No pressure had been put on her to accept it. She'd only just returned from Eastern Europe, where she'd been part of a team that had broken up a cyber-fraud scam, so by rights she was due some downtime.

No, the truth was, she'd actually volunteered to do it. In spite of all the things she'd promised herself. Yes, she knew she ought to spend more time with her daughter, who was the most important person in the world to her. Yes, there were jobs in the flat they shared that badly needed doing, too. And she knew her father was not very happy at the moment. The move to the senior care home had hit him hard – he could do with some serious TLC from his family.

And yet.

And yet as soon as her boss had outlined the assignment, something inside her had gone: "mine". Almost without thinking, she'd heard herself begging to take it on. Even though she knew it would upset her daughter, her plans, her life. So, what was she? Assia asked herself gloomily. The world's worst mother? Hot contender for the award of Most Masochistic Workaholic?

Pulling a face, Assia Dawson sighed and shook her head resignedly. There was so very little point in beating herself up about this. Maybe she was going to make all the usual promises to herself and to her daughter. Again. And maybe she really intended to keep them. Perhaps when she got back from this job, she would. But at the end of the day, she was still going to take the job, wasn't she?

Assia finished her tea, then got up from the table with a little groan. She had a tough evening stretching ahead of her, she thought. She needed to make peace with her daughter. And she had an awful lot of paperwork to do in preparation for her new assignment. She placed her mug in the sink, walked out of the kitchen and into the hallway. Then, squaring her shoulders and taking a deep breath, Assia went to the far end of the corridor, and knocked softly upon her daughter's bedroom door.

THE MORNING SUN SHONE DOWN ON THE SHINY GREY ROOF OF THE INTERCITY BUS. JAZMIN DAWSON TURNED UP THE AIR-CONDITIONER ABOVE HER SEAT AND TOOK A COUPLE OF SIPS OF ICED WATER. She checked once again that her bag was still in the overhead locker – not that anyone was going to steal it, but hey, it was always good to be security conscious. Then she settled back and stared out of the window. She had already been travelling for two hours. Two hours of high-speed motorway. Now there was only a short time to go before she got there.

Jazmin pressed her forehead against the cool glass. She watched the countryside whizzing by and tried to ignore the slight nervous fluttering in her stomach. She hoped she'd get on with her uncle and aunt. And especially, she hoped she'd get on with her cousin Clea. She knew the success of their relationship could make or break her visit.

She also secretly wished that she'd parted on slightly better terms with her mum. She was speaking to her, but the atmosphere was still frosty enough to ski down. She wondered what her mum was doing now. Maybe she should call her? Jazmin felt herself wavering. She got out her micro. Then she recalled the conversation they'd had last night. Her resolution hardened. Hey girl, get a grip, she told herself. This sort of weak attitude would *Not Do*. She put the micro away again. She was not going to call her mum; she was just going to tough it out on her own.

The intercity bus drew into the depot and came to a halt. The driver leaned over and pressed the automatic doors, which swooshed open. They had arrived.

IAN DAWSON AND HIS FAMILY LIVED IN ONE OF THE NEW HIGH-RISE COMPLEXES. IT WAS LOCATED JUST A SHORT DISTANCE OUTSIDE THE PICTURESQUE CATHEDRAL CITY OF YORK, AND WAS THE NEWEST of the so-called sky-cities. The concept had been dreamed up in the 1980s – the brain child of a visionary architect who had realized that as more and more areas of the globe were lost to pollution and climate change, people would need new places to live. Thus the idea of sky-cities –

populations of twenty-to-forty thousand people living in clustered high rises – was born.

Each city community had its own shopping malls, restaurants and recreational facilities. Parks and green spaces planted with trees had been incorporated into the massive structures, as well as schools and medical facilities. Wind turbines and solar panels ensured that the cities were self-sufficient. The first sky communities had been piloted in Japan, then Hong Kong, and had proved so successful that, forty years after the initial idea, the sky-city concept had become a way of life for millions of people throughout the world.

"AND THIS WILL BE YOUR ROOM," IAN DAWSON SAID, OPENING A DOOR AND STANDING BACK. HE SMILED AND JAZMIN SUDDENLY SAW THE RESEMBLANCE TO HER MOTHER. SHE KNEW THEY WERE twins, and she'd being trying to find similarities ever since her serious, business-suited and slightly formal uncle had met her at the intercity bus depot. Now she saw it clearly for the first time. She smiled back.

"Thanks, it looks great."

"Your en-suite bathroom is just off to the left." Ian hesitated, pushing his greying hair from his forehead. "Erm...I need to get back to work, if that's all right with you. I think your aunt and Clea will be back soon. They've just popped down to the deli."

"I'll be fine, Uncle Ian," Jazmin reassured him. "You can leave me to unpack if you want."

Ian nodded gratefully at his niece and hurried from the room. Left on her own, Jazmin prowled round her bedroom. Exploring. Opening drawers and cupboards. Familiarizing herself with her new surroundings. She tried out the bed, bouncing on it a couple of times approvingly, then went into the sparkly clean, white-tiled bathroom. There were a couple of fluffy yellow towels, an unopened bottle of apricot washing-gel. A hot shower would be nice, she thought to herself. Wash away the grime of the journey. And she wanted to make a good impression on her cousin. First impressions were important. She started to get undressed.

When Jazmin finally emerged from the shower, wrapped in one of the soft yellow towels, she discovered a girl sitting on her bed. Jazmin stared at her. It was obvious who she was, the likeness between them was uncanny. They both had the same colour eyes, same shape face and same dark hair (although this girl looked to be a bit taller and quite a lot slimmer than Jazmin).

There, however, the resemblance ended. Seated in front of Jazmin was a Girl Who Groomed. She was buffed and waxed and polished and manicured. Her make-up was perfect, her hair was sleek and shiny and smooth. It was the way Jazmin envisioned her imaginary kick-ass alter ego Jaz Dawson might look. A look she would never achieve in a million years. However hard she worked at it.

"Hi, there," the girl said, languidly. She waved a dainty hand fringed with rose-painted nails. Bead bracelets tinkled musically on her slim wrist. Jazmin stood awkwardly in the en-suite doorway, hitching the towel more securely round her and dripping water on the bedroom carpet. The girl tilted her head to one side picturesquely, opened her long-lashed blue eyes wide, looked expectantly at Jazmin and waited.

"Er...hi. Is it Clea?" Jazmin ventured.

"Actually, it's pronounced Clay-argh," the girl told her.

"Oh, right. Sorry."

"Mummy sent me up to see if you were settling in okay." The girl glanced down at Jazmin's unopened bag on the floor. "Do you want a hand unpacking?"

Jazmin silently checked out Clea's fashionably cut black velvet trousers, her pretty, ribboned cream top, her tiny seed-pearl necklet. Everything her cousin wore shrieked designer. She thought about the contents of her bag. "I can manage, thanks," she said firmly.

"Suit yourself," Clea said, tossing her dark curly mane of hair. She extended one foot and studied the rose-painted toenails peeking out from between her jewelled sandal straps.

There was a silence. Then: "So what is it your mother does?" Clea asked, still studying her feet from every conceivable angle and seeming pleased with what she saw.

"She investigates threats to global security."

"Uh-huh, really? And what's she investigating now?"

"I don't know. She's not allowed to talk about it."

Clea raised her perfectly arched eyebrows. "Uh-huh, really?" she repeated again, transferring her gaze to her fingernails.

"She's on a secret mission," Jazmin boasted, instantly regretting her words as she realized that she sounded silly and childlike.

"Ooh. A secret mission – my, my," Clea murmured politely, a little smile playing about her lips. "How extraordinary."

There was another brief and awkward pause.

"I guess you'll be going to the YLC while you're here," Clea said in a bored tone of voice.

"The what?"

Clea eye-rolled. "Uh. The Youth Learning Centre. It's where all the kids go."

"Oh. Yeah, I guess," Jazmin frowned. She had kind of conveniently forgotten about her education. "Is that where you go?" she asked.

Clea looked shocked. "Lord no!" she exclaimed, waving a dismissive hand. "I have my own ILP."

Jazmin hadn't a clue what Clea was talking about. What on earth was an ILP? A piece of computer equipment? An item of clothing? A pet? Whatever it was, she was getting a bit fed up with her cousin's superior attitude. And the way she was talking down to her as if she was a little kid. She decided, rashly, to bluff her way out. "How nice for you," she said. "I had one of them once."

Clea's eyes widened in astonishment. "You did? And what was it like?"

"Er...I don't remember. I think I broke it when we moved house."

Clea emitted a loud snort of laughter. "An ILP is an Individual Learning Program," she said. "It means I'm so bright I have my own tutor and I don't have to attend class with the sapheads round here."

"Oh, er...I..." Jazmin stuttered in embarrassment. She felt her face flame.

Clea smiled in a superior fashion, uncurled her legs and stood up. "Right, must run," she said, tripping lightly on her high-heeled sandals to the door. She paused on the threshold, spun round. "Oh, by the way, dinner is at seven. Mummy's roasting a dead animal to welcome you. Yum, yum."

Jazmin waited until the tap-tap of her cousin's high heels had faded into the background. Then she threw off the towel and got dressed. So that was Clea. Right. She threw up a mental picture of her cousin as she remembered her – the fat, spotty and silent picture – and then compared it to the Clea she'd just encountered. There was no interface whatsoever. This was not at all the person she'd expected.

As she pulled on her shabby jeans and tried to tame her unruly hair with her brush, Jazmin's mouth set in a thin line. Her cousin Clea was so up herself she could probably brush her teeth from the inside. Jazmin shook her head sadly. So much for first impressions. It was quite clear that she and Clea had absolutely nothing in common. They were not going to get on. She sighed and began to unpack her case. It was definitely going to be a long, long visit.

ASSIA WAITED UNTIL SHE'D RECEIVED THE MESSAGE FROM IAN SAYING JAZMIN HAD ARRIVED SAFELY. THEN SHE BEGAN HER CAREFUL AND METHODICAL PREPARATIONS. FIRST, SHE WENT INTO the bathroom and, taking a pair of scissors from the cabinet, cut her long, curly hair as short as she could. Long hair could be grabbed and used as a restraining mechanism. In a fight-or-flight situation, this could mean the difference between life or death. Then she took a bottle of blonde hair dye and applied it all over her head.

Next, Assia checked the contents of her backpack. She removed her diary, ID card, pictures of her daughter. The small but significant things that, if they got into the wrong hands, could be used to identify her and trace her family. There was no way Assia would ever let her daughter be threatened or put in a dangerous situation. She replaced all her personal bits and pieces with a fake ID, and a small silver pen, which was actually the latest ISA high-tech gadget. It contained a cartridge of disabler spray, a tiny satellite receiver and, when slid apart, opened out into a minute keyboard and screen. This would be her link to the outside world – the way she'd have to communicate from now on.

Lastly, Assia changed into a nondescript pair of workman's overalls and a scruffy padded jacket. She put on a pair of sturdy leather boots. Fading-into-the-background clothes. Then, picking up a tiny but powerful handgun she tucked it into the heelstrap of her left boot. Normally she did not carry weapons, but this time she was taking a Beretta .32. As a precautionary measure. Finally, satisfied that she'd done everything she needed, Assia Dawson closed her front door and stepped out into another life.

JAZMIN SAT AT HER UNCLE AND AUNT'S TABLE, EATING HER DINNER. YOU COULD LEARN A LOT ABOUT A FAMILY BY OBSERVING THEM AT MEAL TIMES, SHE THOUGHT TO HERSELF. ONE THING she'd definitely learned was that her uncle and aunt, who seemed on the face of it to be two very nice, intelligent adults, were totally under the thumbs of their kids. Jazmin marvelled at how a pair of such high-powered people (her uncle ran a highly successful cyber company and her aunt was CEO of a top global management consultancy) could be so completely suckered by one spoiled, fussy fifteen year old and one unreliable nineteen year old.

"Why don't you take Jazmin out and show her around?" Dee suggested to her daughter after they'd finally finished eating what, in Jazmin's opinion, was an excellent roast dinner. (Veggie Clea had picked at a plate of salad and complained that there wasn't any of her favourite dressing.) For dessert, there had been apple pie and ice cream. (Clea had left the pastry – too soggy, she said – then stirred her ice cream into sauce.) Jazmin, who was used to the "find something in the fridge" type of meal, had enjoyed every bite.

Clea pouted. It was clear that she didn't want to take her cousin anywhere. Then she paused. A thoughtful expression crossed her face. But only Jazmin saw it. Her aunt and uncle were far too busy worrying about where Ed was, when he was coming back and why he hadn't called home.

"All right, Mummy. Maybe I'll take her to look round the mall," Clea agreed.

Dee's eyes shone with amusement as she looked at her daughter. "I might have known you'd want to go shopping, sweetie," she said indulgently.

"Can I borrow your paycard, Mummy?" Clea asked sweetly. "I'd really like to treat my cousin Jazmin to something nice to welcome her, only I haven't got any credits left." Innocence hung from her words like loops of toffee.

Dee gave her daughter a beaming smile. "What a lovely, generous idea. It's on my desk. Help yourself."

"Thanks, Mummy, you're *so* the best," Clea said. She hurried out of the dining room, returning some minutes later with a smug smile on her face. "Coming?" she said offhandedly to Jazmin.

Jazmin nodded. She didn't really want to go shopping on her first evening in a new place, but she knew it was important not to fall out with Clea. She got up from the table. "Thank you for the delicious meal, Aunty Dee," she said politely. Clea stared at her in astonishment. Got you there, rich girl, Jazmin thought grimly. She reckoned her spoiled cousin wouldn't recognize gratitude if it leaped up and bit her on the bum.

CLEA AND JAZMIN TOOK THE ELEVATOR TO THE GROUND FLOOR. CLEA LED THE WAY ACROSS THE LOBBY. JAZMIN TRAILED ALONG BEHIND HER. SHE KEPT FINDING INTERESTING THINGS TO STOP AND look at: a bronze sculpture, a display of bonsai trees, an abstract mosaic on a wall.

"Come on," Clea said impatiently.

"Hang on a minute." Jazmin paused in front of a large tank of scarlet and silver koi carp. Wow, amazing, she thought. She placed her hand flat against the tank and grinned delightedly as all the koi began congregating on the other side of the glass, their mouths opening and closing hopefully.

Clea clicked her teeth and uttered an exclamation of annoyance. "They're only stupid fish," she said. "Honestly, you should have seen our place in Hong Kong. It was so much bigger and better."

Yeah, well, maybe, Jazmin thought. But I'm never going to see it, am I? And I want to look round this place. Only you're not letting me.

"What's the hurry?" she inquired, still staring at the koi. Clea didn't reply. Instead, she waited a few paces ahead, tapping her foot, her arms pointedly folded. The picture of resigned boredom.

"Okay, I'm coming now," Jazmin said, reluctantly tearing herself away from the beautiful fish. She cut Clea a hard stare as she caught her up. This was no fun. It was like being herded along by some pampered pedigree sheepdog. A female sheepdog. Jazmin was *so* trying not to use the B-word quite this early on in their relationship.

Clea hurried her along a covered walkway and through the heavy glass doors that led into the mall. She headed for the escalators.

"We're going up to the fifth floor," she told Jazmin over her shoulder. "All the best shops are up there."

"Great." Jazmin did a face-scrunch behind Clea's back.

Given the choice, she'd have much preferred to stay and annoy the koi carp.

However, as soon as they stepped off the escalator, Clea unexpectedly spun round to face her. "Umm...look Jazmin," she said, "I've actually arranged to do something right now. You'll be okay to look round on your own for a bit, won't you?"

"Oh." Jazmin was startled. She had automatically assumed that Clea wanted to go on a personal spending spree, and was merely using her as a convenient excuse.

Clea fumbled in her tiny jewelled shoulder bag. "Here's Mummy's card, just in case you find something you like," she said. She held it out. "No, take it," she said, as Jazmin hesitated. "Honestly, she won't mind. She'll be pleased you're enjoying yourself." Clea got out her minute gold micro. Her fingers began moving over the keys. "See you back here in two, all right?" she said airily. Then she turned round and strode off purposefully.

Oh, great, Jazmin thought. She hadn't wanted to come shopping in the first place. Now she'd been dumped. She glanced around, swore under her breath. Okay, so she liked shopping – hey, who didn't – although her meagre allowance meant that her trips to the mall back home were usually made up of window shopping rather than buying. But right now, she really didn't fancy spending two hours in a strange environment looking around a bunch of shops that were no different to the ones back home. She wondered fleetingly if she could remember the way back to the apartment. It would just serve her selfish cousin right if she arrived back on her own. Let her wriggle her snaky way out of that one.

Jazmin began to retrace her way back downstairs from the fifth floor, wondering what she should do. The fourth floor, however, was full of shops selling books and computer games. Tempted, she decided to stop off and look around for a bit. Jazmin could never resist a good bookstore. In fact, if she was honest, much of her fantasy life was based on the plots of stories that she'd read in books.

She entered one of the stores and started working her way along a rack of crime and thriller stories. Her favourite fiction. She soon sorted out a pile of books, then took them over to the customer scan screen and sat down. Jazmin decided to play her usual game: read the first couple of chapters to see what the crime was, make a guess who did it, then turn to the end to see if her suspicions were correct. It was uncanny how often they were. Easy to see who she took after, too. She was her mother's daughter all right. A future career as a secret agent and crime fighter definitely beckoned.

After flicking through the books for a while, Jazmin decided to treat herself to a couple. She reckoned she was going to have to find some way to pass the time while she was staying here. She twirled the rack around, looking for ones she hadn't read. Then she carried her chosen books to the paypoint and, ignoring what Clea had said, bought them using her own card. She checked the time. Oh, pig! She still had plenty of it left to kill.

Jazmin made her way upstairs to the bookstore's café. She bought some double-chocolate-chip cookies and a juice, sat down at a table and opened up the first book. Cookies and crime fiction – her favourite combination! Pretty soon, she had entered the imaginary world of the story and was totally lost in a tangled web of fast action, murder and mayhem.

Time passed.

CLEA DAWSON GLANCED AT HER WATCH. THEN SHE GLARED AT HER COUSIN. THEN SHE EYE-ROLLED EXAGGERATEDLY. "WHERE WERE YOU?" SHE COMPLAINED. "I'VE BEEN WAITING AGES."

"I got lost, okay," Jazmin snapped back. "I've never been here before. I don't know my way around, remember?"

Clea shrugged. "Oh well, it can't be helped I suppose," she sighed. "Come on, we'd better get back before they start worrying."

Furious, Jazmin fell into step with her cousin. The expression on her face could have hammered rivets.

"I see you bought something," Clea said finally, breaking the frosty silence.

"Uh-huh."

"That's good."

"Uh-huh."

"Mummy will be pleased."

"Uh-huh."

Clea shot her a quick sideways glance, her eyes narrowing thoughtfully.

Hey, she's getting the message, Jazmin thought sardonically.

The silence fell between them again, leaden and heavy.

"So..." Clea said at length. "Er...looking forward to the learning centre tomorrow, then?"

"Yeah. Can't wait," Jazmin answered, icicles dripping from her words. "I'm sure I'll soon settle in with all the other sapheads. Won't that be great!"

Clea had the grace to look uncomfortable. "Look," she said, turning to face Jazmin, "I didn't mean to suggest...that is..." She paused awkwardly.

Jazmin waited, arms folded, refusing to help her out.

"Okay, I'm sorry I had to leave you on your own," Clea admitted in a rush of words. "But I just *had* to see some people about something. It was important, right? It was nothing personal against you."

"Right," Jazmin said tightly.

They walked back to the apartment in total silence. Clea opened the front door. Without saying a word, Jazmin stalked past her. She handed over the borrowed paycard and went up to her room, where she shut the door and threw herself onto the bed. A great wave of loneliness and misery washed over her. She hated this place. She hated her stuck-up cousin. She wanted to be back home, in her own bedroom, with its dark-blue walls and posters of computer-generated fractals. She wanted to be surrounded by her own things: her scented candle collection, her seashells, the piles of books by her bed. Most of all, she wanted her mum. She wanted her mum so badly that she could almost smell her perfume in the empty air. Suddenly, Jazmin felt that she'd give anything in the whole wide world to be in the middle of one of their really big, shouty, door-slamming rows.

Feeling as if her heart was going to break, she laid her head down on the cool pillow, gave in to her emotions, and had a good cry. Then, feeling better, she got up, went into the bathroom and splashed her face with cold water. She put on her PJs and slipped under the duvet. She and Jaz Dawson, secret agent and crime fighter, were currently inhabiting a hostile alien environment. There was no way out, so they were just going to have to make the best of it. Like her mum always said: when life deals you lemons, you make lemonade. She reached out a hand and turned off the light.

A COOL SUMMER'S EVENING. TWO MEN WAIT IN A NAPLES BACKSTREET. OCCASIONALLY, THEY CHECK THE TIME, SHRUG THEIR SHOULDERS, LIGHT ANOTHER CIGARETTE. EVERY NOW AND THEN, one of the men strolls the short distance to the corner, leans against a house wall, and looks both ways up and down the street. He listens intently.

Nothing much happens for a while.

Then, the sound of a car is heard. The men straighten up, become suddenly alert. The car approaches fast, tyres squealing as it shoots round the corner and screeches to a halt. The driver of the car winds down his window. One of the men says something to him in an urgent undertone. He speaks a central European language. The driver gesticulates towards the rear of the car. By the light of the flickering streetlamps, the men see something large on the back seat. It is wrapped in black thermolin, and occupies most of the room. They exchange a quick, satisfied glance. Then the two men step forward, open the car doors and get in, one in the front, one squeezing into the back. The driver starts the engine. The car roars off into the night, heading north.

Tomorrow morning, very early, the car will be found abandoned near the Porta Capuana, by a woman walking her dog. Its plates will be gone. And there will be nothing on the back seat.

MORNING ONCE MORE, AND THE VIEW FROM JAZMIN DAWSON'S BEDROOM WINDOW WAS OF ENDLESSLY BLUE SKY. OUTSIDE, IN THE REAL WORLD THAT EXISTED JUST BEYOND THE SHINY TRANSPARENT glass, it was going to be another perfect summer day. She could hear the sounds of her uncle and aunt moving around, getting ready to go to work. Soon the smell of freshly ground coffee would filter up to her room, along with the shouts telling Ed to get up. A few days had passed, and she was becoming familiar with this family's routines. She was beginning to feel less homesick.

Jazmin had learned that her uncle and aunt went to work early and stayed at their offices late into the evening. Their jobs were their top priority. They worked long hours, brought work home with them. Same as her mum. They expected their kids to fit in round their busy lives. Then, every now and then, they went on guilt trips and made promises. It was all remarkably similar to home. The big difference was that her uncle and aunt earned so much money they could buy their kids anything they wanted. And they did. Jazmin had seen immediately that Clea had far more and far better stuff than she had. She had also decided that it didn't make her cousin a better person, which was rather reassuring.

Now she listened to the hurrying footsteps in the hallway, the last-minute shouts to Ed, the front door opening and closing, followed by silence. Then she lay back and turned her attention to the world just beyond that front door. Jazmin admitted to herself that although she was starting to get to grips with her cousin's family, she was still having a hard time buying into the vertical-community concept.

It seemed to her that there was something unnatural about living high above the ground. She felt that she was already beginning to lose touch with the real world. The one that contained noise and dirt and the smell of cars and trucks. The sky-city was a beautiful place, but its beauty was deceptive. In many subtle ways, it was like a prison too. Yes, you could leave any time you wanted to – but nobody seemed to want to. Why should they, was the attitude, when they had everything here?

In the short time she had been here, Jazmin had already met kids in the learning centre who had never been outside the complex. Ever. They had been born here, grown up here, and eventually, she guessed, would probably die here too. It was weird and rather scary. Jazmin couldn't relate to it at all. All she knew was that for her, the beautiful steel and glass world, with its immaculate parks and wide spacious malls, was fast losing its appeal. More and more, she longed to walk upon real ground. Real ground that was there because it had always been there. Rather than put there by some upmarket, designer-landscape company.

Jazmin got dressed and went downstairs. In the kitchen, she discovered her cousin Clea grumpily toasting bagels.

She had filled up the kwik-cook and, as usual, had taken over the juicer. This was what she had done every morning of Jazmin's visit, regardless of the fact that she and Jazmin always ate at the same time. So once again, Jazmin would have to wait until Clea had finished, before she could start to prepare her own breakfast. She was beginning to strongly suspect that Clea was doing it deliberately, to send her a subliminal message about how things worked around here. About who was important. And who wasn't.

In the meantime, Jazmin got some milk and took it into the den to drink while she waited. There was no point trying to have a conversation with Clea first thing in the morning. She'd tried when she first arrived, and had now given up. It simply wasn't worth the effort. Her cousin could do to a conversation what treacle did to a watch. Jazmin picked up the remote and began to surf channels, looking for something entertaining to watch.

Eventually, Clea entered the den, balancing a big glass of juice on top of a loaded plate. "Kitchen's free," she said abruptly, without making eye contact.

"Thanks."

Clea attempted to lower herself gracefully backwards into a lounger, miscalculated, and slopped juice all over her beaded, blue silk top. She swore daintily.

Jazmin decided to pretend that she hadn't seen. Or heard. She got up and left the room. Gee, it was clearly tough living life in the clever lane, she thought sarkily.

She grinned happily to herself as she hurried off to prepare her own breakfast, before getting her stuff ready for another tedious day of school.

THE YOUTH LEARNING CENTRE WAS LOCATED IN THE WEST TOWER. JAZMIN REACHED IT BY TAKING A LONG RIDE IN A GLASS-TOPPED ELEVATOR FOLLOWED BY A SHORT STROLL ACROSS A SERIES OF open-air walkways. Jazmin's classes took place on the ground floor. Clea's classes, as befitted her superior status and intelligence, took place in a suite of rooms on the thirty-second floor, where she and the rest of the similarly überbright hung out. They weren't popular.

Jazmin was tolerant of the learning centre. It was pretty much identical to the centre back home – the facilitators kind but distant, the work not too stretching. She'd begun to make a few contacts – once the knowledge that she was Clea Dawson's cousin had been footnoted by the information that she was not like her in the slightest.

Now it was lunchtime. Jazmin sat on her own in the canteen. She was eating the canteen lunch – like institutional food everywhere on the planet, it was luridly coloured and didn't seem to belong to any recognizable food group – and while eating, she was making plans. She decided that after class, she'd take the elevator down to the ground and go for a walk outside the city. Maybe that was where all the interesting stuff happened. Lost in her thoughts, she barely registered when a girl from her geography class dropped into the seat opposite. Jazmin looked up, tried to remember the girl's name, failed, but smiled dutifully anyway.

"Hey ya," the girl said in a friendly fashion. She ripped the top off a vitamin drink and sipped. "Boring class, eh?"

Jazmin shrugged. "It was okay."

"Ecology! Who needs it?" the girl went on. She waved to a couple of her friends queuing at the paytill. "All that stuff about the glaciers melting and sea levels rising?" she continued. "I mean, for freak's sake – who cares?"

Jazmin sighed mentally. Yet another person who didn't get out enough. "Not you, huh?" she said, the words slipping out before she could stop herself.

The girl blinked at her, then frowned.

Uh-oh, irony bypass, Jazmin thought, recognizing the telltale signs. She lapsed into "fit-in" mode. "Yeah," she drawled, shrugging her shoulders and eye-rolling dramatically, "like they should be telling us useful stuff, shouldn't they?"

"Too right," the girl agreed. She crushed her carton and flipped it into a nearby recycling bin. "Coming to check out the boys playing football?"

"Maybe."

"Catch you later, then."

Jazmin finished her tasteless salad roll and started on her brightly coloured jam tart. What was with this place?

Nobody seemed to have any interest at all in what was happening outside their little glass world. They were like the koi carp she'd seen on her first day. Swimming around in their nice, clean aquarium, totally unaware that there was a whole great sea out there to be explored.

Jazmin wondered where her mum was, and what she was doing right now. She hadn't heard from her yet. But that's what she'd expected. That's how it was when her mum worked undercover. She made contact when she could. Jazmin didn't like it, but she had learned to – no, she'd *had* to – adapt. She knew she could always call Hally Skinner at the office if she was worried. However, she chose not to call Hally. She wasn't a little kid (even though her cousin thought she was). She could cope on her own. Anyway, she reassured herself, no news was good news: it meant that her mum was getting on with her assignment and everything was okay.

Though this particular assignment seemed especially weird. Not that she'd been told much. Practically zip. And what she *had* been told sounded so like the plot of a really bad crime thriller. Somewhere on the planet there was a dead body, with no ID, no witnesses, no motive, no suspects. And it was her mum's job to find the body and then work back to discover the rest. Uh-huh. Sounds crazy, Jazmin thought. Even her imaginary detecting diva Jaz Dawson would struggle to fix a lead on this case.

AT THE END OF THE DAY, JAZMIN GOT READY TO QUIT THE BUILDING AND HEAD OFF INTO THE REAL WORLD. SHE PACKED HER BOOKS INTO HER BAG. THAT WAS WHEN SHE DISCOVERED THAT THE KEYS TO HER uncle and aunt's apartment were missing. She hunted frantically through her bag, then her pockets. Then she remembered she'd left the keys on her chest of drawers. Oh pig! She cursed herself for being so careless. Now she had given herself a problem. She knew her uncle and aunt would not be home until very late tonight – they were attending some work function. Ed rarely seemed to be home. Which, sadly, left only one person who could help her out.

Jazmin decided she'd better liaise with Clea and find out what time she was planning to get back. She really didn't want to – Clea was bound to say something sarky. But it was her only option, other than breaking into the apartment. She called up her cousin on her micro. It was switched off. Jazmin thought hard. She really needed to speak to her. Then she remembered that Clea and her exclusive crowd of friends often hung out after class in a particular coffee shop in the food court. Maybe she was there now? Jazmin took the express transporter to the recreation tower, where all the shops and cafés were.

There was indeed a group of girls clustered at a table in the coffee shop. Clea's crowd. Jazmin knew some of them, but only by sight. She had not been allowed to mingle. Clea was definitely trying to keep her at a distance.

Nothing had actually been said, but Jazmin had got the distinct impression that Clea thought she was far too scruffy and stupid for her posh mates.

The girls were loud and brash and brightly dressed, like a flock of squawky parrots. Jazmin went over and stood next to their table for a while. Nobody looked up or paid her the slightest attention. The general assumption seemed to be that she must be merely waitressing staff and so was not worth their notice.

Eventually, Jazmin got tired of being blanked. "Um...hi," she said, almost shouting to be heard above the noise.

A couple of girls looked round. "So...yeah?" one of them inquired.

"I'm looking for Clea Dawson," Jazmin said. "Have you seen her?"

The girl sitting nearest to her stared, frowned, then very slowly and deliberately looked all around the room, under the table, even going as far as to open her bag and peer inside. The rest of the group watched her, grinning.

Finally, the girl did a palms-up. "Well, my oh my, I can't see her *anywhere*," she drawled insolently, tossing back her hair. Her friends sniggered. Jazmin could so see why Clea liked being with these girls. They were all as snot rude and up themselves as she was.

"Do you know where she is?" Jazmin persisted, resisting the impulse to throw hot coffee all over them.

"She's gone shopping with her doofy little cousin, okay," the girl told her. "Now, if you don't mind, this is a private meeting." She turned her back on Jazmin, freezing her out.

Well, that was *interesting*, Jazmin mused as she made her way out of the coffee shop. I'm Clea's "doofy little cousin" and as far as I know, she certainly hasn't gone shopping with me. So where is she? Jazmin tried the micro again. No response. It seemed that wherever she'd gone, Clea did not want to be contacted. What a total pain she was.

Jazmin made her way back to the elevator area, thinking about her cousin. Why should Clea lie to her mates? All at once, she was reminded of her first day, when Clea had dumped her and taken off on her own. She hadn't told her where she was going then, either. Jazmin's eyes narrowed. Mmm-hmm. So what could her cousin possibly be up to that she didn't want anybody finding out? She took the elevator to the ground floor, feeling suddenly much brighter in spirit. There was nothing like a bunch of unanswered questions to whet her appetite and set her brain racing. A mystery! Maybe she'd misjudged things. Maybe her stay here was going to be slightly more interesting than she'd first thought.

SO WHERE DOES ONE BEGIN SEARCHING FOR A DEAD BODY? THE QUESTION TURNED OVER AND OVER IN ASSIA DAWSON'S MIND AS SHE SAT IN A CAFÉ ON A BUSY DOCKSIDE, WATCHING THE SUNLIGHT play lazily on the oily water.

"Another cup of tea, love?" the waitress asked.

Assia nodded absent-mindedly. The waitress fetched a fresh mug of strong copper-brown tea. Assia spooned three heaped spoonfuls of sugar into the steaming liquid. At home, she drank her tea black, herbal and sugar-free. However, in her present job as casual dockworker, she had been unloading crates from a Baltic cargo ship all morning and right now she badly needed a quick energy fix.

Working on the docks might seem an odd thing to do to kick off an investigation, but to Assia it was nothing out of the ordinary. When you have the whole planet to search, you have to start somewhere. And this place seemed as good a place as any. On the docks, you got to hear stuff. Sailors travelled the world and picked up strange stories and they liked to tell them to fascinated audiences. And she was prepared to be as fascinated as it took. Maybe it was a long shot, but Assia believed in long shots. Particularly in her field of operations. More importantly, she had a gut feeling that it was here that, eventually, she'd get her first lead.

For this was not just any old dead body. No indeed. What was different about this body was whose body it was. Or might be. Assia drained the mug of tea and picked up her heavy-duty gauntlets. Another ship was due in later, from Italy this time. Maybe it would be the one to give her that vital first clue.

JAZMIN STEPPED OUT OF THE ELEVATOR. SO WHAT WAS HER COUSIN CLEA UP TO? SHE BEGAN MINDSTACKING SOME POSSIBLE IDEAS: SHOPLIFTING SCAM, DRUG RING, EXTORTION RACKET, BLACKMAIL rap. Or maybe she just had a secret boyfriend and didn't want anybody to know about him yet.

Jazmin crossed the white marble atrium with its tall, indoor palms and tinkling water features. She passed by the security and housekeeping desk. And then she stopped. Perhaps she was imagining it, but she suddenly had the distinct sensation that there were eyes boring into her back. She glanced all around. Nobody seemed to be paying her the slightest attention. Nobody was even *looking* at her. And yet, she was sure that someone not too far away was watching her. Jazmin tried to rationalize the feeling. Perhaps this was just the product of too much detective fiction and an overactive fantasy life.

On the other hand, what if it wasn't?

Feeling curious, Jazmin decided to set a trap. Feigning a nonchalant air, as if she hadn't got a care in the world, she stuck her hands into her pockets and wandered through the revolving doors that led to the outside world. Then, she slipped automatically into the persona of Jaz Dawson, spy girl and crime fighter. Currently being followed by an unknown assailant. She started walking slowly and purposefully around the building. Every few steps, she stopped, listening for the footsteps that, in her imagination, seemed always to be just out of sync with hers.

This was classic, low-level anti-surveillance at its best, she thought happily.

At last, Jazmin spotted what she was looking for: a line of parked vehicles. She quickened her pace until she was pretty sure she was far enough ahead to be out of sight. Without turning round to check behind her, she dived between two shiny SUVs, clumsily catching herself on a sharp piece of metal, which ripped a jagged hole in the knee of her jeans. She crouched down low and waited.

A long, tense minute passed. Then footsteps. And a voice: "Are you all right?"

Jazmin froze, heart pounding. Slowly, she raised her eyes and looked up.

A boy was standing in the gap, staring down at her. He was tall and slender, with short fair hair, a thin face, high cheekbones and very dark, velvety-brown eyes. Jazmin blushed. She was painfully aware that the boy was gorgeous, while she definitely wasn't looking quite her best. Her clothes were untidy, her hair ruffled, her jeans torn at the knee. Oh pig! The boy folded his arms, regarded her quizzically, and waited for her to respond. He wore an amused expression. Embarrassed and scarlet-faced, Jazmin scrambled to her feet, combing down her hair with her fingers.

"Er...I just dropped something," she bluffed.

The boy took a couple of steps towards her. "Can I help?" he asked politely.

"Um...it's okay." Jazmin made a sudden swoop downwards, her fingers clutching on empty air. "Whew, I got it!" she lied. She straightened up, and pretended to put something in her pocket. "Hey! How good is that!" she went on, with fake enthusiasm.

The boy frowned, eyed her curiously. "Are you sure you're all right?"

"Yes, really. I'm perfectly fine."

"You seem a bit jumpy."

"No, honestly. It's nothing."

"Uh-huh? I saw you in the building. You looked very worried about something. And I've been walking behind you for the last few minutes, and you keep stopping and starting. Is there something the matter?"

Shoot! Jazmin thought. So that's who was looking at me. And following me. "I'm fine. Thanks," she said firmly.

The boy looked at her and shrugged. He did a palms-up, smiling a half smile. "Okay, if you're sure," he said, and turned to go.

Whoa, quick, say something interesting, Jazmin told herself. She'd just met a cute boy. She couldn't let him go off like that thinking she was a total lurdo. But the boy was already striding purposefully along the pedestrian walkway towards the carport area. "Hey, I didn't catch your name," Jazmin called after him.

"Hey, I didn't throw it," the boy replied teasingly over his shoulder. He continued walking until he turned a corner and disappeared from sight.

Thunk – mental head slap. Jazmin scolded herself. Hello and goodbye Mr. Braincell. She could have handled that so much better. She swore softly. Her alter ego Jaz Dawson would have had the boy eating out of her hand in no time at all. She'd have charmed him with her witty conversation. Not to mention the eyelash-fluttering and hair-flicking skills that her creator had never managed to master, despite practising in front of the bathroom mirror for ages.

Now she was going to have to start from scratch to find out this good-looking boy's name, how old he was and where he lived. And, most importantly, whether he had a girlfriend or not.

Jazmin waited for a while, in case the mysterious boy reappeared. Then she returned to the building. She entered through the great steel-and-glass doors and headed for the food court. She badly needed something to eat. It was impossible to strategize on an empty stomach, especially when it looked like she had a two-muffin problem on her hands. It was also a way of putting off the inevitable moment when she'd have to find her cousin Clea and confess that she'd managed to lock herself out of the apartment.

Jazmin grabbed some food, went to the paytill, then carried her tray over to one of the tables and sat down. She broke one of the muffins into pieces and began absent-mindedly stuffing them into her mouth, while she thought about the boy she had just met. There was something about the way he spoke that made her think he was not from this part of the world. She wondered what he was doing here – maybe his family had come over to work. She started eating the second muffin. Whatever the reason, it shouldn't be too difficult to track him down again, she decided. All she needed to do was to check out the learning centre. He was bound to be a student there. Problem solved. Jazmin glanced down at her plate: it was empty. She checked her watch and sighed. Reaching into her bag, she fumbled for her micro. Reluctantly, she called Clea. Again.

TIME WORKS IN A LINEAR WAY. THINGS BEGIN, CONTINUE AND FINISH. THERE IS A FIXED ORDER. BIRTH OCCURS AT ONE END OF THE SPECTRUM, DEATH AT THE OTHER. BUT SOMEWHERE ALONG THE spectrum, time intersects with place. And at every intersection, a different story is created. But which story it is depends upon where you are at the time.

Perhaps this is the story of a bunch of intrepid polar research scientists collecting core samples at Vostok, who stumble upon something so amazing that it blows their minds. Or maybe it is the story of a deregistered ship docking at a long disused South African port. The story of a mysterious crate unloaded secretly at midnight onto a deserted quay and an expensive car with foreign plates speeding away into the night. The story of a Neapolitan sailor and a female dockworker from England who share a drink and a chat in a bar one rainy summer afternoon.

Or maybe the story goes back even further. To the birth of all stories. When there was an awful lot more space and time than anybody could imagine. And an unheard voice that might have said: let there be light.

THE WORLD IS FULL OF STORIES. HOWEVER, THERE ARE ALSO FACTS. SOME OF THESE FACTS WERE GIVEN TO ASSIA DAWSON IN A REPORT, WHICH SHE READ BEFORE EMBARKING ON HER ASSIGNMENT.

And the facts were these...

Science states that the Earth was born 4.6 billion years ago. This statement is supported by radiometric dating, which dates the earliest known rocks to 3.7 billion years. To a time known as the Precambrian, when continents were forming, and a newly emergent oxygen atmosphere allowed the first primitive life forms to exist. With this information, scientists over the centuries evolved a clear picture of how the Earth came into being, the way it developed and the evolution of plant, animal and human life.

Of course there were other theories; you couldn't expect there not to be. These other theories usually involved the intervention of a god or divine being of some sort (although there was one interesting theory that the Earth emerged from the backside of a giant kangaroo). But none of these theories were scientific, so they could only be classified as speculative assumptions. They could not be proven. And therefore, as speculative assumptions, they were easily discountable and largely dismissed as non-rational, superstitious or just plain damn wrong.

Then some Antarctic research scientists found a body in the ice. Intact and perfectly preserved. A body that should not have been where it was. Indeed, *could* not have been where it was, because the strata that contained it (recently reachable thanks to the effects of many years of global warming) had been dated to sometime pre-Precambrian. Whereas palaeoethnological and palaeobotanical research stated categorically that man did not appear on Earth until 200,000 years ago – the final link in a chain of evolutionary processes.

Scientific bewilderment increased even more when preliminary tests carried out at the site proved that the body was not a hoax. It was not an ape, not some humanoid. It was a man. *Homo sapiens*. Absolutely real and authentic. A man in a layer of ice that dated back so far it had probably been laid down at the moment when the Earth was first formed. And suddenly, centuries of accepted factual knowledge were tossed up in the air. It looked as if the whole bitter, controversial, centuries-old science-versus-religion argument was about to re-ignite. Only this time, instead of science winning hands down, it seemed as if those who had always posited that there was a creator god might just have had a valid argument all along. Many in the worldwide scientific community held their breath. And then, the body suddenly disappeared. Along with the three researchers who had made the discovery.

So what had happened to it?

The ISA was currently running with a couple of possible theories, the most obvious being that the group had met with a terrible accident somewhere out in the perilous ice deserts. But a rescue team dispatched to look for them had so far found nothing – except for a top-of-the-range Snokat mysteriously abandoned on an ice floe.

A second theory assumed that some unscrupulous scientific establishment had taken the body because it wanted to be the first to examine it and publish its results. Most regrettable. But such things happened in the cut-throat world of scientific research. Investigations were currently in progress. Places were being visited. Questions asked. So far yielding nothing.

Thirdly, there was the inevitable theory that involved the so-called X factor. The unknown group or organization, the individual not affiliated to anything legitimate, who had stolen the body for some strange and possibly dangerous purpose of his/her/their own.

And this was where Assia Dawson and her team came in. Dealing with the unknown, the individual and the strange was their particular field of expertise.

No stone was being left unturned. Wherever its current location, it was imperative that the mysterious body was quickly located. A resurrection of primitive non-scientific ways of thinking was...unthinkable. It simply could *not* be allowed to happen.

"WE THOUGHT WE'D TAKE YOU OUT TO DINNER IN A NICE RESTAURANT TOMORROW," AUNT DEE SAID TO JAZMIN THE FOLLOWING EVENING. "YOUR UNCLE AND I WOULD LIKE TO GET TO know you a bit better. It's been rather a busy time at work for both of us, and I wouldn't want you to think we're neglecting you!"

"Oh, great," Jazmin said, trying to look suitably enthusiastic. She did a quick mental scan of her meagre and rather basic wardrobe. Deliberately ignoring her mum's advice – They're bound to take you out somewhere posh to eat; make sure you pack something suitable – she had only brought hanging-out clothes and casual clothes. Not Nice Restaurant Clothes. "Uh, only I don't think I've got anything to wear," she confessed.

Aunt Dee smiled. "You sound just like Clea. She always

claims never to have anything to wear!" she laughed. "Tell you what, maybe Clea could lend you something. She's got closets full of clothes she never wears."

Yeah, I bet she has, Jazmin thought miserably. And I bet she'll so love lending me her stuff!

She sat in the lounge and listened while her aunt called up to Clea. She heard her cousin coming slowly and reluctantly downstairs. A hurried and low-voiced conversation then took place in the hallway. It terminated in Clea entering the lounge, tossing her long curly hair. "Okay, Mummy says you have to borrow some of my clothes, yeah?" she drawled.

"I don't *have* to—" Jazmin began, but Clea cut her short.

"Come," she commanded, spinning on her heel.

Reluctantly, and strongly resisting the urge to go *woof*, Jazmin got up and followed her. Clea led the way to her huge and lavishly furnished bedroom. She threw open one of the mirrored floor-to-ceiling closet doors that ran all along one wall. Racks and racks of clothes, all coordinated by colour, were packed tightly on hangers. Boxes and boxes of shoes, each with a picture of its contents on the front, were piled high on side shelves. In spite of herself, Jazmin was impressed. Clea had elevated shopping to an art form. Clearly, she was in the presence of a serial retail therapist.

Clea studied Jazmin's figure, her eyes narrowing. Then she rummaged through her extensive clothes collection, picked out a strapless lemon top and held it up against her cousin. She pursed her lips, did a face scrunch, then shook her head. "Too small," she said. "What size are you anyway?"

Jazmin told her.

Clea tutted. "Never mind," she said consolingly. "I remember I had puppy fat too when I was your age. Don't worry, you'll grow out of it."

"Excuse me!" Jazmin declared indignantly. "I do not have puppy fat!"

Clea looked her up and down, her eyebrows gently lifting. "Oh, really? Sorry. My mistake. Must be just fat then," she said.

Jazmin glared at her.

"Hey, whatever." Clea shrugged. She waved a dismissive claw. "You'll have to look in the end closet. I think there's some big stuff in there that might fit you." She opened the far door, then sank gracefully back into a chair, grabbing a glossy fashion mag. Ignoring Jazmin's baleful expression, she began flicking through the pages. "I'd check out the black stuff at the far end of the rail if I were you," she suggested from behind the magazine. "Black's generally supposed to be slimming."

What was with that girl? Jazmin asked herself angrily some ten minutes later, when she'd finally escaped from Clea's room clutching an armful of black items. She was such a cow! And somewhere along the line, she seemed to have undergone a total tactectomy. Puppy fat indeed! Jazmin's eyes narrowed. Her cousin's superior attitude was really hacking her off. Their relationship was definitely on the slide. And it had hardly kicked to start off with.

Back in her own room once more, Jazmin stood sideways in front of her bedroom mirror, frowning at her reflection in the glass. She sucked in her stomach. She'd never visualized herself as fat before. Before she'd tried on Clea's thin clothes, that was. She pulled a face. Ewww! Maybe there *was* a bit too much hip and not enough hooray, she decided. She should cut back a little on the canteen lunches and the pre- and post-meal snacks.

Sighing, she laid the pile of black clothes on her bed and began to try them on. She was fed up with being treated like she was some dumb little kid. She tried on a skintight pair of black trousers, wincing painfully as she hauled up the zip. And it wasn't even as if her cousin really cared where she was, or what she was doing. The reality here was that Clea was only looking out for her because she had been told to do so. Given the choice, she couldn't have cared less.

And yet they were supposed to be family, Jazmin reasoned, gritting her teeth as she tried unsuccessfully to back-button her cousin's elegant, lacy top. Families should be there for each other. There was a ripping sound. Jazmin laid the torn top back down on the bed with the rest of Clea's funereal cast-offs. Maybe there was a metaphor here. She didn't fit into Clea's life like she didn't fit into Clea's clothes. Or this place. And it looked like she never would. Period.

JAZMIN DECIDED TO DEDICATE AS MUCH OF THE NEXT DAY AS SHE COULD TO TRYING TO FIND OUT ABOUT THE STRANGE BOY SHE'D MET. SHE BEGAN BY CHECKING OUT ALL THE PLACES IN THE LEARNING centre that were favourite stopping-off areas: the foyer, the canteen, the resources room, the water cooler and the area behind the Humanity and Ethics block where the older male students gathered to smoke. He wasn't there. She asked around. No joy.

She even lowered her standards and joined the boy-worshippers, who spent every recess walking round the perimeter of the fake-grass football pitch and who knew every boy in the school. He didn't play football. She spent all day searching. But there was no sign of the boy anywhere. Nobody seemed to know who he was either. It was a total mystery. Clea had told her that all the kids in the city went to the learning centre. So why didn't he?

As soon as her last class ended, Jazmin hurried to the learning-centre entrance for a last try at finding the mystery boy. She positioned herself in a quiet corner and watched the students leaving the building. The boy she'd met was not amongst them. Bummer. Now there was nothing left to do, nowhere to look. She had run out of ideas. Jazmin set off back to the apartment to get ready for the meal out. This had not been a good day, she decided. She'd totally failed to locate the boy – and she never liked to admit defeat. She had two assignments to do over the weekend. Her stomach was growling because she'd missed lunch. And she hadn't heard from her mum yet. A real un-beach of a day.

Jazmin kicked an empty can along the walkway. When she had a bad day, she liked to cheer herself up with the comforting thought that at least she got to go home at night. Whereas now, she thought gloomily, she didn't. She liked to remind herself that there was always a welcoming fridge full of leftovers waiting for her to raid. Whereas here, although there was a fridge (a capacious one), she still didn't feel comfortable raiding it. And tonight she'd have to make polite conversation with her relatives over dinner, when all she really wanted to do was curl up with a good book and a bag of cookies and sleep in her own bed again. And to cap it all, she was going to have to wear an unflattering long black dress that belonged to Clea and made her look like a finalist in a Miss Mortuary Contest. Gee, sometimes life really sucked!

Feeling extremely sorry for herself, Jazmin cut across the shopping atrium. At least she was beginning to know her way around. That was something positive. She stood and waited for the elevator to take her to her uncle and aunt's apartment block. And then, as she was standing by the doors, she suddenly felt a familiar prickling feeling on the back of her neck. As if somebody, somewhere, was watching her.

Jazmin looked round. There *was* someone watching her! Lurking in the shadows by one of the steel pillars, she saw a strange, unearthly figure dressed from head to toe in glowing white. It had a chalk-white face, deep, sinister, black-rimmed eyes that were staring straight at her and a strange, blood-red mouth. White hair curled like smoke around its head. Jazmin gasped. Her heart skipped a beat. She froze, felt her throat tightening. Was it a ghost? Suddenly, the figure came straight towards her, the grotesque mouth widening into a scarlet-gashed grimace.

She opened her mouth and screamed at the top of her voice.

The white figure stopped. It spoke. "My, you *are* jumpy, aren't you!" it said.

There was something familiar about that voice. She recognized it, had heard it somewhere before. Jazmin paused, stared a bit more closely at the strange white-clad form, and suddenly realized who it was. "Oh, it's you!" she gasped. Then she paused, frowning in disbelief, "But you're..."

"An entertainer?" The boy produced three shiny silver balls from a pocket, spinning them above his head. "A master of magic, a paragon of prestidigitation?"

"A clown? Uh – you're dressed as a CLOWN???"

The boy pocketed the spinning balls and performed an elaborate and courtly bow. "Correct. Today I am Tonda the white-faced clown, at your service. And tomorrow? Who knows who I shall be."

Jazmin gaped at him.

The strange boy held out his hand. There was a bunch of bright paper flowers in it. "For you," he said simply.

Blushing furiously, Jazmin accepted the flowers.

"Your name is Jazmin, isn't it?" the boy said.

"Oh, wow! How did you know that?" she gasped.

The boy grinned and pointed to her bag. The luggage label was still dangling from the zip. JAZMIN DAWSON, it said, in big black letters.

Der, Jazmin thought. How dumb am I! "Right. Er...and your name is Tonda," she said brightly.

"You can call me Tonda if you like."

"Isn't that your name?"

"It can be, if you want."

Jazmin pulled a face. For pig's sake! This boy could vague up a conversation better than her cousin. Tonda's soft, teasing brown eyes held hers for a brief second. Then he glanced down at the impossibly large cardboard watch attached by a giant safety pin to his baggy white trousers. "Ah. Sorry Jazmin, I have to go now," he said. "Kid's birthday party on the eighty-third floor. Mustn't keep my public waiting."

He shot her a smile – at least Jazmin presumed that's what it was.

"Look, tomorrow my group's doing a show in the east atrium forecourt," he told her. "Perhaps you'd like to come and watch?"

Jazmin nodded. "Yeah, why not?"

"Ten o'clock. See you there," the boy said.

Jazmin stood and waited for her elevator to arrive. Hey, mission accomplished, she thought smugly. She had met up with the good-looking boy again and now she knew his name. Although she wasn't absolutely convinced about the clown thing. Clowns did not feature high on her list of good people to hang out with. But it was probably only a part-time job, she reassured herself. Something he did after school and at weekends. Still, she'd been invited to see his show – which was practically a date, wasn't it? Suddenly, Jazmin felt much happier. It had been a bad day. But it was getting better by the minute.

THE NONDESCRIPT WOMAN BREAKFASTING AT A CAFÉ ON THE BOULEVARD ST. MICHEL BARELY REGISTERED A SECOND GLANCE FROM THE PARISIANS BUSTLING BY AS SHE DIPPED A MORNING-fresh croissant into her aromatic black coffee. Nobody paid her the slightest attention as she keyed in some numbers on a minute keyboard and stared intently down at the sleepy-eyed face that materialized onto the tiny screen.

"Did I wake you? Sorry," she said.

"No, it's okay, Mum. I'm up, really," Jazmin lied, stifling a yawn. "Hey, where are you? How's it going?"

"I'm in Europe," Assia told her. "I'm sitting outside a little café having breakfast." She focused the screen on her white china plate, the big gold-rimmed cup.

"Looks nice. Are you coming home?"

Assia Dawson smiled ruefully. She had guessed her daughter would ask this question. She also guessed her daughter already knew the answer. "Not just yet," she said.

Jazmin's face fell.

"Maybe soon, though. Listen, are you having a good time? Are they spoiling you?"

"We went to a posh restaurant last night. Chinese. I had duck pancakes."

"Mmmm...lucky you. And Clea? I bet you're both getting on like a house on fire."

"Yeah, something like that."

"What are you planning to do today?"

"Nothing much. Shopping, the usual stuff."

"Great. See, I said you'd enjoy yourself. Look, I'll speak to you very soon. Have a perfect day. Bye, sweetheart. Love you."

Assia Dawson finished her call just as the waiter brought over a tiny silver plate. On it lay a folded-up piece of paper. She unfolded the paper, read the contents. Then, placing a couple of coins on the red-checked tablecloth, she pushed back her chair and hurried off in the direction of the Quai de Montebello, deftly sidestepping the open boxes of fruit and vegetables piled up all along the pavement.

She was on her way to find a bookshop in the Rue de la Bucherie. Someone was waiting for her there. Someone she'd arranged to meet. Someone with important information. The search for the missing body was rapidly narrowing down, becoming more focused. The net had been cast.

JAZMIN SLID OUT FROM UNDER THE DUVET, AND GOT UP. SO HER MUM THOUGHT SHE AND CLEA WERE GETTING ON LIKE A HOUSE ON FIRE, DID SHE? UH-HUH. JAZMIN THREW UP A MENTAL PICTURE of a house on fire. Flames shooting everywhere. People shouting and yelling and running in all directions. Right. Perhaps it wasn't such a bad description after all.

She dressed and made her way downstairs. There was nobody in the kitchen. Her uncle and aunt were not up yet. On Saturday, they usually had a lie-in before they went into work mid-morning. Jazmin guessed Ed and Clea were also still in bed. Good. She didn't want to have to tell Clea where she was going. Jazmin was beginning to bitterly resent the way her cousin kept tabs on her all the time, like she was a wayward pet or a little kid who couldn't be trusted out on her own. Clea seriously needed to get a life and stop ruining other people's. Jazmin grabbed herself some breakfast, then set off to find the venue where the show was going to take place.

In the east atrium, an impressively large crowd had gathered to watch the clown show. Rows of kids squatted at the front, some waving coloured flags or bright balloons. Behind them, parents stood indulgently handing out sweets or reprimands as the occasion demanded. Jazmin noticed a posse of seniors sat on benches to one side, probably mumbling on about how clown shows were much better in the old days. And there were the inevitable gangs of younger boys buzzing about, maintaining their distance and wearing suitably bored expressions on their faces. Jazmin also recognized several students from Clea's classes. Instinctively, she positioned herself well away from them. She didn't want some busybody snitching to her cousin.

As soon as the big steel-and-glass clock struck ten, sounds of discordant music could be heard in the distance. Small children started to wriggle excitedly. Suddenly, a side panel in the wall slid back and a motley group of clowns, gaudily dressed in oversized patchwork trousers and impossibly shaped hats garnished with droopy flowers, marched solemnly into the centre of the crowd. Each clown was playing a musical instrument and they were doing it very loudly and badly.

Jazmin spotted Tonda instantly. He was dressed in the same sparkling-white costume as before, his face once again garishly painted chalk-white, with black triangles under his eyes. Today, however, he had discarded the curly, white candyfloss wig. His hair was greased flat and he was wearing a tiny white conical hat with black pompoms. Tonda was leading the parade of clowns. His instrument was a silver toy trumpet and he was pulling a green and yellow striped handcart behind him. Sitting in the cart was a mournful-looking little mongrel dog, wearing a pink ruff round its neck.

The crowd laughed, catcalled. The clown band circled a couple of times, playing their crooked music. Then, to the accompaniment of loud applause, they formed a ragged line and bowed. They piled their instruments into the cart. The dog jumped out and began racing round and round, barking. The show had begun.

Jazmin had never reckoned much to clowns before, but over the next hour, her negativity underwent a severe change. Juggling, somersaulting, leaping, play-fighting, the clowns delighted the watching crowd. The pace was fast and frenetic. Everything was done in mime, but so skilful were the actors that the audience understood every nuance of their performance. And when the show culminated in the staging of a mock clown wedding, complete with clown bride and groom and a couple of comic (male) bridesmaids, the little dog carrying a cushion on which reposed a pair of golden handcuffs, the crowd roared its approval.

Custard pies were thrown at the happy couple as a grand

finale. Then the clowns lined up once more and solemnly bowed. The performance was over. The audience continued applauding as the little dog trotted round carrying a small bucket in its mouth, which was soon filled with coins and tokens. The clowns, their faces streaked with runnels of sweat, started loading up the cart with their props.

Jazmin edged forwards through the crowd, until she reached the front. Tonda was demonstrating his juggling skills to a group of small boys, who watched in wide-eyed amazement as the bright silver balls circled like tiny planets above his head. As soon as he saw her, he palmed the balls and came straight over. "Hey, Jazmin, you made the show," Tonda greeted her. He looked pleased to see her there.

"Yeah, and it was great. Really good. I enjoyed it," Jazmin told him.

Tonda gave her his weird, shiny, crimson grin. "We have another performance this afternoon," he said. "But right now I have some time-out. Would you like to go and get lunch somewhere?"

Oh, wow, Jazmin thought. I just got asked out by this good-looking, older boy. She paused, savouring the moment. She'd like to take this moment, press it in a book so that she could take it out every now and then and remember it. She flashed Tonda a dazzling smile.

Tonda nodded briefly. "Okay, that's good. I'll just help the others tidy up," he said. "Meet you back here in fifteen minutes?" His dark, velvety-brown eyes met hers, then glanced swiftly over her shoulder. Suddenly, his expression altered, became wary. "Ah. Don't look now, but I think someone is watching you," he said.

Jazmin groaned. Not again! She spun round and her heart sank. Oh, pig! Why was there *never* a runaway truck when you wanted one? There, standing a couple of feet away, with her arms folded and a very sour expression on her face, was her cousin Clea.

"HELLO, WHAT WERE YOU THINKING ABOUT?" CLEA DAWSON SCOLDED. "YOU JUST WALKED OUT OF THE APARTMENT WITHOUT TELLING ME WHERE YOU WERE GOING."

"You could have called me," Jazmin said sulkily.

"I called you. Believe me, I called you. I tried for ages, but your micro's off," Clea said exasperatedly. "Look, I thought I made it quite clear to you that you must tell me where you're going. I'm supposed to be looking after you. If it wasn't for Xinna spotting you in the crowd, I'd never have known where you were." As she spoke, Clea gestured towards a pretty blonde girl standing nearby. She was talking away avidly into her own micro. Jazmin recognized her as one of Clea's group of nasty girlfriends. Gloom descended.

"Well, I'm sorry," she muttered, tight-lipped. Which was true, she thought. She *was* sorry. Sorry her cousin was treating her like a little kid who couldn't be trusted out alone. Sorry she had turned up to spoil things.

The blonde girl finished her call and strolled over to join them.

"*Ewww,* clowns are *so* not discreet," she drawled languidly.

"You were watching them," Jazmin countered. "I saw you."

The girl eye-rolled. "Oh *puh-leease*!" she protested. "I was *not* watching them. I was minding my *little brother* who was watching them. *Big* difference."

Jazmin blinked at her. She'd never met anybody who talked in italics before.

"Whereas you were actually speaking to one of them!" Clea exclaimed. "What were you doing talking to a stupid clown?"

Damn, Jazmin thought. "He's not a stupid clown. His name's Tonda," she said defiantly.

"*Tonda!*" Xinna shrieked. "*Ewww!* What sort of a name is *that*?"

Jazmin glared at her. "It's his sort of a name, okay? What sort of name is Xinna?"

Xinna looked from Jazmin to Clea and shook her head. "You *so* have your work cut out for you," she told Clea sadly.

"Meaning what, exactly?" Jazmin inquired icily. She gave Xinna a look that could have performed surgery.

But Xinna merely grinned, brushing her aside like an annoying fly. She flipped open her micro, keyed in a number and spoke a couple of curt commands. A second later, a small boy detached himself slowly from the eager crowd of little kids still hanging hopefully around the clowns. He trailed towards them, glancing longingly back over his shoulder.

Xinna issued another order into her micro. Sighing heavily, the little boy fell obediently into step a couple of paces behind her, holding his own micro in one hand, a purple balloon in the other. His mouth was turned down at the corners. Jazmin felt sorry for him. She noticed that Xinna never looked at her little brother once. She just strode off fast, talking to him on her micro as if he wasn't really there.

As soon as the two of them had gone, Jazmin furtively checked the time. The minutes were ticking away. Soon, Tonda would be back. She needed to get rid of Clea and fast. She had no intention of introducing the two of them. Apart from the way Clea snubbed her and put her down all the time, there was the undeniable fact that her cousin was very pretty. And better dressed. And probably much nearer the boy's age. And if she chose, Clea could turn from Nasty Clea to Nice Clea in an instant and do the charm thing like a professional. She definitely didn't want Clea muscling in on Tonda when she'd scarcely got to know him herself.

"Right, er...I'm going to the library now," she told Clea. "Got assignments to do." She sighed exaggeratedly. "Honestly, you'd think they'd let me off because I'm only visiting, wouldn't you?"

Clea pursed her lips. She eyed Jazmin, frowning slightly.

"Quadratic equations – ugh! Hey, maybe you could come and help me?" Jazmin suggested. She was fairly sure that doing somebody else's maths homework was not top of Clea's to-do list for a sunny Saturday morning.

"Well..." Clea hesitated, the tension between duty and desire almost palpable.

"And then I thought I'd go home and tidy my room," Jazmin continued brightly, her face poker-player blank. "Oh, boy, is it ever messy! You can hardly see the floor. And this afternoon, I might go to the park to read my books – unless you'd like me to do something with you, of course?" she finished up, assuming a keen and innocently helpful expression.

Just as she hoped, Clea instantly backed off. "Uh – no, it's okay," she said. "You do whatever you want. Just as long as you're all right. Actually, I have stuff I need to get on with."

Yeah, I bet you do, Jazmin thought. She mentally promised herself once again that, some day soon, she was going to find out exactly what it was Clea got up to when she was supposed to be with her friends or minding her cousin. Soon, but not right now. Out of the corner of her eye, she saw Tonda making his way towards her.

"Okay, have a nice day," she said meekly. "And I'm sorry for upsetting you."

"Right. I'll see you later, then," Clea said. She adjusted her tiny shoulder bag and, to Jazmin's intense relief, set off quickly in the totally opposite direction to Tonda.

CLEA DAWSON HURRIED ACROSS THE CROWDED ATRIUM. NOW SHE WAS GOING TO BE LATE, AND IT WAS ALL HER STUPID COUSIN'S FAULT. WATCHING A CLOWN SHOW, SHE THOUGHT DISGUSTEDLY. Honestly, what was the drelby girl like! She had told her parents right at the start, when they'd first informed her that her young cousin Jazmin was coming to stay for a couple of weeks, that okay, she was prepared to show her round, be polite, but she was not prepared to act as an unpaid babysitter. And, as she had feared, just look what she'd ended up doing! She had her own life to lead, Clea thought resentfully. And, right now, her whole family seemed to be conspiring to prevent her from leading it.

THE CIRCUS HAD FASCINATED TONDA FOR AS LONG AS HE COULD REMEMBER. HE'D BEEN TAKEN TO SEE HIS VERY FIRST SHOW WHEN HE WAS ONLY THREE YEARS OLD. HE COULD STILL RECALL THE occasion clearly: the blaring music, the ringmaster in his top hat and long striped coat. The white ponies trotting round and round the ring, their bright harness jingling, their black shiny hooves lightly touching the yellow sawdust. The beautiful lady in a pink tutu who rode bareback, cracking her long whip. There were daredevil acrobats, defying gravity as they tumbled and leaped, high-wire walkers performing incredible balancing feats on a length of wire so fine it looked almost invisible to the small boy far below.

And then, just when Tonda thought that he had seen and experienced everything, in came the clowns, juggling plates, riding unicycles, creating their own zany world of madness and make-believe. And he was transfixed. It wasn't just their amazing costumes and the distinctive make-up, it was the sheer brilliance of their performance. Tonda saw at once that the clowns were much more than just funny guys – each clown could juggle, tumble, wire-walk, ride. They could do it all. They were the supreme circus performers. In that one moment, the boy knew exactly what he wanted to be when he grew up: a clown. But not just any clown. Not the knockabout Auguste, or the tramp-like Charlie. He wanted to be the white-faced clown. The mysterious, sinister clown. He wanted to wear the white spangled suit and the white conical cap and be in control of everyone.

Big dreams for a small child. In the meantime, however, there were other things to fill his time: school and friends and growing up in a big family in a small village in the countryside. Still, every year, when the circus came to town, Tonda was always there, watching the acts from the front row and, as he got older, helping out behind the scenes. This was where he learned the art of the circus: to juggle using an instinct faster than rational thought, which made his hands act almost by themselves. Where he learned the timing that allowed his body to somersault through the air at astounding speed and still land upright on his feet.

This was what Tonda told Jazmin as they ate lunch together in one of the gleaming food court cafés. The more he practised his circus skills, he explained, the better he got. And the better he got, the more he knew he simply had to join the circus. It was the only place he wanted to be. And then one day, when he was sixteen, his parents dropped the bombshell: they had arranged for him to leave school and go to the nearest technical college. It was time to get some qualifications, they told him. Time to learn a trade and start earning a proper wage. It was time to abandon his dreams.

"It was difficult," Tonda admitted. "So many rows, so much unhappiness. So I waited until autumn, when the circus came to town again. Then I ran away from home to join them. And here I am. I haven't been back to see my family since."

"Oh, wow!" Jazmin breathed, gazing at Tonda with wonder-wide eyes. This was so far and away the most romantic story she'd ever heard.

Tonda smiled across the table at her. "The way I see it, your dreams are the most important things in the whole of your life. More important than anything or anyone in the world. You must follow them, wherever they lead."

"You are so right," Jazmin agreed, nodding fervently.

There was a pause.

"But," she added, "don't you miss your family sometimes?"

The boy shrugged. "A clown laughs because he does not cry," he remarked elliptically.

Then Tonda told her about the rest of the group. How they were all performers like himself, students at the Moscow Circus School. How, every summer, the students toured round, putting on shows, earning money to support themselves through college. Two weeks ago, he said, his group had been in Venice, entertaining the crowds in the Piazza San Marco as part of the celebrations of *La Sensa*. Now they were here, in the biggest sky-city in the western hemisphere. In a short time, they would return to Europe and then, in September, go back to the school to continue their training.

"And you?" Tonda asked when he had finished explaining all this to an enthralled Jazmin. "What about your life?"

Jazmin pulled a face and did a palms-up. "Hey, my life's very ordinary," she said dismissively. And it was so true, she thought sadly to herself. Compared to Tonda and his friends, she had done nothing, been nowhere.

"Well, I think you are a very interesting person," Tonda said and he smiled across the table at her.

Jazmin felt her cheeks going bright scarlet. I wish, she thought. I so wish. She gave him an embarrassed smile, then buried her burning face in her ice-cream sundae. Jaz Dawson, secret agent and crime fighter was an interesting person, she thought to herself. Jaz Dawson's creator was a grey, vanilla person. She sighed, letting her shoulders sag. She really had to stop living her life inside her head. The boy was absolutely right. She should Follow Her Dreams, and Stop Using Them As A Substitute For Real Life.

ASSIA UNDERSTOOD THE SIGNIFICANCE OF DREAMS. DREAMS WERE THE BRAIN'S WAY OF SORTING AND FILING. MAKING SENSE OF THE EVERYDAY STUFF THAT HAPPENED IN ONE'S LIFE. WHICH WAS interesting, she thought, because she didn't remember any of the stuff currently featuring in her dreams ever happening to her.

Right now, Assia Dawson's dreams had a fragmented quality to them. There was no narrative. They were like bright mirror-shards of nightmare: the sound of huge wings beating, as if a great imprisoned bird was struggling to free itself; a falling into vortical darkness, this always accompanied by terrible screaming and howls of agony; feelings of total despair and loss.

She tucked her jacket behind her back, trying to protect her body from slamming against the sides of the lorry. They had been on the road for hours. What was the time now? 3.00 a.m. Too early in the morning to be early in the morning, she thought ruefully. Assia eased herself into a more comfortable position. All around her, people were sleeping. She marvelled at their ability to ignore discomfort. Still, most of them were university students, she reminded herself. Discomfort was part of the deal. What did they care? As long as they got fed and paid at the end of the day.

Assia closed her eyes, tried to rest. She thought about her daughter. Jazmin was so unlike Assia had been at the same age. When she'd been a young girl, she'd been quiet, studious, a conformist. It had been Ian, her twin brother, who'd always tested the boundaries. Jazmin was far more like him – continually questioning, never satisfied with superficial answers. It was good to be like that.

Good, but problematic for those around her.

Assia breathed a sigh. Suddenly, she felt very lonely and very far from home. And she missed her daughter. Missed her terribly. But at least she knew Jazmin was safe. That was the important thing. Safe, where nobody could find her. She closed her eyes, surrendering her weary body to the jolting movement of the lorry.

The lorry thundered on through the night on its way towards the Czech border. They were all going to pick cherries on the estate of some rich countess, near Prague. Nothing special about that. Except that the countess and her husband owned the Roztok Institute, an independent, non-governmental scientific research establishment. And the Roztok Institute, she had been reliably informed by her Paris contact, had recently taken a midnight delivery of something unusual that they were keeping very quiet about.

The net was closing.

THE ALARM SHRILLED LOUDLY, WAKING JAZMIN UP WITH A SHOCK. IT WAS 6.00 A.M. FOR A BRIEF MOMENT, SHE DIDN'T HAVE A CLUE WHERE SHE WAS. SHE STARED ROUND THE UNFAMILIAR WHITE room. Hospital? Accident? Then normality kicked in and she remembered. She was in her uncle and aunt's house. It was Monday morning. Follow Your Dreams time. And hey, she was going to start off with a healthy run.

Groaning, Jazmin rolled out of bed and pulled on her sweats. She really didn't want to do this, but she had no choice. She'd been doing some hard thinking over the weekend, and she'd come to the regrettable conclusion that although her mind was totally razor sharp (as befitted a secret agent and crime fighter), her body did not quite match up. It was flabby and unfit. So she had decided that if she ran twice a week and maybe had fewer snack attacks, she'd bear slightly more resemblance to the sleek, glamorous person in her head and slightly less to the untidy, chubby person in the mirror. *Swift*, *leggy* and *kick-ass gorgeous* were not currently words you could truthfully apply to her. Although right now, neither were *keen* and *enthusiastic*, she thought grimly, making her way quietly downstairs. Funny how good intentions always turned out to be bummers when you tried to carry them out for real.

Quietly, Jazmin let herself out of the apartment. She did a few hamstring stretches, jogged on the spot for a while and then set off at an optimistically brisk pace along the walkway. It was surprising how many people were out and about this fine summer morning. She passed fellow joggers who waved jauntily at her as they sped by, dog walkers, seniors limbering up gently for their morning doze, and, in the local park, the obligatory group of super-fits in shiny spandex working out to high-energy music.

For the next thirty minutes, Jazmin ran round the neighbourhood. Then she pulled up, bent double and sucked in air. Her face was pouring sweat and her hair was plastered to her head. She held her knees and gasped. Maybe she wasn't cut out to be this healthy, she thought, trying to wipe sweat away from her face but discovering that she couldn't lift her arm that high. She forced herself to straighten up. No pain, no gain, she told herself grimly. She took a couple of deep, painful breaths, then jogged slowly back the way she had come.

When Jazmin got in, the apartment was still early-morning quiet. She went straight to the kitchen area. She had only managed to push herself the last part with promises of a really nice breakfast. Ignoring the fact that this was not her kitchen, not her fridge, she opened the door and began foraging about inside. Desperate times required desperate measures. She discovered some fruit and some leftover double-layer chocolate cake from Sunday's dinner. Boy, what a tough decision. Clea entered the kitchen just as she was licking the last of the chocolate off her fingers.

"You've been running?" Clea exclaimed, her big blue eyes widening even further in astonishment.

"Yeah," Jazmin told her. She decided to stay sitting down, because her legs were too wobbly to stand up.

Clea looked almost impressed. "My, my," she murmured. "Do you run when you're back home?"

"Oh yeah, all the time," Jazmin lied. "And I work out at the gym."

Clea helped herself to juice and a small piece of fruit. "My, my," she murmured again.

Jazmin guessed the only exercise Clea ever did was jump to conclusions.

"You can come with me next time, if you want."

"Umm...thanks. I'll certainly bear it in mind."

The usual awkward silence fell between them. Clea sighed. She sipped her juice in an exhausted fashion, as if she'd been the one out for the early-morning run and not

Jazmin. "So...I guess your mum is still on her 'secret mission' then?" she remarked languidly.

Jazmin nodded. "Uh-huh. I guess." She suspected which way her cousin's thoughts were heading. Yeah, Miss Designer Princess, you're going to have to put up with me for a bit longer, she thought acidly.

Clea finished her minuscule breakfast and rose with graceful fluidity out of her seat. "You'd better hurry up and get ready for school," she said reproachfully. "You don't want to be late, do you?"

"No, Clea. Of course I don't," Jazmin murmured meekly, flashing her cousin a smile so thin it could have strolled down a catwalk and modelled designer clothes.

Jazmin went up to her room, peeled off her sweaty tracksuit and hit the shower. Actually, she had no intention of going to school today. She had far more important stuff to do. She'd arranged to meet up with Tonda later. He had promised to introduce her to his friends. Jazmin really wanted him to like her. She wanted his friends to be impressed with her too. Which meant she was going to have to find something good to wear. On the face of it, this was going to be a problem, because as well as No Nice Restaurant Clothes, she had also failed to bring any Meeting Cute Boys Clothes. And she didn't have time to shop. But in reality, it actually wasn't going to be a problem. Luckily for her, she could source what she wanted right here on the premises. Jazmin waited until she was quite sure that the apartment was empty. Then she snuck out of her own room and made her way quietly to Clea's room.

EVERYONE HAS A CONDITIONAL CLAUSE IN THEIR LIFE. AN UNSPOKEN ADD-ON TO THE RULES. PHRASES LIKE "UNLESS I REALLY HAVE TO" OR "EXCEPT FOR...". JAZMIN DAWSON WAS NOT IN the habit of helping herself to other people's stuff without their permission. But she was desperate and this was one of those conditional-clause moments. So she pushed open the door of her cousin's bedroom and stepped inside.

Clea's room smelled faintly and not unattractively of the expensive floral scent she used. And it was very, very tidy. Jazmin stood in the centre of the room, shaking her head sadly. No girl in their right mind should live like this. It was so unhealthy.

She opened the end closet door and began to rummage among Clea's clothes. She reminded herself that she was only looking through the unwanted stuff. It was unlikely that Clea would really care. After all, she never wore any of this stuff now, and she'd kind of given her permission anyway, hadn't she? Finally, after much searching, Jazmin found a couple of nice tops and some trousers that both fitted her and weren't black. Result!

Jazmin shut the closet door. She paused, then gave in to temptation. She opened up the other closet doors and started to have a good nose around the rest of her cousin's stuff. Amazing. There wasn't a single item that didn't have a designer label. She must spend thousands on her clothes. She was so lucky. And her shoes. Jazmin had been dying to investigate Clea's shoes. She lifted down a few boxes and took a look inside. How did she walk in these things? Whoa – and see the prices! Jazmin didn't spend in a year what Clea spent on a pair of wispy leather straps held together on scarily high heels. They surely lived in different worlds.

Shaking her head in total disbelief, Jazmin replaced the boxes carefully, making sure they all faced outwards with the pictures of the shoes clearly visible. Her cousin was such a major control freak, she thought. One look inside her closet said everything you needed to know about her. (And she wore bum-flossing underwear too – she'd seen some of it in the dryer. Yechhh!) Jazmin took a quick final look around the room, checking that she'd left everything just as she'd found it. She didn't want to face any awkward questions when Clea got in later.

She was just about to zap back to her own room to change when she noticed a tiny dazzling shimmer of light on one of her cousin's walls. The morning sunlight streaming through Clea's window had caught a tiny silver pendant in the shape of two wings that was hanging from her dressing-table mirror.

Jazmin paused. She stared at the pendant. It was very

unusual. She couldn't recall ever seeing Clea wearing it. Tempted, she took a couple of steps towards the dressing table. That pendant would look good with the stuff she was planning to wear... For a second, her hand hovered over the dressing table. Then she drew back. It was one thing to help herself to her cousin's cast-offs. Her jewellery was something else. Jewellery was personal. Maybe this pendant meant something special to Clea. Perhaps, Jazmin thought, grinning to herself, it was a gift from her secret boyfriend!

Leaving the pendant exactly where she'd found it, Jazmin quit her cousin's room and went to get herself ready.

"...AND THIS IS PIERRE, THAT IS AUGUSTE PLAYING WITH SAUSAGE THE DOG, AND OVER THERE DOING THE PAPERWORK IS TONI," TONDA SAID. "I THINK CHOCOLAT IS GETTING SOME DRINKS." HE MIMED putting on the kettle and Pierre nodded, pointing to Jazmin and raising his painted eyebrows in exaggerated puzzlement.

"He wants to know if you would like something to drink," Tonda translated. Jazmin nodded. The clown picked up an imaginary cup, held a non-existent spoon over an invisible sugar bowl and raised his eyebrows once again.

"Two spoonfuls of sugar, thanks," Jazmin told him, grinning.

The clown called Pierre regarded her sadly through his huge owl-like spectacles. He was dressed in an oversized green and red check suit, the trousers held up by red and white striped braces. His black hair was tipped with bright rainbow colours, and stood out in spikes all over his head, giving him the appearance of a myopic hedgehog who'd had a fight in a paint factory.

"Doesn't he speak?" Jazmin asked Tonda as Pierre shuffled off in his extra-large boots. Tonda looked at her with a puzzled expression on his painted face. "I thought he just did."

"Oh. Ah. Right. I see," Jazmin lied.

However, as the morning progressed, she began to understand what Tonda meant. The clowns communicated with each other as they did with the audience, by using a seamless mixture of words and mime, both of which appeared to have equal status in their eyes. It was just another aspect of their strange and bizarre world. Like the way they called each other by their clown name, not their real one. (Although Tonda told her that was totally logical. After all, when you were in costume, it *was* your real name.)

The clowns were rehearsing in a quiet area just off one of the shopping malls. Nobody was paying them much attention – it was late morning, so people were either at work or shopping for groceries, and all the kids were in school or nursery. For a while, Jazmin sat on the floor, hands clasped round her knees, watching them. The clown called Auguste, who wore blue overalls, a red rubber nose, had bright red hair and was – she suddenly realized – female, was throwing a small ball to Sausage the dog, who cleverly caught it and balanced it on his nose. Suddenly, Auguste looked at Jazmin, and asked her something in a foreign language.

Jazmin stared at her, felt confused. "I'm sorry," she apologized. "I don't understand."

"Auguste wants to know how old you are," Tonda translated.

"Oh, right. I'm sixteen," Jazmin told her smoothly. She'd decided over the weekend she was going to have to lie about her age. She didn't think Tonda would be interested in her if he knew how old she really was. Auguste glanced pointedly down at her, a quizzical look on her bulbous-nosed face.

"But I'm a lot taller than I look," Jazmin added quickly.

Auguste shrugged. She asked something else.

"Auguste wants to know if you're still at school."

"I'm leaving school this term," Jazmin said. It was partly true, she reminded herself – she would be leaving this school as soon as her mum got back.

"And what will you do then?" Tonda asked.

Jazmin shrugged. "Hey, who knows? Maybe I'll get a job, maybe work abroad, like my mother does. I haven't really thought that far ahead."

Auguste held out her hands towards them, palms-up. Then crossed them over her heart. She looked at Jazmin, head on one side, then flicked a lightning glance at Tonda, her blue eyes under their long fake red lashes dancing mischievously.

"Auguste says she hopes you achieve your heart's desire," Tonda told her solemnly.

Jazmin felt herself blushing. To cover her confusion, she picked up a couple of spare juggling balls and began throwing them clumsily into the air.

"Would you like to learn how to juggle?" Tonda inquired, after watching her efforts for a few seconds.

"Yeah – definitely," Jazmin agreed enthusiastically. Anything to deflect attention, she thought. That Auguste was a bit too clever!

Jazmin stayed with the group for the whole morning, watching them practise and getting to know them. Then she joined the clowns for lunch in their rented flat and got to know them a bit better. Pierre was the mute clown, she discovered, never speaking a word the whole time she was visiting with them. Toni was the tramp clown who rode a tiny unicycle and stilt-walked. Auguste was the only girl; she had a wicked sense of humour, teasing the others and laughing a lot. She talked non-stop in her own language. Chocolat was very tall and striking. He wore a red cap perched on one side of his head, a red coat and black trousers. He and Auguste seemed to be an item.

Sausage the dog appeared to belong to all of them.

But Tonda was by far the nicest of the group, Jazmin decided. He was the most talented too – his juggling and acrobatics were amazing. Jazmin was lost in wonder at his dexterity. And every now and then, Tonda would glance across to where she was feebly throwing the bright silver balls and dropping them, and his face would light up into a smile of encouragement, his dark eyes would shine, and Jazmin's heart would perform a backflip with happiness.

JAZMIN MADE SURE SHE GOT BACK TO THE APARTMENT BEFORE CLEA FINISHED SCHOOL. SHE DIDN'T WANT ANOTHER INTERROGATION. SHE WENT STRAIGHT TO THE KITCHEN, HELPED herself to a healthy snack of fruit and took it up to her room, where her school books lay unopened on the desk. The Homework Fairy was obviously not making house calls. She changed her clothes, folding them up and placing them at the back of her wardrobe. Then she eased off her shoes and lay down on her bed. It had been a good day, she thought. The best since she'd got here. She'd missed a whole day's boring school and almost mastered the one-ball cascade. And most important of all: she had fallen in love.

A few minutes later, Jazmin heard the front door open, which meant that Clea had returned. She slid off the bed and quietly closed her door. But her cousin's return prompted the thought that she still hadn't found out what Clea got up to in her free time. Jazmin sat up, pursed her lips and frowned. She didn't like Clea. In her opinion, her cousin's nose was so up in the air it was probably snowing on her face, but that didn't stop Jazmin from having a major curiosity overload about her secret life. She really wanted to find out where Clea went and what she did there.

Jazmin heard her cousin's high heels tappity-tapping up the wooden stairs. She did some mental knuckle-crunching. So, what would the professionals do? They'd mount an undercover surveillance operation. It was always the best way to get at the truth. Right, she thought. That was exactly what she'd do. All she needed now was a really good disguise.

MEANWHILE, ON A BIG COUNTRY ESTATE JUST OUTSIDE THE CITY OF PRAGUE, IT WAS CHERRY-PICKING TIME. THIS WAS STILL CARRIED OUT IN THE OLD TRADITIONAL WAY. CENTURIES OF TECHNOLOGICAL advancement had never been applied to, and therefore had never solved, the cherry-picking problem. So it was simply a case of climbing up a long ladder, carrying a basket and a wooden pole with assorted cutting devices.

Assia Dawson was undeniably a skilled secret agent. Nobody doubted it. One of the best. She could blend into her surroundings, virtually disappear from the face of the earth. She was a highly trained professional who had never failed to deliver on any mission she'd undertaken. However, she was not a skilled cherry-picker. Far from it.

For a start, she had no head for heights. So she was finding it virtually impossible to juggle all her picking tools and her basket, while at the same time balancing on a tall ladder. And the trouble was, if you lacked the necessary skills, or failed to acquire them quickly, it was all too easy to fall off the ladder.

As she was just about to do.

Assia had a brief, exciting glimpse of the world rushing past her at speed. Then her head made contact with the ground and suddenly, dramatically, everything went black.

NEXT DAY, AFTER HER CLASS ENDED, CLEA MADE YET ANOTHER EXCUSE TO HER FRIENDS. SHE GAVE THEM A LITTLE FINGER-WAVE AND BLEW THEM AN AIR KISS. THEN SHE TURNED HER BACK ON them and hurried away, leaving them to make their leisurely way over to the coffee shop. Round her neck, but at this moment hidden beneath her top, Clea was wearing her silver-winged pendant. Not because it was the latest fashion accessory. Or because it was a gift from a friend. Wearing the pendant was a secret sign. It meant you were a member of the small, select group known as the Angels.

The Angels were very, very exclusive. You did not find the Angels, they found you. That was how it worked.

It wasn't like a store, or a club. You did not choose, you were chosen. Clea had been chosen some months ago. She could not quite remember the exact details of how it had happened. She only knew that something had made her take the elevator up to the top floor of the mall, an area she never usually frequented because it was full of shops that didn't sell clothes.

Then the same weird magnetic force had pulled her into a mysterious little shop crammed with candles, lightballs, ancient healing stones, dream catchers and jars of strange Chinese herbal medicines. Once inside, she had somehow been irresistibly drawn to the back of the shop where a door, painted deep blue with white fluffy clouds, stood invitingly open. Without even thinking, she had gone through the door and into the room behind it. And a whole new world had opened up to her.

Now Clea was a member of the Angels. Not that the name of the group was strictly correct. "Angels" sufficed as a generic term, but within the group itself there were many layers of hierarchy. Angels were actually located right at the bottom – Clea was an angel. Above her were people known as archangels, and at the top, the powerful cherubim and the three seraphim leaders.

Clea stood outside the shop. She became aware of someone coming up behind her. She turned and saw a small clown dressed in a baggy yellow costume, its face painted with a sad grin. Clea glared at it. The small clown stopped, smiled hopefully, and juggled a couple of balls. Clea cut it a look indicating that if asked to distinguish between a clown and a puddle of cat sick, she'd be hard pushed to tell the difference. She swept into the shop, her nose in the air. The small clown shuffled its oversized boots and peered through the window.

Clea slipped into the darkened back room. Immediately, she was surrounded by a crowd of people hugging her, greeting her, caring about her, making her feel welcomed and special. It had been like that from the first – this great wave of love and acceptance flowing out to her, engulfing her. That was why she had been drawn to the group at the beginning. And it was why she was here now.

Thinking back, Clea couldn't remember anybody ever telling her they loved her. It certainly wasn't the sort of thing her parents said. They told her lots of stuff: what they'd bought for her, the sacrifices they'd made for her, how lucky she was and what they expected from her in return, but the actual word "love" was never mentioned. Okay, maybe it was implicit in all those other things, but they'd never actually *said* it. Whereas here, everybody told her they loved her. They actually said it. It was what drew her back, time after time. Love was a powerful drug. Now she had returned once more to get another fix.

Ambient music was playing in the background, as it did before every meeting, and light boxes projected swirling coloured patterns on the walls. The three seraphim, each wearing the long grey robes of leadership, were moving round the room, smiling, greeting and welcoming.

Eventually, one of the seraphim, a tall man in his late thirties with long black hair, deep-set eyes and an intense, serious expression, made his way to the front. This was Seraph Gray, the group's leader, teacher and visionary. He had founded the Angels and he normally led the main meetings. Seraph Gray had an air of authority about him. The rest of the angels felt instinctively that when he spoke, it was the truth. Now, people scurried to find seats. The room fell expectantly silent. It was time to begin.

Seraph Gray raised his arms above his head. "Exult," he intoned in a high sing-song voice.

Everyone raised their arms and responded, "We exult."

"EXULT!" Seraph Gray repeated, louder this time.

"WE EXULT!"

This went on for some time, each repetition faster and louder than the last, until all at once, when the room was ringing with the sounds of exultation, Seraph Gray solemnly raised his left hand. Silence fell. He opened his mouth to speak, then suddenly paused, frowned, his eyes drifting over the heads of the people. Something was happening at the back of the room. Clea turned round to look. It seemed that the small clown had somehow managed to slip into the meeting. Two burly archangels were throwing it out. Seraph Gray waited patiently until the archangels returned, and took up their former positions, arms folded, on either side of the doorway. Then he resumed speaking.

Clea hunched down in her seat in the darkened room and let all the love and the promises flow over her like golden syrup, let them enter her soul and soothe her hungry spirit. Within two seconds, she had forgotten all about the irritating small clown, the boring world outside, and her own pampered, but completely empty life.

ASSIA DAWSON FELT HERSELF SLOWLY REGAINING CONSCIOUSNESS. IT WAS NOT AN UNPLEASANT SENSATION, SHE DECIDED. RATHER LIKE DRIFTING TO THE SUN-DAPPLED SURFACE OF a deep pool. She became aware that she was lying in a comfortable, soft bed. She stretched out a hand and encountered crisp linen sheets, a quilted cover. The air smelled pleasantly of rose petals. She opened her eyes. Sunlight was streaming in through wooden shutters. Well, wherever this was, it bore no resemblance to the rather basic comforts of the student hostel, she thought. This was a very nice, clean, and most of all, a very quiet place. She sat up and looked around.

Instantly, almost as if she had been waiting just outside the room for Assia to wake up, the door opened and a plump, middle-aged woman entered. She wore her auburn-dyed hair pinned up in a neat French pleat and was elegantly dressed in a loose, red silk shirt over navy casual trousers. She nodded when she caught Assia's eye. "Ah, you are awake. How do you feel now?" she asked briskly.

"Fine," Assia said. Was this woman some sort of doctor? "I've got a bit of a headache, but that's all."

"You were very lucky, my dear," the woman told her. She spoke slowly, in a heavily accented voice, as if English was not her native tongue. "That was a nasty fall you had. You could have broken many, *many* bones."

Assia lifted the sheets, and saw for the first time that her left foot and ankle were heavily bandaged. "What happened here?" she cried.

The woman advanced to the foot of the bed. "You broke your ankle, my dear. And fractured a couple of bones in your foot. Still, it could have been worse. My private doctor has taken care of everything, and with a bit of rest, you should soon be fine."

Cursing inwardly, Assia lay back on the pillow. This was not in the plan. This should not have happened. Particularly now, when she was so close to making that all-important discovery.

The woman continued to regard her placidly. There was something a little disconcerting about her expressionless stare. "So," she said finally, "now you will have some breakfast? I shall supervise it personally. After all, it is the least I can do."

Assia frowned. "Sorry, I don't quite understand. Who are you? And where am I?"

"You are in my house," the woman explained. "Allow me to introduce myself. I am Countess Valentina Markova. My husband, Count Eduard Marek, and I own this estate. And you, I believe are Violet Smith? You are thirty-six, single, you work as a teacher in England and you are on holiday in our beautiful country."

Assia's head began to spin wildly. "My clothes, my things..." she said faintly.

"You will find that they are all on the chair by your bed," the countess reassured her. "I'm sure you don't mind, but we had to look through them to find out who you were." She paused. "And I'm afraid we have taken the precaution of removing your gun. Such a *very* unusual thing for a teacher to take on holiday, we thought." The countess gave Assia the sort of smile that lay on sand banks, waiting for unwary swimmers. "My husband and I are so looking forward to getting to know you better, Violet Smith," she purred.

"HER REAL NAME IS ASSIA DAWSON. SHE IS A WIDOW WITH ONE CHILD – A FOURTEEN-YEAR-OLD DAUGHTER CALLED JAZMIN. SHE IS FORTY-THREE, LIVES IN LONDON, ENGLAND AND WORKS FOR THE ISA," Valentina Markova declared triumphantly. She spread cherry jam thickly on a slice of newly baked rye bread.

Marek raised his eyebrows. "How on earth did you find that out?"

The countess smiled complacently. "I have my methods," she said. Her hand slipped down and patted her pocket, which contained the silver pen, picked up and given to her by one of the students.

"You know, I didn't think she looked thirty-six," Marek replied thoughtfully. He shook a finger playfully at the countess across the breakfast table. "Funny how ladies always like to tell little fibs about their age."

The countess shot him a stern glance.

"Except for you, *milenka*, of course," Marek added hastily, lifting the lid of a silver serving dish and helping himself to grilled sausages. "You will always be young – whatever age you are."

Mollified, Countess Valentina nodded graciously. "You know what ISA stands for?"

"Suppose you tell me, *milá*."

"It stands for the International Security Agency. Which means our so-called teacher is not here to pick our cherries. She is in fact a secret agent, probably sent here to spy on us."

Count Marek looked genuinely indignant. "Why? What could we possibly have done?"

The countess sighed. She reminded herself that her beloved husband, for all his irritating little ways, was a brilliant and dedicated scientist. This meant that he did not live in the real world. All that mattered to him was the pursuit of scientific knowledge. In this, he was a purist. Things that bothered everybody else, like the legality, the morality, the ethics of something, were to him merely trivial and inconsequential details on the way.

"I think she may have been sent to ask questions about..." Here, the countess deliberately dropped her voice to a low whisper.

Marek leaned across the table to catch her words. Then straightened up, his face soberly grave. "I am shocked," he exclaimed. "Deeply shocked! Why, this may be the most important scientific experiment of the century." He waved a fork at her. "The march of scientific progress cannot be halted, you know."

"Oh, it won't be," his wife reassured him. She smiled grimly. "Nothing will stand in your way. You can be absolutely sure of that."

MEANWHILE, BACK IN JAZMIN'S HIGH-RISE COMPLEX IN ENGLAND, IT WAS 4.30 P.M. ON A HOT SUMMER'S AFTERNOON AND THE CROWD IN THE EAST ATRIUM WAS WAITING FOR THE CLOWN SHOW TO START. People were getting ready to marvel at the juggling, to be amazed by the fire-eating, to roar with laughter at the slapstick, mayhem and anarchy. They wanted to see the scary white-faced clown, the funny red-nosed clown, the big black clown, the clown with the spiky hair and silly glasses. And, of course, they all wanted to see the brand-new clown: Lemonade.

Lemonade was a sad little yellow clown who wore a pineapple-coloured wig. Lemonade was totally useless. She couldn't do anything right. Lemonade always fumbled the balls she tried to palm-spin. She was such a dweeb that she couldn't even juggle a single club without dropping it on her foot. When Lemonade opened her tiny parasol, it rained on her head. Lemonade was the most pointless, hopeless waste of a clown's costume ever. And the kids loved her.

Jazmin wasn't quite sure where the character of Lemonade had come from. It seemed to have arrived fully formed from the first moment she'd tried on the yellow clown costume and had been shown by Pierre how to apply the distinctive make-up. Suddenly, she had become Lemonade the endearing idiot, the loveable dunce. It was slightly worrying, because Tonda had told her that a clown's character always came from inside, and Jazmin was certain she was nothing like the ditzy yellow clown.

Now she stood waiting at the back of the group, as they prepared to begin the afternoon's performance. She could hear the excited chatter of the kids on the other side of the door, the atmosphere building nicely. She was not nervous at all; after all, things going terribly wrong were all part of the show's appeal and of her particular character.

Jazmin watched the other clowns as they did warm-ups, mimed rapid conversations, or ran quickly through a new routine. She felt a warm glow inside. She was so much part of this. She seemed to have found her niche, the place where she belonged. When she was with Tonda and his friends, she was included, accepted for who she was: a small clown called Lemonade.

All at once, the white clown put a white-gloved finger to his painted lips. The group quietened, focused. The dog, who had been curled up asleep in the cart, suddenly awoke and sat upright, pink tongue lolling. Then Tonda circled his thumb and forefinger, gave a quick nod of his head and said, "It's show time." The clowns raised their assorted musical instruments to their painted lips. Another performance was about to begin.

A COUPLE OF EVENINGS LATER, CLEA DAWSON SAT AT THE FAMILY DINNER TABLE AND STARED DOWN AT HER DINNER PLATE IN DISGUST. SPINACH LASAGNE. HOW REVOLTING, SHE THOUGHT TO HERSELF.

"Is there something wrong?" her mother asked anxiously. "You don't seem to be eating much."

"No, Mummy. It's fine." Clea sighed. She took a tiny bite, washing it down with water. All around her, the rest of the family ate contentedly. Clea felt her gorge rise. The goldfishing mouths. The chewing sounds they were making. Ewww! It was disgusting!

She stole a quick glance around the table. Her father had

his head down over his plate. He was methodically forking the food into his mouth. Her brother Ed was eating at high speed, shovelling dinner in and glancing every now and again at his watch. Clea's upper lip curled. She could just about remember a time when she used to enjoy family dinners. But that was in the past. Now, she simply couldn't wait to get away from her family. They got on her nerves, they set her teeth on edge. They were like a long, sharp fingernail drawn slowly down the blackboard of her soul.

Sadly, Clea knew this was all quite normal, because she had recently had a long conversation with a girl called Gabi, one of the cherubim. Gabi had told her exactly why she felt this way about her family. "They are nephilim, Clea," Gabi had said, and when Clea had looked at her, puzzled, Gabi had carefully explained that everyone who was not one of the Angels, was one of the nephilim. The nephilim, she'd said, were the people who originally inhabited the Earth, before the angels came. They were fierce and warlike and were responsible for killing all the original angels. That was why an angel could never feel at ease in their company.

Well, it made total sense, Clea thought gloomily. She felt so ill at ease, she was finding it hard to remain in her seat. She glanced quickly across the table at her dopey cousin, who was tapping her knife absent-mindedly on the side of her plate and grinning to herself. Urgh! Did she have to be so childish?

"More salad, darling?" Her mother's voice broke into her thoughts. Clea shook her head.

"So, what have you two girls got planned for the first week of the holidays?" her father asked. "Going to spend some time together doing exciting things?"

Clea didn't answer. Actually, she had lots of plans, none of them involving Jazmin. She looked up. Her cousin was staring at her in that strange way again. She'd been doing it quite a lot recently. As if she'd got hold of some big juicy secret that she was keeping all to herself. Stupid kid – what was her problem? Clea stared straight back until Jazmin dropped her eyes and began fiddling awkwardly with her cutlery.

The nephilim, Gabi had told her, having driven out or killed all the angels, had continued to live on Earth, fighting each other and polluting or destroying everything. "Just look around you," Gabi had said. "We live in a broken world. You can see the results of their handiwork everywhere, can't you?" It was all so clear, the way she put it. Gabi had also told Clea that to be a true angel, she had to make choices. She had to loosen the ties that bound her to the world. She had to create distance between family, friends, everything in her past. She had to move on.

Clea moved food around her plate and listened half-heartedly to the conversations happening around her. So boring. Meaningless, nothing words uttered by people who did not matter. She didn't bother to participate when her parents spoke to her or asked her questions, she replied in grunts or in monosyllables. She was creating distance, she thought. Just like Gabi had told her to.

"And it will be so worth it, believe me," Gabi had said, her eyes gleaming as she leaned forward, her hand resting lightly upon Clea's. "Because one day – and Seraph Gray believes that day is coming very soon, Clea – angels will take their rightful place in the world. One day," Gabi had said, her voice taking on a low, reverent tone, "Seraph Gray says, legions of angels will come down to Earth, and we will all fight the nephilim and drive them away. And then the Earth will be free." Then Gabi had spoken to the three seraphim and they had all gathered round Clea and each one had laid a hand on her head or on her shoulder and they had told her how special she was and how important and how loved. And then they had chanted stuff. Clea had felt something like warm lightning shooting through her and had experienced a great sense of peace and purpose.

This wonderful experience had happened after the last meeting, but it had been such an astonishingly vivid event that she could still feel the effect of it today. And now, sitting at the dinner table, physically close but yet so distant from her family, Clea knew deep in her heart and soul that everything Gabi had told her was absolutely and unconditionally true. She was an angel, a chosen one. She was special. Her family were nephilim, polluters of the planet and her sworn enemies. The only question remaining was: how much longer could she go on living with them, now that her eyes had been opened to the truth?

THE ROZTOK INSTITUTE, THE PLACE WHERE ASSIA DAWSON BELIEVED THE STOLEN BODY WAS CURRENTLY LOCATED, WAS SITUATED ON THE OTHER SIDE OF THE MAREK'S VAST ESTATE, quite close to their magnificent country house. Both house and institute were reached by a single main entrance.

The institute consisted of two low, featureless, whitewashed concrete buildings. It was linked to the house by a small, wooded access road and, from the outside world, through a set of electronically operated steel gates. The institute looked to all intents and purposes like some sort of private hospital. Both white buildings were joined by a windowless corridor and the whole complex could only be entered by going through an insulated metal cube. Inside this, the worker or visitor to the site was carefully screened by a set of micro-filters, to prevent any particles from the outside world getting in. This was an important procedure, always rigidly adhered to. Roztok was a biotech and nano-engineering company. Contamination had to be avoided at all costs.

Countess Valentina Markova, carrying a covered glass Petri dish, stepped into the metal cube. She stood and waited. It was always a two-stage procedure: directed blasts of air blew off any contaminated material, then a vacuum sucked the debris away and expelled it via an air vent. The countess didn't move until the final whoosh signified that the vacuum pumps had completed their task. Then the heavy metal door in front of her slid back. She walked out of the cube, followed the corridor round and down and entered one of the busy, white-walled labs.

A middle-aged, bearded scientist looked up from his screen of data banks, and smiled affectionately at her over the top of his titanium-rimmed glasses.

"*Dobrý den, milenka*," he sang out gaily.

The countess pursed her lips disapprovingly. She wished (not for the first time) that her beloved husband would refrain from calling her "sweetheart" in front of the research staff. It undermined her authority.

Count Marek eyed the Petri dish in his wife's hand. His eyes lit up. "Aha!" he said.

The countess set the dish down carefully upon the workbench.

"This is it?" the count asked. "You have managed to copy the DNA?"

The countess nodded.

Marek picked up the Petri dish and held it to the light. His eyes gleamed.

"So, now we can begin," he murmured.

NANOTECHNOLOGY WAS NOT A NEW SCIENCE. ITS ROOTS LAY AT THE END OF THE LAST CENTURY, WHEN SCIENTISTS HAD MANAGED TO CREATE TINY MICROSCOPIC ROBOTS THAT WOULD PERFORM simple but useful tasks: powering household gadgets, flying aircraft, carrying out low-level surveillance, and programming computers. Nobody could have dreamed of the future advances in micro- and nano-research. Nor guessed at the ingenuity of the scientific minds now working in these complex and frontier-extending fields of research.

The Roztok Institute specialized in the production of nano components for medical research. The company had been the first to create cancer-killing nanoparticles. Tiny nanoscopic molecules had been programmed, like an invisible guerilla army, to search out and destroy mutating cancer cells. Roztok had also developed the use of self-assembling molecules that could mimic cell and molecular structures in the human body.

Marek's pioneering work had focused upon the creation of tiny particles that could be used in surgical procedures. These micro fabricated devices had the ability and intelligence to create, assemble or rebuild organs and limbs actually *in* the body. Roztok held the worldwide patent, and was now producing them in sufficient commercial quantities, so that the need for invasive surgery was already becoming obsolete in many hospitals around the globe. The Roztok Institute was small, notoriously secretive, but universally recognized for being at the forefront of biomedical nano-research.

Living nano-symbiosis. It was a complex but highly successful procedure. And now, Marek was about to take it a step further. A step into unknown and unwalked territory. What he was about to do had never been tried before – except in the pages of the more lurid gothic fiction of the past. Marek was going to use a combination of cloned DNA and nano-engineering to restructure an entire body. Piece by piece. Every cell. Every organ. Every tissue. But not a living, breathing human being. This was a body that had not drawn breath since the dawn of time.

Marek was going to attempt to bring the primeval dead back to life.

CAT AND MOUSE. THAT WAS THE NAME OF THE GAME THEY WERE ALL PLAYING, ASSIA DAWSON THOUGHT. EACH WAITING FOR THE OTHER TO MOVE. AND SHE HAD TO ADMIT THAT THE MAREKS WERE very good at playing it. Experts, in fact.

Of course, they were still calling her Violet Smith, still maintaining the fiction that she was a teacher. But Assia knew they didn't believe her story. Why else was she being kept prisoner in their house? Not that either of them was admitting for a moment that she *was* a prisoner, it was just that every time she suggested it was time to leave, ornate and elaborate excuses were found to keep her there.

And on the one occasion when she'd managed to drag herself slowly and painfully to the front door, it had been locked, which was rather a giveaway, although the Mareks had come up with a charmingly apologetic excuse – something about keeping summer dust off the expensive Persian carpets.

Meanwhile, Assia was becoming increasingly concerned about her foot and ankle – they did not seem to be healing fast enough, and until they did, she couldn't hope to make a run for it under cover of darkness. She had to get away before one or other of the Mareks discovered who she really was. If only she had the silver pen, she thought, she could communicate her whereabouts to the outside world. But the pen had gone – she guessed it had probably fallen out of her pocket and broken when she fell out of the cherry tree.

Naturally, the countess had asked her, several times, if there was anybody she needed to contact. But Assia had always said no. She wasn't fooled by her hostess's fake kindness. She did not want any of her calls listened to and her identity traced. So, for the time being, Assia Dawson was resigned to playing the game too. She was also pretending. She was pretending she was Violet Smith, thirty-six, single, a teacher, and that she was enjoying the count and countess's generous hospitality, while waiting for her tiresome injuries to heal. She lay back in the bed, in the alien room, and breathed a silent prayer of relief that neither of her two jailers had yet discovered her true identity.

"THROW THE FIRST BALL...*C'EST ÇA*... NOW THE SECOND," CHOCOLAT COMMANDED.

JAZMIN FOLLOWED HIS INSTRUCTIONS. "HEIGHT AND WIDTH," SHE muttered to herself.

"Now raise your other hand, show the ball to the audience, but don't throw."

"Like that?"

"That's good. Now do it every time you throw the first ball...concentrate...get a rhythm going...*oui, c'est super*!"

Chocolat was teaching Jazmin a very easy one-handed juggling pattern called the Dummy. It involved moving a palmed ball up and down in one hand to mimic one of the two balls being thrown by the other hand. This gave the audience the impression you were juggling all three balls. A good trick. Particularly if you juggled like a complete klutz anyway. Throw vertically, she told herself silently. Chocolat watched her for a while, then nodded in a satisfied way.

"So, your mother is still working abroad?" he asked chattily.

Jazmin stopped practising because, with the best will in the world, she couldn't concentrate on two things at the same time. "Yeah, she's still there, I guess," she replied.

"Somewhere in Europe, you said?"

"Umm...yeah, last time I heard," Jazmin told him. Wasn't she? Or had she moved on to somewhere else? She tried to remember. Now that school was out for the summer, her life had somehow slipped into a routine. A different routine from back home. At home in the summer, everything focused around her mum: where she was, what she was doing, when she'd be back. Jazmin would wake to find a note telling her how her mum's day was panning out, and a list of chores that needed to be done before she went out to meet friends or do whatever she'd planned.

Whereas here, there was no list, no routine. Nobody cared what she did, and as long as she checked in with Clea occasionally, she was a free agent. So Jazmin usually began her day by running or doing some exercise. Then after breakfast, she left the house, telling Clea she had some shopping to do, or the library to visit. But of course, she spent the day with Tonda and his friends, rehearsing, or helping them put on shows. She'd also managed to go clubbing with them, and take in the latest movies, while Clea was at one of her weird meetings and her aunt and uncle were out. And best of all, she and Tonda had gone for a couple of late-night walks together.

Those had been the most magical times, Jazmin thought dreamily. They talked about their lives and hopes. Tonda had held her hand. Once, on the way back, he had bent over and brushed her cheek with his lips. And somehow, in all of this, her mum seemed to have faded into the background. Now Jazmin mentally scrolled back, and realized to her surprise that she hadn't actually heard from her for some time. This thought was followed by the equally worrying one – that she hadn't even noticed.

"Jazmin? Hello?" Chocolat was staring at her. He snapped his fingers.

"Oh, huh? What?"

"You kind of dozed off. Maybe it's time for a break now, huh?"

Jazmin followed Chocolat over to one of the "outdoor" café tables, where the rest of the clowns were relaxing under a red and white striped umbrella. Auguste pulled out a chair for Chocolat, and gave Jazmin a thumbs-up.

"She's right, you are getting good," Tonda said, smiling. He poured her a glass of bottled water. "Maybe we should come up with a new routine for you – something special to end our time here. What do you think?"

Jazmin looked round at the now familiar faces of her friends: Pierre with his funny-serious expression; Toni, the sad tramp, always frowning, always worrying about something; and mischievous Auguste and handsome Chocolat, who spent every spare minute holding hands and gazing into each other's painted eyes.

She suddenly realized how much she had grown to like them over the past few weeks. And especially Tonda, with his snow-white face and smoke-blown hair. Tonda, who had taught her how to juggle, had accepted her for who she was, and in sharing his life with her, had become a very special part of hers. She wondered what she was going to do without them all, and bit back the sense of sadness that lingered, like a bitter aftertaste in her mouth.

Jazmin knew the clowns were getting ready for their final week of performances. All too soon, they'd be gone and there were no words to express how much she was going to miss them. Their lives would move on; new places, new audiences. And she'd be left with a huge hole in her world, with nothing to fill her empty days, and no real friends to hang out with.

The time spent with them had been so special, so precious. It had been like walking a line that radiated light. Now a darker, uncertain, more jagged line was stretching into the future. But she fought back the tears and smiled bravely. "Yeah, a new routine would be great," she said, and was rewarded by Tonda putting an arm round her shoulders and smiling his heart-stopping smile.

"You'll see, it will all work out somehow," he murmured, as if reading her deepest thoughts.

Jazmin made a conscious effort and lidded down her feelings. Maybe he was right, she thought forlornly. Perhaps it *would* all work out. Although right now, her heart was so brimful of sorrow that she really couldn't see how.

MIDNIGHT. OF COURSE, IT HAD TO BE MIDNIGHT, MAREK REASONED. IT WAS THE ONLY TIME TO PERFORM SUCH AN EXPERIMENT. SHAME ABOUT THE WEATHER THOUGH, HE THOUGHT WRYLY. TRADITIONALLY, these things should be accompanied by thunder, lightning, and torrential rain pouring out of gloomy dark clouds. Not a warm summer night with bright stars twinkling overhead in a clear sky. Should there not also be a ruined castle, wolves howling in the background and a sinister cackling figure dressed in black? Ah, well.

Marek contemplated the body. It currently lay encased in a giant glass pod. The domed roof panel revealed the flattened, but recognizable outline of a human body, its skin yellowy-black and slightly shiny in texture. The eye sockets were hollow and staringly empty, the nose reduced to an arch of splintered bone. But from the size and weight of the thigh bones, and the prominent musculature still visible under the leathery skin, Marek had calculated that the man had stood well over two metres when he'd walked the Earth. Quite amazing. Marek liked to imagine from this, and the haughty set of the bony skull on ruined shoulders, that when alive, the man had been a truly noble creature. Maybe a king or leader of his tribe.

The body had been allowed to thaw slightly, and was currently being kept at a temperature of minus seven degrees centigrade, and in a totally isolated, stringently sterile environment to prevent any deterioration or contamination from outside. The insulated room in which the glass pod lay was also maintained at a constant cold temperature.

Marek paused, thinking about what was shortly going to happen. On such a night as this, he thought to himself, Rabbi Loew, the sixteenth-century Prague scholar and magician, had created a golem out of clay and made it come alive. Perhaps he too had stood in silent awe, looking at his handiwork and meditating upon the moment when he would give it the greatest miracle of all: the gift of life.

But this was now, Marek reminded himself. And he was not some ancient Jewish mystic about to wreak havoc on an unsuspecting city. He was a scientist: he observed; he tested; he experimented. And for him, and for his team of two, this was just another scientific experiment, although its potential significance had not escaped him. And it was time to begin. He checked his watch, made a note of the start time on his handheld computer. He was going to observe, note down every procedure. The application of the scientific mind.

Marek checked the valves connecting the pod to the nanoparticulator, the machine responsible for producing the billions of particles that would flood into the body and begin the work of reconstruction. The process of revivification was beautifully simple: as each group of nanoparticles entered the body, they would be programmed to seek out and attach themselves to an individual organ, bone or body part. Once in place, they would surround and absorb the dead or decaying matter, rebuilding it as a new, living organism.

The only unknown part was the time factor. To achieve complete revivification might take many hours. The experiment had never been carried out before. But Marek was prepared for that. He and his assistants would stay for as long as it took.

Carefully, Marek went through the final safety and control checks. Then he sent a signal from his handheld to his two assistants, instructing them to switch on the nanoparticulator.

"And now," he declared dramatically, "let there be life!"

TIME	COMMENT
12.15	Nanoparticulator assembly line on and working at full capacity. Billions of molecules being pumped into the body, ready to carry out task of revivification.
12.55	Switched computer to differential subprogram. Molecules now instructed to carry out differentiated tasks within the body.
02.30	Body seems to be altering shape, filling out.

	Checked program, all proceeding well.
03.10	Epithelial layer beginning to crack and reform. Colour lightening. Internal organs breaking down and reforming.
03.58	Epithelial layer complete. Skin colour normal. Veining beneath skin clearly visible. Outlines of internal organs visible on monitor screen. Some lung movement detected. Faint irregular heartbeat and pulse.
04.00	Filip sets up ventilator to initiate breathing. Heartbeat louder and more regular. Rapid eye movement detected.
05.05	Heart rate 155. Blood pressure 110/75. Body temperature 37°C. Ventilator turned off. Jan sets up intravenous dextrose drip to nourish and aid hydration.
06.03	Revivification complete. Jan releases pod lid.

Countess Valentina Markova calmly finished reading her husband's notes on the handheld. She stared round the empty lab. Everything was very still, very quiet. Only the hum of the air-conditioning units broke the deep silence. The countess slipped the handheld into the pocket of her white labsuit and looked around, frowning perplexedly. So where was Marek? And where were the rest of his team?

Suddenly, as if on cue, the door at the back of the room was flung open. A man stood on the threshold. The countess gasped. Her hand flew to her mouth. It was her husband, but his features were terribly changed. Marek's greying hair was now snow white. His round, amiable face looked hollow and skull-like; the skin stretched thinly over protruding cheekbones, had turned the colour of old parchment.

Marek saw his wife and his lips drew back from his teeth in a rictus of fear. "*Dobrý den, milenka*," he whispered hoarsely. He stared straight ahead, his eyes wide with fear. The countess glanced down and gasped in horror. Blood splattered her husband's white labsuit and stained his shaking hands.

"IT TORE OUT JAN'S THROAT WITH ITS BARE HANDS," MAREK GASPED. HE HAD COLLAPSED AGAINST A WORKBENCH, BURYING HIS FACE IN HIS HANDS. "AND THEN IT LIFTED HIM UP AS IF HE WAS a feather and threw him against the wall and then it..." The rest of his words were lost in great shuddering sobs. "What am I going to do, *milá*? How am I going to tell his wife what has happened?"

The countess, always the strong, practical one, whatever

the circumstances, cleaned the cloth she'd used to wipe the blood from his hands. "Where is Jan's body now?" she asked.

Marek moaned, shaking his head. "Don't ask. Don't try to find out." He raised his head slightly and stared at her, his eyes wide. "Filip has fled. He escaped while I was...and then I locked the main gate and sent a message to all the staff telling them not to come in. We can't let anybody enter the complex while that...thing is here." He glanced round. "Where is it now?" he whispered, his eyes bright and alive with terror.

"I don't know. It, he, seems to have vanished," the countess replied. Her brow furrowed. "But I don't understand. Can he really have done this? Are you sure you didn't imagine it – you haven't been sleeping much recently. Maybe you dozed off and dreamed it."

Marek gave a harsh laugh, then shuddered. "You want to think that, don't you? I wanted to think it too. Because the face is so, *so* beautiful. You will see. But look deeper, *milá*. Look right into its eyes, if you dare, and you will see power and evil beyond anything you can ever imagine." Marek wailed aloud. "I am like Rabbi Loew," he cried. "I am Victor Frankenstein. I tried to create human life and instead I have created a madman – a monster!"

As he spoke, the sliding door to the lab moved. Marek clutched hold of his wife's arm and pulled her behind the workbench. A tall, broad-shouldered figure stood in the open doorway, filling it with its presence. Light streamed around the figure and lit up the room with a blinding brilliance. Marek whimpered and hid his face.

"Who are you?" the countess whispered, shielding her dazzled eyes.

"I am Azazel, Lord and Standard Bearer to Lucifer, the Prince of Light," the figure announced grandly. It advanced into the room and pointed at them. "Get down on your knees, miserable Earth creatures and crawl. Crawl before your new Lord and Master."

ONCE UPON A TIME, THE STORY GOES, AT THE BEGINNING OF THE CIRCLE OF EARTH, BEFORE THE PORTALS OF THE WORLD WERE IN PLACE, BEFORE THE WIND BLEW AND THE THUNDER RUMBLED AND the flashes of lightning shone, there were a number of angels who, out of envy and pride, decided to raise a rebellion against God himself.

Led by their prince, a seraph once called Lucifer the Light-Bringer, the apostate angels fought and lost and were hurled headlong out of heaven. As they plummeted through the empty, bottomless air, their bodies stung by sulphurous hail, the rebellious angels saw the newly created Earth hanging from heaven by a silver chain, looking like a tiny, bright azure bead in the endless night sky.

And as soon as he saw the beautiful, brand-new world, Lucifer resolved to get his revenge upon God. He determined that he would secretly go and visit the Earth to learn all about it, so that he and his followers might one day bring evil and destruction there. He knew there were people living there. His one fixed objective now was to turn them against their creator, and then to drive them out, just as he and his followers had been driven out of heaven. So, filled with this intent, Lucifer selected one angel, a former prince amongst cherubim, to accompany him, and under cover of night the two fallen angels flew silently towards Earth on their great wings.

It is said that Lucifer landed somewhere between the rivers Tigris and Euphrates, in a place referred to in the Bible as the Garden of Eden. Where the other angel landed remains a mystery, for he was never seen or heard of again.

THE HEAD OF THE LONDON BRANCH OF THE ISA WAS VACATIONING WITH HIS FAMILY AT THE COPACABANA HIDEAWAY HOTEL IN HAWAII WHEN HALLY SKINNER PUT THROUGH A VIDEOCALL TO HIM.

"I'm so, so sorry to bother you on holiday, sir," Hally apologized, "but I'm really worried about Assia Dawson. She hasn't filed a report and I can't seem to get hold of her at all. It's as if she's vanished, sir."

Like many men who spend their working days straitjacketed in a formal three-piece business suit, the head of the ISA had gone overboard on the tasteless beachwear. Sitting under a coconut awning, sipping some exotic cocktail, he was wearing dark wrap-around sunglasses and a bright blue luau shirt featuring rows of jolly, dancing pineapples. "You were quite correct to contact me," he said solemnly. "Where was Agent Dawson when you heard from her last?"

"She was staying in a student hostel just outside Prague," Hally told him, trying hard not to be distracted by her boss's garish clothing. "According to her last report, she was just about to check out a tiny research establishment called Roztok. We think that's where they are storing the body. I have a bad feeling about this, sir. Assia's always meticulous about logging in and keeping in touch, wherever she is."

The head of the ISA frowned. "Surely we've got people out there who can locate her?"

"I've asked around, sir. Trouble is, she's gone into deep cover, so she's probably changed her appearance dramatically. You know how good she is at doing that. You said yourself that you've walked past her on the street and not recognized her! And of course, she'll be operating under an alias. We've got nobody in the European branch of ISA, right now, who'd be able to ID her." Hally pursed her lips and frowned. "And there's another problem, sir. These people aren't stupid – they've managed to get a body out of the Antarctic in midwinter and transport it halfway round the world. And we haven't been able to do a thing to stop them. They'll be on their guard, watching for us. Maybe they even have a list of our agents. We need a clean skin. Somebody they won't be looking for."

"So what do you suggest?"

Hally paused, took a deep breath. "There is somebody we could send," she said slowly. "It would be unusual, totally unorthodox even, but in the circumstances..."

"Oh, yes? And who's that?"

Hally gave him the name.

There was a long pause.

"Yes. I see. Totally unorthodox. As you say."

There was a further pause while the head of the ISA mulled over the suggestion and Hally Skinner held her breath, crossed everything she could think of and prayed.

Then, unexpectedly, the head of the ISA nodded. "All right Hally, go ahead. You have my permission," he said. "Agent Dawson is one of our best. We've lost a few agents over the years, and we certainly can't afford to lose someone of her calibre now. But be careful. The girl's role is solely to locate her for us. Then we take over. I don't want the girl involved any further than that. And for goodness' sake, make sure she is accompanied every step of the way. Nothing, I repeat, *nothing* must go wrong."

Hally Skinner pressed the cut-off button, let out a sigh of relief. She'd got the permission she needed. Now all she had to do was set the wheels in motion. She punched up the Dawson file and began scanning it for a contact number.

A SHORT TIME LATER, THE PHONE RANG IN IAN DAWSON'S OFFICE. HE PICKED UP. THERE WAS A FEMALE VOICE AT THE OTHER END OF THE LINE, A WOMAN HE DIDN'T RECOGNIZE. SHE EXPLAINED THAT she was his sister's work deputy. Ian listened as the woman, who gave her name as Hally Skinner, told him she'd be in the area later that day. She had some important stuff to tell Jazmin. The woman's tone was light, casual. She was just checking it was okay to contact Jazmin. A courtesy thing. Ian agreed. The woman said thanks, then rang off.

After the call had ended, Ian sat for some time staring out of the window thinking about his sister and her work. She was truly amazing. He was full of admiration. He reckoned his sister could discover a crime taking place in an empty room! He visualized Assia, and wished he could still work out what she was thinking, the way they used to do when they were little. He'd love to know what she was up to right now. But sadly, he knew that trick had been lost long ago in the dull grey mists of growing up.

Ian then turned his thoughts to his niece. He hadn't really managed to spend much time with her, but he'd got the impression that she was rather shy. A nice enough kid, but a bit gauche. No trouble, but quite difficult to talk to. He wondered how she'd react to Hally Skinner's arrival. She was certainly nothing like Clea, he thought, although the facial resemblance between the two girls was quite striking.

Smiling, Ian glanced at the many framed photos of Clea on his desk, and felt his heart swell with pride. His beautiful daughter. His pride and joy. He made a mental note to buy her something nice on the way home that evening. To show how pleased he was with her for the way she had taken so much trouble to look after her mousy little cousin during her visit.

MEANWHILE, JAZMIN WAS SITTING AT THE CLOWNS' FAVOURITE TABLE, TRYING TO COME TO TERMS WITH WHAT SHE'D JUST BEEN TOLD. THERE WAS A BIG BLOCK OF ICE PRESSING DOWN ON her heart. Time had stopped.

Tonda had gone.

A message had apparently arrived totally unexpectedly, very late last night, from one of his sisters. It said that his father had had a stroke and was in hospital. Tonda was needed back home. So the white clown had packed a few things and left on the first plane out. Jazmin was in shock. There had been no warning, no contact from him. The first she'd realized something was wrong was when she'd turned up to rehearse as usual and discovered he wasn't there.

Toni explained to her, in his halting English, that Tonda intended to meet up with them all at their next venue: a theatre and puppet festival.

But I'm not going to be there, Jazmin thought, trying to

hold back the tears. This is as far as it goes for me. It suddenly dawned on her that they had spent all this time sharing the bright, floaty bubbles of their hopes and dreams, but they had failed to share the practical things like their contact numbers and where they lived.

Seeing her downcast expression, Chocolat lifted one of the menu cards and picked up a small parcel hidden underneath. "Tonda left this for you," he said.

Jazmin tore open the parcel. The clowns sat silently, watching her. Under the wrapping, she found a letter and a wooden box. She opened the letter first.

Dear Jazmin
Please look after this for me until we meet again.
Take good care of yourself.
Love to you
Tonda

Her eyes misting over with tears, Jazmin put the letter on the table. Then she opened the box. Inside was an egg. It was painted to represent the white-faced clown. Jazmin remembered Tonda explaining that, traditionally, every clown painted an egg with his or her face. It was a record of their uniqueness, a sign that they existed. A kind of clown DNA. No other clown would ever use that face once it had been recorded. Naturally, there was a cyberfile of all the clown faces in the world, he said, but many clowns still liked to have their own personalized egg with them. Jazmin had never seen Tonda's painted egg before. Now she marvelled at what she saw. The tiny face was so lifelike, she almost expected it to open its scarlet mouth and speak to her – it even had its own miniature, white-smoke wig.

Jazmin stared down at the delicately painted egg and felt her heart lift as she understood the significance of the gift. Tonda cared. He had not forgotten her; he had been thinking about her and had left her something that was very precious and important. He had left her himself.

Auguste grinned. She leaned forward, and said something.

"Auguste says you must take good care of this," Chocolat interpreted.

Jazmin felt that her heart was suddenly almost too full. She nodded. "I will do," she breathed, cradling the little box in her cupped hands. "I promise. I'll never let it out of my sight."

THE OWNER OF THE ANTIQUE MODEL-CAR SHOP HAD GOT USED TO THE STRANGE WAYS OF THE STORE OPPOSITE. IT SEEMED TO HAVE NO REGULAR OPENING HOURS. WHEN IT *WAS* OPEN, IT OFTEN STAYED open long after the other stores had closed. It sold strange stuff like healing crystals, Tarot cards and jars of dried herbs. Weird music could be heard floating out through the doorway. Sometimes, far more people went in than could comfortably fit inside and when they came out, they weren't carrying gift bags or boxes. It was as if they weren't going to the shop to buy anything.

Not that he was criticizing, mind. Each to his own, okay. Live and let live, that was his motto. After all, this was the thirteenth floor, home of the small specialist or esoteric retail outlet. Nevertheless, he was curious. He was making a reasonably good living, largely thanks to the current revival of interest in all things antique and retro. But how those guys over the way could afford to pay their rental was a continual mystery. The thirteenth floor was scarcely at the cutting edge of retail therapy.

Recently however, the model-car store owner had observed a sharp increase in activity taking place opposite. There were more comings and goings. He had seen animated conversations taking place outside the store. The light had been left on late into the evening. But still nobody seemed to be buying anything. The store owner tutted to himself as he tidied and arranged his merchandise, prior to opening the store. That was not the way to run a successful business. He'd give them a couple of weeks, he decided. Then surely they'd either have to have a major stock clear-out, or close down altogether.

LATER THAT SAME DAY, HALLY SKINNER SAT AT A TABLE IN THE FOOD COURT, NURSING A DOUBLE SKINNY VANILLA LATTE AND WAITING FOR JAZMIN TO ARRIVE. SHE HAD ARRANGED TO MEET HER at 2.30 p.m. Downstairs in the car park, a driver was poised to take them both to the airport. From there, Jazmin and her two ISA minders would be flown on to Prague.

Everything was set up and ready to roll.

Hally stirred her coffee and congratulated herself on getting it all together so speedily. As long as things went according to plan, and Jazmin did exactly as she was instructed, Assia should be back in touch by Friday at the latest. Which would mean Hally had got it sorted before the head of ISA returned from his vacation. She exhaled air. This really needed to go well. There was a lot riding on it. The integrity of the department for one. The safety of Assia, her boss. And her job and future promotion was on the line too.

Hally sipped her coffee. She was quietly confident. She'd only met Assia's daughter a couple of times, when she visited the office, but she'd always given the impression that she was polite, biddable. She wasn't one of those awkward teenagers; she wanted to please. Jazmin Dawson was the sort of kid who'd do what she was told.

Hally didn't know how wrong she was.

AT 2.25 P.M., JAZMIN SLIPPED INTO THE SEAT OPPOSITE HALLY. SHE WAS BREATHLESS, A WORRIED EXPRESSION ON HER FACE. "HI, HALLY," SHE PANTED. "WHY ARE YOU HERE? IS IT MUM? I HAVEN'T HEARD from her in ages. Has something happened?"

Hally stretched out a reassuring hand and patted her arm. "Hey, slow down, Jazmin," she said. "Nothing's happened. Your mum is fine. Absolutely fine, okay?"

"So why hasn't she rung me? Why are you here?"

"We think your mother may have lost her communicator," Hally said, launching into her carefully prepared speech. She fished around in her bag, then held up a tiny silver pen. "She has one like this. It's very easy to mislay it. That's what we think has happened. That's why nobody's heard from her for a while."

"So where is she?"

"She's staying in a student hostel just outside Prague."

"Prague? Hey, that's..." Jazmin began excitedly.

Hally looked across at her. "Yes? That's what?"

"Nothing." Jazmin lowered her eyes. "It's nothing. I heard someone mention Prague the other day, that's all. It's just a coincidence. Go on."

Hally placed the pen on the table between them. "Jazmin, I'm here to ask you a big favour," she said. "What I want you to do is deliver this new communicator to her – it's got some updated information on it that she needs." Hally smiled widely. "Believe me, I'd go myself, but someone has to keep things ticking over in the office.

I'm asking you to go because your mother will be working in disguise, so you're probably the only one who'd recognize her. That's why I need you to do this, Jazmin. You know it's important we stay in touch with her."

Jazmin looked relieved. "Sure. I understand. So Mum's all right?"

"Absolutely all right. You have my word."

Jazmin expelled air. She reached across the table, picked up the silver pen. "And you want me to go to Prague and give her this?"

"That's right." Hally handed her a sealed envelope. "Here is your plane ticket, the address of the hostel where you'll find her and some money. Are you okay with all of this?"

Jazmin nodded. "Yeah, I'm good. So, do I get a gun?"

"Of course not." Hally sounded shocked. "Absolutely no way, Jazmin."

Hey, lighten up, Jazmin thought. It was a joke. Ha ha.

"There's something else you need to know: you'll be accompanied by two of our ISA people."

"What?" Jazmin stared at Hally. Her face fell.

"They're there to look after you and to liaise with your mother. It's really important that you stay with them the whole time. After all, we can't have a fourteen-year-old schoolgirl travelling all on her own to a foreign country, can we?"

"Can't we? Why not?"

"Look, Jazmin," Hally said, in a talking-to-the-hard-of-thinking voice, "I'll level with you – it was my idea to send you and it's my responsibility that you remain safe. You know your mother would never forgive me if anything happened to you. Now, you'd like to help your mother, wouldn't you? Of course you would. So cooperate, huh? That way you get to see your mother, maybe take in a few days' sightseeing, and you help us out at the same time. Now, how good is that?"

Jazmin shrugged and did a face scrunch. For a moment, Hally thought, it looked as if she wasn't going to play ball after all. Then a thoughtful, speculative expression flitted across the teenager's face. As if her mind was running way ahead of events. Unexpectedly, she grinned. "I need to pack my stuff," she said. "And I need to write a note to Uncle Ian and Aunt Dee to say thank you and tell them where I am."

Hally smiled back at her, relieved. "Of course you do. We don't want them to think you've been kidnapped by aliens!" she laughed gaily.

"Ha, ha." Jazmin forced a laugh. She stood up, pocketing the pen and the envelope. "See you in a bit, then," she said.

"Take as long as you like," Hally reassured her. "I'll be here waiting for you."

Heisenberg's Uncertainty Principle states that there is no such thing as a foolproof plan. Unfortunately, Hally

Skinner was not familiar with this important concept. So she ordered another coffee and waited.

AS THE CAB SPED AWAY TOWARDS THE AIRPORT, JAZMIN DAWSON CHECKED SHE HAD ALL THE RELEVANT DOCUMENTATION IN A SAFE BUT ACCESSIBLE PLACE; THEN SHE SAT BACK TO ENJOY THE RIDE. She wondered how long it'd take Hally Skinner to realize she'd been scammed. Cooperate, huh? Yeah, right. Just who did Hally think she was talking to?

As soon as she got to the airport, Jazmin planned to make a few alterations to her appearance, in case anybody from the ISA was scoping out the check-in desk. Then she'd get herself straight through to the Departure Area to wait for the flight. Tactics. She was going to play it by the book. (The book that recommended: always cheat, always win.)

Cooperate, huh? It was the story of her life. Do this, Jazmin, do that, Jazmin. No, you can't stay home alone. Don't go out without saying where you're going. Too many people had jerked her around for too long. *Not any more*. Those three little words had suddenly set her free.

Jazmin felt a shiver of excitement as the cab pulled into the terminal. From now on, *she* was in charge. It was a good feeling. In a short time, she'd be in Prague. Once there, she'd find her mum and hand over the communicator. Then, and this was the totally amazing bit, she'd be able to meet up with Tonda and her friends again. They were on their way to Prague too, to the theatre and puppet festival. Jazmin couldn't wait to see Tonda's face when she turned up. This was not just some lucky coincidence, she thought to herself gleefully as she paid the driver and entered the terminal. This was Meant To Be. Jazmin glanced swiftly around the complex. Then she headed purposefully straight for the restrooms, stopping off briefly to make a purchase at one of the shops on the way.

Twenty minutes later, and now almost unrecognizable, Jazmin Dawson emerged from the restroom and set off across the concourse. She was wearing a long black dress (courtesy of her cousin Clea's discards). Her long unruly hair was tied back and completely hidden under a brightly coloured headsquare. Her face and hands were brown in colour, and her eyes were rimmed with black kohl. To the casual passer-by, she looked just like a young woman from the Middle East.

Jazmin scanned the departure board. The first boarding call had just been posted for her flight. She made her way to the check-in desk. Mingle, smile, eye contact, she reminded herself. More tactics. She joined the rapidly forming queue waiting to be checked through.

Back at the food court, Hally Skinner was beginning to get impatient. Just how long did it take to throw a couple of things into a backpack? She drummed her fingers on the table. It was another thirty minutes before the suspicion began to grow that Jazmin was not coming back. Hally started to recall her negative response when she was told about the two ISA agents. Then she remembered the way Jazmin had grinned at her. It was the sort of grin that was planning something. The suspicion became a certainty. Hally called the airline, wanting answers.

The trouble with wanting answers is that you have to ask the right questions. The airline informed Hally Skinner that nobody called Jazmin Dawson had left on the evening flight to Prague. What they did not tell her, because she did not ask, was that a passenger with the same name had boarded an earlier flight, having obtained a last-minute transfer. So, while Hally Skinner was frantically making calls and restructuring her carefully laid plans, Jazmin Dawson stepped off a plane onto the tarmac of Ruzyně airport and caught a bus into town.

FOR ASSIA DAWSON, TIME HAD CEASED TO HAVE ANY MEANING. SOMETIMES SHE SLEPT, SOMETIMES SHE LAY DROWSILY, HALF AWAKE. SOMEWHERE IN THE BACK OF HER MIND, THE THOUGHT kept recurring that this was not normal, this was not how she was meant to be, that they must be doing something to her to keep her in this passive state. Whoever "they" were. That information was currently eluding her. In her more lucid moments, she tried to remember why she was here and what was actually wrong with her.

Occasionally, a woman dressed in a white labsuit came in, fed her, bathed her, then left her alone again. Once, Assia awoke to see a tall man by her bedside. He was standing absolutely still, looking down at her. She remembered the man clearly, because he had long, fair, curling hair and the most beautiful face she had ever seen. But his eyes were dark and cold, and as he stared at her, the pupils glowed fiery red.

Sinister eyes. Evil eyes. She could not forget them.

She hoped the man would not come back.

WHILE ASSIA WENT ON FITFULLY SLEEPING, HER DAUGHTER JAZMIN WAS EATING DINNER AT THE FOREIGN STUDENTS' HOSTEL (ITS ADDRESS HELPFULLY SUPPLIED BY HALLY SKINNER). There, using a combination of family photos and her recently acquired miming skills, she was finding out exactly what had happened to the woman the students referred to as Violet Smith.

AND AT THE SAME TIME AS JAZMIN WAS QUESTIONING THE STUDENTS, CLEA DAWSON'S PARENTS WERE ENJOYING A LATE SUPPER AND A GLASS OF WINE AFTER A BUSY DAY AT THEIR WORKPLACES. The apartment was very quiet. Ed had gone away on vacation with a bunch of his rowdy male friends, and Clea was up in her room.

Ian smiled fondly at his wife. His business was doing well. He had a good marriage, a nice apartment in a prestigious location, two great kids. What more could anybody want out of life? He cleared his throat. Dee looked up expectantly.

"You know, I was thinking," Ian said, "we really ought to try to arrange some kind of special treat for Clea. It must be hard for her, what with her brother on a summer break, and now her cousin's gone too, while she's stuck here on her own. What do you think?"

Dee ran her finger thoughtfully round the top of her wineglass. "Funny you should mention it," she said. "Clea and I were only talking about this earlier. She asked me whether she could go on holiday with one of her school friends – Gabi Foster."

Ian frowned, shook his head. "I don't recall a Gabi Foster," he said. "Who's she?"

"The family only moved to the city this term, Clea says. Apparently they are all going scuba-diving in the Cayman Islands for a fortnight, and they've invited Clea to go with them. What do you think – should we let her go? It would be a wonderful opportunity for her."

"Sounds fantastic. But what do we know about this family?"

"Well," Dee said, "I spoke to the mother – Clea gave me her number. She sounds extremely pleasant – quite young, I thought. The trip seems very well planned. I think we should let her go. After all, she's nearly sixteen. She'll be with a friend, and I'm sure she'll be well supervised and looked after."

Ian nodded. "You're right. And it's better than her hanging around here on her own. Shame you can't take any time off work."

Dee shook her head. "I know, but I really can't. Wish I could, but we're snowed under. I can possibly find a window in October, but that's the earliest I can manage. What about you?"

"Same," Ian agreed. "Oh, well. It looks as if it's the Cayman Islands, then. Lucky girl!"

"Clea will be so excited," Dee said, rising from her seat. "I'll tell her the good news right now!"

MUCH LATER THAT SAME NIGHT, A MAN SLUMPED AT A CORNER TABLE IN A QUIET BAR IN THE MALÁ STRANA RAISED HIS HEAD AND STARED VACANTLY AROUND HIM.

"*Pivo!*" he commanded.

The waitress brought him another beer. The man mumbled a slurred thank you. The waitress returned to polishing glasses and eyeing the fake-antique gold clock on the wall above the door. It was very late.

Every evening for the past few days, the man had come to this bar. He was not a local, the waitress was pretty sure of that, because she'd never seen him before. Nor was he a tourist, although Prague was full of tourists at the moment. No tourist would drink himself into oblivion night after night. He must be from out of town, she thought.

The waitress wondered about him. Why was he here? What drove him to drown his sorrows in this way? She concluded that the man must have been unlucky in love. He was not that old, not that bad looking. And he did not wear a wedding ring. Yes, he had definitely been jilted, the waitress decided. His heart had been broken. It was very sad, *velmi tragický*.

The man finished his beer, then staggered to his feet, clutching the table for support. He started to make his way towards the door.

"*Dobrou noc*," the waitress murmured politely.

The man turned and stared at her for a few seconds. He made no reply. Then, opening the door, he launched himself unsteadily out into the night. The waitress paused, cloth in hand, staring wordlessly after him. The expression in his eyes, she thought to herself. She had never seen anyone look like that before. She shuddered. She was wrong. This man had not loved and lost. This man had stood at the mouth of hell and seen terrible things. Things no human being should ever have to see.

The waitress went to the door and looked out into the silent, deserted street. Then she shut the door and bolted it firmly against the night and the man and the ghosts of the alchemists and astrologers who walked the cobbled streets at night and loitered in the grey mists swirling about the mysterious Charles Bridge.

A little wind rustled the leaves on the trees as the drunken man crossed Charles Bridge and headed towards Josefov, the Old Jewish Quarter. The slice of silver moon was almost hidden behind clouds as he cut down the narrow street that ran alongside the Klausová Synagogue and the Old Jewish Cemetery with its lichen-covered gravestones and thousands of ancient, closely-packed bodies.

The man quickened his unsteady, erratic pace, deliberately keeping his head down and his eyes on the uneven paving stones. He did not see the tall figure as it stepped silently out of the shadows by the iron cemetery gate. He did not hear the footsteps coming up behind him.

The subsequent police autopsy report would give the man's name as Filip Henshall, aged thirty-nine, and unmarried. It would also state that he worked as a lab technician at the Roztok Institute. The report would indicate that death had occurred as a result of massive haemorrhaging of blood from a wound to the throat. Blood high up on one of the synagogue walls would also suggest that the man had been somehow hurled against it with tremendous force, smashing most of the bones in his body.

THE CHERRY-HARVESTING SEASON WAS OVER FOR THE YEAR, BUT THERE WAS ALWAYS PLENTY OF SOFT FRUIT LEFT TO PICK. AFTER A SUBSTANTIAL EARLY BREAKFAST OF BREAD AND TEA AT the hostel, all the students piled into the battered lorry that took them from site to site. Today, they were picking grapes at a vineyard in Mělník, a town some thirty-three kilometres from Prague.

Before they set off, however, the students had a quick word with the driver and as a result, a short distance out of the city, the lorry unexpectedly groaned to a halt. An individual hopped down from the back and waved cheerfully as the driver revved the ancient engine and drove off in a fume-filled dust cloud along the deserted country road.

Jazmin stood and looked up at the set of heavy steel gates, clamped firmly shut. She looked at the high razor-wired walls and the security cameras. She looked at the notice in Czech that she didn't understand but she guessed was telling her not to waste her time because she didn't stand a snowball's chance in hell, okay?

However, a short distance along the road, and set slightly back from it was a rough unmade track, almost hidden by high grass and overarching trees. Jazmin decided to follow it and see where it led. Given the choice, she told herself, she usually preferred the scenic route anyway.

COUNTESS VALENTINA MARKOVA CARRIED THE BREAKFAST TRAY TO THE KITCHEN. THINGS WERE BAD. FOUR DAYS AGO, HER BELOVED HUSBAND HAD WALKED INTO HIS OFFICE OVER AT THE COMPLEX AND locked the door. He was now refusing to come out. She had tried talking to him, coaxing him, pleading with him. Even shouting and raging at him, but all to no avail. Three times a day, she walked across, placed a tray of food outside the office door, and fifteen minutes later, collected it. Each time, he seemed to have eaten less. She had also heard him sobbing on a couple of occasions. He was a broken man.

Meanwhile, the angel – if that's what it really was, and every rational, scientific bone in her body fought against the concept – roamed around and came and went, doing whatever it pleased. It did not appear to eat, nor did it sleep and it possessed the uncanny ability to manifest itself or disappear whenever it wanted to.

The countess knew she was a highly intelligent and rational scientist, but there was something about that thing that defied and went beyond her human understanding. All she knew was that she was absolutely terrified of it. Terrified of what it was capable of doing. And terrified that someone would find out that it was here. Soon.

The countess placed the tray down on the kitchen table and began to stack the dirty dishes in the sink. Just how much worse could it get?

She was about to find out.

The front doorbell rang.

"OH, HI!" JAZMIN GUSHED. "YOU DON'T KNOW ME, BUT I'M A FRIEND OF VIOLET SMITH – YOU KNOW, THE TEACHER FROM ENGLAND YOU'VE GOT STAYING WITH YOU. ANYWAY, THE THING IS, I'M supposed to be meeting her in Prague, only she contacted me and said she had fallen and hit her head and was having to rest up here for a couple of days. So here I am!" Jazmin smiled winningly.

"Pardon? I'm sorry?" The woman standing in the doorway stared blankly, as if the girl on her doorstep was a visitor from another planet.

"I'm looking for my friend, Violet Smith," Jazmin repeated slowly and loudly in case the woman didn't understand English. She paused. Smiled. "Violet Smith. My friend. Is she here?"

For a brief moment, Jazmin thought the woman was going to be sick. Her skin went a nasty grey colour and her pale, expressionless eyes bulged. Then she swallowed hard. "No, she is not here," she said abruptly. "She has gone now. I don't know where she has gone. So sorry, I cannot help you. Goodbye." And she shut the door.

Jazmin stood outside on the step. Uh-huh, she thought. So that's how it is. She turned and walked back along the path for a short distance. Then she sat down under a tree from where she could see, but hopefully not be seen, and started reviewing her options.

STUPID! COUNTESS VALENTINA MARKOVA THOUGHT TO HERSELF. STUPID! STUPID! WHY HAD SHE SAID THAT? WHY HAD SHE ALLOWED HERSELF TO BE CAUGHT OFF GUARD? SHE SHOULD HAVE INVITED THE girl in, made up some plausible tale and then sent her happily on her way. Instead, she had just automatically blurted out the first lie that came into her head. It was not good enough! She stood in the silent hallway, cursing herself.

After she had calmed down a bit, the countess went back to the front door, opened it, and peered out. No sign of the girl; she had gone. A friend of Violet Smith. Oh yes, as if she believed that for one moment! She suspected exactly who the ingenuous caller was. And she would be back, the countess thought grimly. Assia Dawson's daughter was not going to give up just like that. She would be back. And next time, maybe she would not be on her own. And then what?

The countess took a couple of deep breaths to steady her wildly beating heart. She reminded herself that she was a member of the Czech aristocracy; the blood of Bohemian nobility ran in her veins. Her ancestors had fought at the Battle of the White Mountain. Then she went to look for her micro. Affirmative action. She was not going to be intimidated by a mere schoolgirl.

WELL HEY, THAT WENT ABOUT AS WELL AS COULD BE EXPECTED, JAZMIN THOUGHT TO HERSELF. SHE LEANED HER BACK AGAINST THE TREE AND TOOK A SIP OF BOTTLED WATER. HALLY SKINNER HAD NOT told her the whole story. Not even a fraction of it. So that explained why she'd wanted to send people with her. Hally Skinner had lied. Her mum was definitely *not* all right.

This was going to be a lot trickier than she'd thought.

MEANWHILE, IN HER FAIRY-TALE CITY IN THE SKY, CLEA DAWSON, THE BEAUTIFUL PRINCESS WHOSE EYES HAD NOW BEEN OPENED TO SEE THE WORLD FOR WHAT IT TRULY WAS, STOOD IN FRONT OF HER mirror, which also never told a lie, and she stared at her flawless complexion, her blue eyes and her long, dark, curly hair.

This is me, Clea thought breathlessly. The real me. About to embark on my journey to a new life. Behind her, on the wide hand-carved white bed, was her overnight case. Just take essentials, Gabi had instructed. We must leave as much of the old life behind as possible. Earlier, she had said goodbye to the two nephilim. (*Don't think of them as "parents"*, Gabi had instructed her. *Think of them by their real names. It will help you move on.*) Also on Gabi's instructions, Clea had emptied her bank account – the money, a considerable amount, was tucked away safely in a zipped inner pocket of her shoulder bag.

Clea took one last look around her lovely bedroom,

with its floor-to-ceiling closets filled with designer clothes, and realized to her surprise that it all meant nothing to her now. It was just things, she thought dispassionately. Things bought by the nephilim to entrap her, keep her in ignorance and blind her to the truth. She slipped the silver-winged pendant round her neck. Then she closed her case and picked up her bag. She went through the apartment and, after placing her house keys on the hook by the door (she didn't need them any more), she slammed the front door shut behind her and walked away.

She was free.

THE LORRY PICKED JAZMIN UP AGAIN AT 4.30 P.M. THE STUDENTS WERE PLEASED TO SEE HER, ASKED AFTER HER MUM, AND TALKED ABOUT THEIR DAY IN A MIXTURE OF SIGN LANGUAGE AND BROKEN English. Jazmin sat in a corner, nodding, smiling, pretending to be interested. She had spent all day watching the house, hoping to catch a glimpse of something to confirm her mother was there. But she'd seen nothing.

Once, the woman had driven off somewhere, returning twenty minutes later. Other than that, nothing had happened. Nobody came, nobody went. The house seemed lifeless, its shuttered windows were like eyes closed to keep the world out. It had been a disappointing day. And she wasn't sure that tomorrow was going to pan out any differently, either.

The lorry dropped its passengers near the hostel. Jazmin trailed behind the chattering student group, feeling very down. At the back of her brain, the unwelcome thought was beginning to surface that maybe this had not been such a good idea after all.

She had almost reached the hostel when she suddenly noticed that there was a small black ATV hugging the kerb right outside the door. It had darkened windows, foreign plates, shiny steel hubs and a lot of scary antennae on the roof. Jazmin's heart flipped. She knew, without a shadow of a doubt in her mind, that its presence was somehow connected to her. Trouble had come looking – and it had found her. She broke into a run, trying desperately to reach the hostel door before anything happened.

Instantly, the ATV doors shot open. Two people leaped out. One male, one female. They stood in front of her, arms folded, blocking the sidewalk. They were young, but their faces wore the same stern, forbidding don't-mess-with-me-huh expression. They were dressed in identical white tees, black work pants and high tops and, from the bits of them that were exposed, it looked as if they both did a lot of working out. Jazmin skidded to a halt. She felt a flutter of fear in the pit of her stomach.

"Well hello, Jazmin Dawson," the man said softly.

"So good to meet you at last," the girl purred.

Jazmin gulped. She felt her mouth going dry.

The man checked her out. Slowly and deliberately.

Then he said, "Hey, Jazmin, the flight transfer idea – neat strategy."

"And getting an upgrade too – very nice," his female companion added. "You really go the whole nine yards, don't you?"

Jazmin stared at them, her jaw dropping open. "Who...w-what?" she stuttered.

"Oh, sorry." The girl's face suddenly relaxed, broadening into a wide smile. "We didn't do the intro." She held out her hand. "I'm ISA Field Agent Suki Smith and this is Field Agent Stash McGregor."

The man called Stash gave Jazmin a high five. "Welcome to Prague, girlfriend," he greeted her, "a city with more history than it knows what to do with." He gestured towards the ATV. "So let's move," he said. "I'll drive, you'll talk, we'll listen, okay?"

FOR THE NEXT TWO HOURS, STASH DROVE AROUND THE OUTSKIRTS OF THE CITY WHILE JAZMIN SAT IN THE BACK AND TOLD THEM EVERYTHING SHE KNEW, WHICH WASN'T VERY MUCH AND DIDN'T take long. Then Suki took over and shared their knowledge. She told Jazmin about the Roztok Institute, what it did and how the ISA had become increasingly suspicious about what Marek was up to inside his impregnable white fortress.

She explained about the body and its significance, the

number of deaths that had already occurred since it had been discovered and how it was vital that both it and Assia Dawson – "one of our best undercover agents" – were located and retrieved.

Then, as soon as Suki had finished talking, and answering Jazmin's many questions, Stash headed back into the centre of town. He parked the ATV in a side street, and led the way to a restaurant. The three of them slotted into an empty booth. Stash looked at Suki inquiringly. "Beer?"

"Beer, please."

Stash pointed to Jazmin. "Beer?"

Suki eye-rolled. "She's fourteen, Stash; she's not allowed to drink alcohol."

"I drank beer when I was fourteen."

"Yeah, I bet you did." Suki laughed.

"I'd like a juice, please," Jazmin said.

"Of course you would," Stash said. He got up and went to the bar. Jazmin buried herself behind the menu, which was in Czech, with no translation.

Stash soon returned with a tray of drinks. "I ordered food," he told them. "Pork and dumplings. We'll need a good solid meal inside us."

Suki nodded. "I agree. Best to be prepared, huh."

Jazmin looked from one to the other. "Why?"

"You ask too many questions," Stash said. He grinned mischievously. "You know what happens to little girls who ask too many questions?"

Jazmin thought for a while. "No," she said, eventually. "What?"

Stash threw back his head and laughed. "That's very good," he said. "I like your style. Right then, here's the plan: after we've eaten, we'll run you back to the hostel. You can take a shower, have a rest, whatever. Then we'll pick you up at...oh, let's say 12.30. Should be late enough for what we have to do. Make sure you're wearing something dark."

"We're going to rescue my mum from that place?"

"We're going to check it out first. Then we'll take it from there."

Oh wow! Jazmin thought. She spent a lot of time in the fast-paced fantasy world of her kick-ass gorgeous heroine, Jaz Dawson. Now here she was, about to do the same stuff for real. How good was that!

"Will we have guns?" she asked hopefully.

Suki shook her head sadly. "You watch too many gangster movies," she said. "Like Stash said, we are looking. And that's 'we' as in Stash and me. You're coming along so we can keep an eye on you, and in case we need an ID, got it?"

"It's back to the script for you I'm afraid, girlfriend," Stash said, grinning.

"Whatever." Jazmin shrugged. She saw the waitress making her way over to their table with three big plates of food. She picked up her knife and fork. Suki and Stash were okay, she decided. They did not treat her like a child and, unlike Hally Skinner, they had told her the truth. She'd do what they wanted. For now. At least until the opportunity arose to apply some creative misunderstanding. At which point she might jettison the script for a little solo improvisation.

AT 12.15, JAZMIN WAS READY AND WAITING OUTSIDE THE HOSTEL. AS INSTRUCTED, SHE WAS WEARING DARK-COLOURED CLOTHES. SHE HAD ALSO BROUGHT WITH HER THE TUBE OF BROWN FACE-PAINT Auguste had given her. Just in case. At 12.30 on the dot, the black ATV pulled up alongside her. Jazmiň jumped in and they sped north, taking the freeway to Melník. Soon, Stash turned off onto a minor road, then pulled to a halt outside the Roztok complex. Jazmin peered out of the darkened rear window at the high, forbidding steel gates. They were still firmly shut.

"Where's this scenic route you mentioned?" Suki asked.

"It's over there." Jazmin pointed over Suki's shoulder into the pitch-dark undergrowth. "But it's only an unmade track."

"Hey, this baby can climb trees if it has to," Stash informed her proudly. He restarted the engine and touched a switch on the dashboard. Instantly, the windscreen darkened, the lights cut out and a screen lit up, showing the trees and undergrowth in ghostly outline.

Stash manoeuvred the ATV along the overgrown track, using the night vision to guide him. Finally, they came within sight of the house. It was in complete darkness. Stash let the ATV glide soundlessly forward until it was practically up against the house wall.

"Okay," he murmured, "now let's see who's home this evening." He pressed another switch, and the small screen now showed an internal plan of the house.

Suki leaned forward and watched the screen intently. "There," she said, pointing. "And there. And look, up there right at the top of the house."

Stash nodded. "I see them."

"See what?" Jazmin whispered, straining to get a closer glimpse of the screen from her back-seat position.

"People," Suki told her. "Follow my finger – here? Where there's a solid shape that seems to almost glow in the dark, that's a person. The thermal imager on the roof's picking up heat from their bodies and transferring it to the screen. Looks like there are three people inside the house. Question is – is one of them Assia?"

"The room at the top?" Jazmin queried in a whisper.

"That's what I'm thinking too," Stash agreed. "The others must be the Mareks."

Jazmin peered out of her window at the darkened house. "So, do you have special tools to break open the front door?" she asked.

Stash chuckled quietly. "You are so great, you know

that? No, it's not quite how we do things nowadays." A large square panel directly overhead lit up. Stash touched it lightly with his index finger. There was a humming noise, then, to Jazmin's amazement, the roof slid back and began to unfold. It moved swiftly outwards and upwards on intersecting metal struts, extending itself up the wall of the house.

"Whoa – it's like a ladder," Jazmin exclaimed.

"Welcome to the real world of high-tech illegal entry," Suki grinned. She handed Stash a pair of black gloves and a black fitted helmet with a smoked-grey front vizor. Tucking a stray strand of blonde hair behind her ear, she lowered an identical helmet over her own head.

"This is how we'll stay in touch," she said, giving Jazmin an earpiece. "When we get into the room, I'll send an image of whoever's there to the screen, okay? You say if you recognize them."

Jazmin nodded, too thrilled to speak.

"And you tell us if you see any lights coming on, or anybody moving around, right?"

Stash made a circle with his thumb and forefinger. Suki gave him a thumbs-up. Next minute, they had both climbed onto the roof of the ATV and were scrambling up the ladder.

THE YOUNG WOMAN HURRYING HOME THROUGH THE DARK STREETS WITH A BAG OF LATE-NIGHT GROCERIES WORE A WORRIED FROWN. NEARLY A WEEK NOW AND STILL SHE HADN'T HEARD WHEN SHE could return to her cleaning job. What was going on? She'd tried banging on the gates; she'd called the Mareks' private number. Nothing. Had she been sacked? Why? She'd done nothing wrong, as far as she knew. Okay, maybe she'd helped herself to the odd bit of food, but that wasn't a sackable offence, was it? After all, everybody had their little "perks", didn't they? And it wasn't as if the countess couldn't spare it. After all, look at her – furs up to her eyeballs and beautiful diamond jewellery. She'd never done a day's hard work in her life. Never had to go down on her knees to scrub a dirty floor. Lazy rich cow!

The young woman pulled her thin coat more closely round her. The nights were drawing in now. August, and it was already getting cold when the sun went down. Soon it would be autumn time. More worryingly, soon it would be rent time. And how was she going to pay it, with no money coming in? She cut across Wenceslas Square, still brightly lit and noisy, with music blaring from the many all-night clubs and bars. She paid no attention to the hooting horns and shouts from cruising cars. It was always busy on the square after dark.

Deep in thought, the young woman headed for one of the quiet back streets behind the big tourist hotels. Even if the footsteps behind her had made any sound, it was unlikely that she would have heard them. Nor was she aware of what was coming closer and closer, until it was too late.

A truck driver collecting rubbish from the back of the hotel would find her mutilated body in the early hours of the morning. He would report it immediately to the police, but for a long time afterwards, would not speak of what he had found. He'd seen some gruesome things in his line of work, but nothing like this. Ever.

BACK AT THE MAREKS' HOUSE, JAZMIN WAS STANDING BY THE ATV LOOKING UP. RAIN RUSTLED SILVERLY, MASKING THE SOUNDS FROM THE TOP OF THE LADDER, WHERE STASH HAD JUST FINISHED CUTTING a neat hole in the glass, and was now probing with a long metal rod for the latch. The next second, the window was open and Suki had climbed through. There was a pause, then Jazmin heard her voice in the earpiece.

Jazmin slid into the driving seat and gazed at the screen, which now showed the image of a woman with very short blonde hair, lying on her back fast asleep. Her arms were flung back in the trusting, vulnerable position small children sometimes sleep in. Jazmin's heart skipped a beat. The hair colour was different, the face thinner, more lined, but she recognized the woman at once. It was her mum.

Having confirmed her mother's identity to Suki, Jazmin watched as Stash now disappeared into the room. She waited impatiently for them both to come back. Time suddenly seemed to have slowed, each second was taking an unbearable age to pass.

At last, Stash and Suki climbed back through the window. Stash was carrying something wrapped in a blanket over his left shoulder, Suki had a backpack. They descended the ladder carefully, then between them, lowered Assia's sleeping body gently through the roof into the back of the ATV.

"Is she all right?" Jazmin whispered.

"She seems fine," Suki said, swinging herself into the front passenger seat and taking off her gloves and helmet. "I think she must be drugged, though, she hasn't woken up once."

Stash retracted the ladder and closed up the roof. He started the engine. "Right, let's get out – fast," he muttered. "I've got a bad feeling about this place. Something's not right here."

The jeep rolled forwards and headed towards the rough track. Jazmin put out her hand and touched the blanket-wrapped body. She listened to her mother's deep, even breathing and felt an infinite sense of relief.

The ATV had almost reached the shadowy entrance to the track when some instinct made Jazmin turn and look back out of the rear window. There was somebody standing outside the house, staring at them. Jazmin felt her breath catch in her throat. The figure was tall, broad shouldered, and as it stood silently watching them, its face seemed to shine with a strange, almost luminous glow.

But what fixed her attention were the man's eyes. Cold and dark, they held her gaze, penetrating right into the car, right into her soul, and as she stared back helplessly, the pupils suddenly glowed fiery red. A bright comet's tail of fear ran down Jazmin's spine. "Guys, there's someone watching us," she whispered urgently.

"Where?" Suki replied, glancing up into the rear-view mirror. "I don't see anyone."

Jazmin looked again; the watcher had vanished.

ASSIA WAS HAVING THE STRANGEST DREAM. FIRST SHE APPEARED TO BE CLIMBING UP AND UP A STEEP HILL. THEN SHE WAS FALLING DOWN AND DOWN AGAIN. IT WAS VERY CONFUSING AND disorientating. Also, she could hear voices whispering somewhere above her head. To begin with, they seemed to be scared voices, hushed, panicky, now they were much calmer. She tried to force herself to wake up, but the waves of soft black darkness came rolling over her again, pushing her back down and down into infinite blackness.

Assia opened her eyes. She was lying in bed in a hotel room, and there was a young woman she did not know sitting by her side. The young woman smiled at her. "Good morning, Assia," she said. "Welcome to the world!"

"Who are you?" Assia asked warily.

"Field Agent Suki Smith. I work for the ISA, like you. Hey, it's good to have you back with us!"

Assia attempted to sit up, then shut her eyes and groaned. She felt as if something had hatched inside her head and was trying to dig its way out. The young woman called Suki put a hand on her shoulder and gently guided her back down again. "Take it easy, huh? You've had a pretty rough time."

"No." Assia shook her off. She struggled into a sitting position. "I'll be fine, thanks. It's just my ankle." She lifted the duvet and looked at her leg, then gave an exclamation of surprise. "Where's the bandage gone?"

"I don't know. You didn't have any bandage on when we liberated you," Suki said.

"But I thought... They told me I had broken my ankle and a couple of bones in my foot. That was why I had to stay in bed and rest all the time."

Suki smiled sardonically. "Uh-huh. Sounds like a good way to keep you compliant."

Assia stretched her leg, rotating her foot. Then she wriggled her toes. "There's nothing the matter with them!" she exclaimed.

Suki said, "It must have been the drugs they were giving you."

Assia swung both legs over the side of the bed. "I have to get dressed," she said. "I have work to do."

"All in good time," Suki nodded. "First, you have to eat something. Then you'll need to do some gentle exercise – you haven't left your bed for some time, so your muscles will be pretty wasted. And while you're doing all that, we'd really like some information about what's going on at the Roztok place."

"We?" Assia queried.

"My partner Stash McGregor and I. We were sent by London to locate you. You've been out of communication for some time, you see."

"I see." Assia covered her face with her hands. "This is not good," she groaned. "This is really not good. I shouldn't have let this happen."

"I wouldn't beat yourself up about it," Suki advised her. "It wasn't your fault. Accidents happen. You're here now, and so are we. Oh – and there's someone else here who's very glad to see that you're alive and well." Suki got up and went into the adjoining room for a moment. When she returned, Jazmin was close behind her.

"Jazmin?" Assia exclaimed, her eyes widening. "Oh, my goodness! I don't believe this! What on earth are *you* doing here?"

"She's been working with us," Suki said calmly. "I tell you, we couldn't have liberated you without her. And she has something special for you."

Suki stood aside as Jazmin rushed over to the bed, threw her arms round her mother and hugged her tight. "I missed you," she said. "I missed you so much."

Suki waited for a moment and then said, "And the other something special?"

"Oh, yeah," Jazmin straightened up, fumbled in her pocket. "Hally gave me this for you," she said, and placed the silver pen on her mother's pillow.

Suki winked at them. "I guess you two could really do with some catch-up time," she said. "So listen, take as long as you need. When you're both ready, we can all grab a bite to eat. Then we'll talk."

THE OWNER OF THE ANTIQUE MODEL-CAR SHOP STIRRED HIS MUG OF TEA AND SMILED GRIMLY BUT WITH A CERTAIN SENSE OF COMPLACENCY. HE'D SEEN IT COMING. OH YES. YOU CAN'T RUN A business without some sort of system. Regular opening hours. A sales policy. Monthly and six-monthly targets. Whereas over the way, well, they were amateurs. He'd bet they probably didn't even have a proper sales ledger. Playing shop like a bunch of kids. He'd predicted weeks ago how it would end.

He peered through his shop window at the unlit and locked-up shop opposite. Two days now and still closed. No sign to indicate what had happened, when they would reopen. There was a pile of post on the mat.

Some kids had grafittied rude words on the wall. Hadn't spelled them properly, of course. So much for education nowadays.

The owner of the model-car shop drained his tea and went to rearrange a nice little display of metallic-grey Toyota Corollas. He wasn't going to lose any sleep over his neighbours' apparent demise. After all, it wasn't as if they ever came into his shop and bought anything, was it?

JAZMIN DAWSON WAS IN LOVE. WITH THE HOTEL'S RETRO-STYLED ELEVATOR. IT HAD LITTLE, BUILT-IN, RED PLUSH SEATS AND A GOLD GRATING IN ONE OF THE SHINY ROSEWOOD WALLS. THROUGH THE frosted glass door, sandblasted with cupids, you could see the cable and counter balance sink into the depths below. It was an elevator to die for!

She and Stash were currently riding the hotel elevator from the ground floor, where they had lunched in the elegant restaurant, up to the two agents' suite of rooms, where Suki had ordered room-service for herself and Assia.

"Your mum's doing well," Stash observed.

Jazmin agreed. A hot bath, fresh clothes and some gentle stretching exercises and her mum was almost back to her old self. It was great to see her looking so much better. And the other thing that had really surprised her was how glad Assia was to see her daughter. After the initial welcome, and the hugs-and-kissage, Jazmin had fully expected the storm clouds to break. But so far, they hadn't. There had also been no mention of sending her back to England. Mind you, she reminded herself, the way Stash and Suki kept praising her up was certainly helping. She owed them.

Assia and Suki were watching the lunchtime news when they entered the sitting room. Suki had clipped a small black box to the side of the screen, and it was busily translating what was being said into English.

"Hey, it's my special-agent daughter," Assia said, smiling at her.

Jazmin felt her heart swell with pride. "You reckon?" she said.

"Definitely," Assia nodded. "She's part of the team now, isn't she?" she said, glancing from Stash to Suki.

"For sure," Stash said.

Oh, wow! Jazmin thought. Did it get much better than this? She gave her mum a radiant smile. Then flopped into an easy chair and stared idly at the screen. A female newsreader, eyes firmly on the autocue, was ploughing through some trade figures. Nobody in the room was really paying much attention to what she was saying. And then, suddenly, everybody stopped chatting and sat bolt upright, eyes glued to the screen.

"We interrupt this news bulletin to bring you a story just breaking," the newsreader announced. "A scientific research establishment on the outskirts of Prague has been invaded overnight by an unknown terrorist group. The Roztok Institute, which specializes in biomedical research had been shut down for some time and..."

The newsreader paused, obviously listening to some message in her earpiece. Then she continued smoothly: "We are now going straight over to the Roztok Institute, and our local affairs reporter Pavel Zeman... Pavel?"

The screen was now filled by a young, dark-haired reporter wearing a suit and tie and an expression of incredible self-importance. He gestured dramatically over his shoulder.

"Marta...I'm standing outside the gates of the Roztok Institute, which are, as you can see, firmly closed. It is not known how the group, which we are told numbers some forty individuals, gained access to the site, but it seems to have happened in the early hours of the morning. It is believed that the director of the institute, the distinguished scientist Count Eduard Marek, and his wife Valentina are both currently being held hostage by the group somewhere inside the complex."

The camera panned away from the reporter, focused on a green and white police jeep travelling at high speed along the road. The camera followed the vehicle as it roared up to the gates. There was a fleeting glimpse of a stern-faced man in uniform sitting in the passenger seat, staring straight ahead of him. Then, without slowing, the jeep shot through the gates, which had been hastily opened to let it through, but immediately closed again behind it. The camera refocused on the reporter, now stationed directly in front of gates once more. He was adjusting his earpiece, straightening his tie, and looking red-faced and breathless.

"Behind this supposedly impregnable wall of steel, a family is under siege from unknown terrorists," the reporter announced. "At this moment in time, we do not know who they are, or what they want. All we know for sure is that the police are doing everything that they can to bring about a safe and speedy ending to this terrifying situation." He paused, clearly savouring the dramatic effect of his words. Then: "This is Pavel Zeman, live from outside the Roztok Institute, returning you to the newsroom."

Assia flicked the remote. "Damn...damn...damn!" she swore softly. "This is not good. This is really not good."

Suki expelled air. "Wow!" she breathed, staring at the blank screen and shaking her head in disbelief.

"I think we'd better get straight round there and liaise," Stash said. "It'll be Havel in charge. I've never worked with him personally, but I gather he's okay as long as you don't push him around."

"Should we take the flak jackets?" Suki inquired.

Stash nodded. "Might as well. You know what they always say: there are old agents, there are bold agents..."

"But there are no old, bold agents," Suki finished. She cut Assia a glance. "Flaks – what do you think?" she asked.

Assia nodded in agreement.

"I'll try to contact Havel on the way over, and warn him we're coming," Stash continued, getting to his feet.

"Good idea," Assia agreed. She stood up as well. "Right, let's go then, shall we?"

Jazmin stood up. "What about me?" she asked. "You're not leaving me here on my own. No way!"

Stash paused, looked down at her thoughtfully, then flicked his eyes to Assia, who gave a little nod. "Okay, you can come too," Stash said. "But only—"

"Yeah, yeah, I know: so that you can keep an eye on me and in case you need an ID," Jazmin said resignedly.

She followed the others out to the hotel car park. The four of them got into the black ATV, Assia in front, next to Suki, who was driving. Stash got in the back with Jazmin, where he immediately began punching numbers on his micro and speaking in an urgent undertone.

The ATV pulled out of the car park and began weaving in and out of the busy lunchtime traffic. Suki drummed her fingers on the dashboard. "This is going to take ages," she complained.

Stash finished his call, reached under the seat and produced a yellow light. He opened his window, leaned out and attached the light to the roof. Then he flicked a switch. Immediately, there was a loud siren noise and the light began flashing and rotating round.

"Not strictly legal," Stash grinned at Jazmin, "but hey, if it gets us where we want to go..."

As if by magic, the traffic parted, allowing the ATV to surge through.

TEN MINUTES LATER, AND AFTER A PRACTICALLY CLEAR RUN, THE ATV SLOWED TO A HALT OUTSIDE THE GATES OF THE ROZTOK INSTITUTE. NEWS OF THE SIEGE HAD SPREAD. MORE MEDIA PEOPLE were hanging around, being deliberately blanked by a couple of big, grey-uniformed police officers, who looked as if they'd trained in the I-don't-kiss-ass school of public relations.

Stash drummed his fingers on the edge of the lowered window. "Okay, Havel. Where are you?" he muttered. "We're here. Get these gates open."

One of the cops stepped up to the ATV, grunting the Czech equivalent of: "Yeah punk, whaddya want?"

"ISA," Suki said, smiling and producing her ID tag. "My partner has spoken to Commander Havel. We're expected."

The cop eyed her suspiciously, then stepped back and had a quick conversation with his companion. They both went into a huddle outside the gate, casting the occasional beady-eyed glance over their shoulders. Their attitude clearly indicated their reluctance to let Suki and her team enter the complex. Fortunately, just in the nick of time, one of the steel gates swung open.

"*Děkuyi*," Stash called out. He waved cheerfully and smiled at the two surly faced cops as the ATV sped through the gate, nearly knocking a pushy photographer off his feet as it went. "Always be sincere," he told Jazmin, "whether you mean it or not!"

"Stash!" Suki said disapprovingly, but Stash merely shrugged and grinned unapologetically.

The ATV bucketed at high speed along an unmade road. After 500 metres, the road suddenly forked in two separate directions, and Suki slowed. "Which way, guys?"

"I'm pretty sure the house is that way," Assia said firmly, pointing left. "Go right."

"You got it," Suki said, accelerating. They drove for a short distance, following the twists and turns of the road, until finally, with a screech of brakes, the ATV pulled up outside the main building of the Roztok Institute.

COMMANDER HAVEL OF THE CZECH POLICE WAS A GOOD OFFICER, CURRENTLY UNDER GREAT PRESSURE. HE DID NOT LIKE DEALING WITH MEMBERS OF THE ARISTOCRACY (AS THEY TALKED OUT OF their backsides most of the time), and what he knew about biomedics would fit onto the back of a smallish matchbox and still leave room for a couple of paragraphs from the Police Handbook on Conflict Resolution. Havel was becoming reluctantly familiar with this book, thanks to his eager young deputy, who had recently graduated (with full honours) from the Brno Police Academy.

On the domestic front, it just so happened to be his daughter's eighteenth birthday today, and he had promised his wife faithfully that he would be back in time to ride shotgun at her party tonight. A promise that was receding further and further into the distance as each hour passed.

And now this lot had showed up.

"Tell you what, Jiří," Havel growled at his deputy, as he watched the ATV disgorge its passengers, "why don't you go to the house and make a hot drink for our visitors?"

"Yes, sir." Jiří's heels almost clicked together with enthusiasm.

"Go on then, off you go. What are you waiting for?"

"Sir, I have a question, sir," Jiří said.

"Yeah? Which is?"

"Do you think we ought to enter a property without the owner's permission?"

Havel took a deep breath. Didn't he have enough problems on his plate without Mr. Let's-Do-It-Strictly-By-The-Rules? "Look lad," he said slowly, "think of it this way – we're here to sort this mess out. Agreed? It's our public duty to rescue these people – yeah? They're relying on us, aren't they? Okay? Following me so far? So given all that, I'm quite sure they won't mind us borrowing a couple of tea bags to help us in our rescue mission, right?"

Jiří hovered hesitantly, apparently still unconvinced.

"Oh, just go and make some tea," Havel growled. "You can check the legality of it in your rule book later."

Jiří saluted smartly, got into the jeep and roared off. Havel sighed wearily, letting his shoulders sag a little. Then he strolled slowly across to the ATV, stopping within a short distance of it, keeping space between himself and the four occupants. He stuck his thumbs into his belt loops and nodded a guarded greeting. "I see you made it then," he remarked. "I'd like to say that my men on the gate mean well. But they don't. That's why they're out there. Now, what can I do for you?"

Assia stepped forward. "I'm Senior Investigation Officer Assia Dawson, ISA – London branch. These are my colleagues, Officers Smith and McGregor. We're here in an official capacity to ask Count Eduard Marek some questions."

Havel gave a short, humourless laugh. "Join the queue, lady. I've got a whole long list of questions for our good friend the count in there," he said jerking his thumb over his shoulder as he spoke. "I've got two dead bodies – and believe me, you don't want to know how they died. Both connected with Marek in some way or another. I've got Roztok staff on my back wanting to know why they're locked out of their place of work, and how they're going to be paid and what am I going to do about it. I've got a pile of paperwork you could mountaineer up. And the rest. And now, I've got a bunch of quasi-religious fanatics who think they've been told to come here by an angel. What's *your* problem?"

Assia, Stash and Suki stared at Havel.

"Excuse me," Suki queried, "what did you just refer to them as? We understood they were terrorists. That's certainly what it said on the news."

Havel's eyes went cold and hard. "No," he said. "They're not terrorists. Believe me, young lady, I wish they were. Terrorists I can deal with. There's a standard procedure. You talk, they talk, then either they give in, or you shoot them. Fanatics – they're a whole different ball game. I don't understand them. I don't know how to get through to them. They scare me. So, if there's anything helpful you lot can input at this stage, it would be very welcome, believe me."

AS SOON AS JAZMIN GOT OUT OF THE CAR, SHE BEGAN SLOWLY MOVING AWAY FROM THE OTHERS. THEN, WHEN SHE WAS SURE SHE WAS OUT OF VISUAL CONTACT, SHE SCOOTED OFF TO RECCE the area. She had noticed there were a few cars and two police vehicles parked in a line. She walked round the back of them, peering into each one. They were all empty. From what she could also see, by pressing her face to the glass windows, not much appeared to be happening inside the building either. The reception area was deserted. Some police equipment was stacked outside the building – surveillance and communication stuff, she thought, but nobody was doing anything with it.

Jazmin was very disappointed. After the dramatic news report, she'd expected a bit more than this. Everything looked to be very low key. Where were all the police in riot gear, the negotiators and armed-response teams? It was a complete non-event. The whole operation seemed to be being conducted by one grumpy, middle-aged police officer who, as far as she could tell, wasn't even carrying a firearm. This was so *not* how they did it in all the books.

"Jazmin?" her mum called out. Reluctantly, Jazmin tore herself away from the building and walked back to the ATV. Assia slipped an arm round her shoulders. "My daughter," she said to the police officer, who looked Jazmin up and down curiously. "You recruit them young," he remarked drily. As he spoke, the police jeep drove up and stopped directly in front of them. The young officer sprang out, then carefully lifted a basket from the passenger seat. "I brought a selection of nice herbal teas, sir," he said. "Hope that's all right for everyone."

Commander Havel, whose idea of a nice drink involved a tall glass filled with something cool and amber-coloured, with froth on the top, sighed wearily. "That's perfect, lad," he said. "Just perfect. Now why don't you go and get it all ready for us."

Jazmin stood a little way off, watching the adults

sipping their drinks and calmly discussing the situation. She shook her head sadly. They were acting as if they were at a tea party. What was going on? And now, as if things weren't static enough, Stash had taken the young police officer over to the ATV, where they were playing around with the sophisticated gadgetry like a couple of kids in a toy shop. A clear case of Severe Loss of Perspective Syndrome, she thought disgustedly.

Assia finished her tea and came over. "Ready to go?" she asked.

"Now? Why?"

"We've set up a liaison arrangement. They'll call us when there are any developments."

"But shouldn't we be *doing* something?"

Assia looked down at her daughter's impatient face and smiled. "Hon, one of the first things you learn in this business is when to do nothing," she said, walking her back to the ATV. "I know it all looked very dramatic on the news, but believe me, that's not how it is in reality. Reality usually involves a lot of waiting around. Commander Havel's done the right thing. He's made an assessment of the situation and now he's waiting to see how things develop."

Jazmin clambered into the vehicle. She felt let down.

"Hey, girlfriend," Stash nudged her, "did you think there'd be SAS men coming down on ropes and blowing out the skylights?"

Jazmin felt herself going red. How did he know?

Stash grinned. "Like I said, you watch too many movies."

Suki drove the vehicle out of the gates. While they'd been talking to Havel, the area in front of the Roztok Institute had grown sightseers. A large crowd had gathered. More press had arrived. Flashlights popped in their eyes as Suki turned left and took the road back towards Prague.

Assia pulled a resigned face. "Let's hope Havel has something positive for us soon," she said. "I really don't fancy running the gauntlet of this lot, day in, day out."

They entered the outskirts of the city and headed for the centre, where the hotel was located. Jazmin leaned forward, rubbernecking at the beautiful, old yellow and ochre coloured buildings and scanning the faces of the people. Suddenly, she felt her heart leap. She saw a face she recognized in the busy crowds passing along the street. "Stop!" she yelled. "Stop the car! I have to get out!" Obediently, Suki screeched to a halt. Cars behind her instantly began hooting, drivers leaning out to curse.

Jazmin threw herself out of the ATV and ran back along the road. It was him – she was sure of it. She elbowed her way through. And amazingly, there he was, standing at a crossing, waiting for the lights to change and speaking to somebody on his micro. Jazmin paused. Took a couple of deep breaths to steady her furiously beating heart. Then she walked forward and tapped the white clown on his shoulder.

A WAITRESS ENTERED THE HOTEL SUITE, CARRYING A TRAY WITH COFFEE AND A PLATE OF DELICIOUS-LOOKING CAKES. "*PROSÍM?*" SHE MURMURED POLITELY. SUKI TOOK THE TRAY, PLACING IT ON ONE of the tables. Then she followed the girl to the door, locking it after her.

"So, Jazmin," Stash said, grinning slyly and grabbing a piece of cake. "Tell us all about your *friend* again."

Jazmin eye-rolled. This was worse than school! "He's just this boy I met while I was staying with my cousin," she said dismissively.

"Uh-huh. We understand. 'Just this boy'," Stash nodded, his eyes dancing merrily. "Keep talking..."

Jazmin felt her face going red. "Umm, it's no big," she shrugged. "Mum knows all about it, don't you?" she went on, cutting her mum a meaningful glance.

"Yes, I vaguely remember you describing him," Assia said. "Tonda – isn't that his name? So what's he doing in Prague?"

"His group is performing at a theatre festival in the city," Jazmin said. "He's here to sort out where they're going to stay and arrange rehearsal times."

"Bit of luck meeting him like that," Stash said

innocently, as he poured coffee and handed it round.

Jazmin shrugged nonchalantly. "I guess."

It certainly was a bit of luck, she thought to herself happily. In all the excitement of scamming Hally and then everything that had followed, she'd barely had time to put her mind to the problem of how she was going to make contact with the group again. She just sort of automatically thought that as they were all in the same city at the same time, it would happen. And, hey, now it had. Jazmin helped herself to a piece of cake and bit into it hungrily. For once in her life, everything was so working out, she decided.

"Are you going to meet him again?" Assia asked, eyeing her daughter curiously.

"Oh...um...well, we kind of agreed to meet a bit later on," Jazmin fluffed, feeling the colour rise to her face. She stuffed the last remnants of cake into her mouth. "Err, I think I'll go have a shower and change now," she told her mum. She got up and headed for the door.

"Okay, hon," Assia said calmly. She pulled the silver pen out of her pocket, flipped up the lid and began dialling.

"Whoa – got to look good for your *friend*," Stash called out teasingly.

"Stash!" Suki said, shooting him a warning look.

Jazmin showered, then put on some of her cousin's better cast-offs. She did the moussing and curling thing with her hair and applied as much make-up as she thought she could get away with. Finally, she surveyed herself in the hotel mirror. Looking good, she thought. Another few centimetres in height wouldn't go amiss, and she'd never be catwalk-slim, but there was nothing she could do about that right now. Anyway, Tonda wouldn't notice little details like that. He was only interested in the Real Her.

Feeling pleased with what she'd achieved, she went out into the hotel corridor and tapped lightly on Stash and Suki's door. "See you all later," she called, then headed swiftly towards the elevator before they could say anything in reply.

SUNLIGHT DRIFTED DOWN LIKE DUST ONTO THE RED PANTILED ROOFS AND THE YELLOW AND OCHRE COLOURED BUILDINGS. PRAGUE WAS SUCH A BEAUTIFUL CITY, JAZMIN THOUGHT, AS SHE HURRIED ALONG THE streets of the old town in the direction of the Charles Bridge. And romantic too. She was going to enjoy exploring it with Tonda.

The white clown was waiting for her on the bridge. "Jazmin!" he exclaimed, holding out both arms and giving her a hug.

"Sorry I'm late," Jazmin puffed breathlessly. "I kept getting lost."

"But you're here now."

Jazmin glanced at her watch. "Yeah, but I can't stay too

long," she said ruefully. "I'm expected back for dinner in an hour."

Tonda leaned on the parapet. The late afternoon sun danced quicksilver on the dark waters of the Vltava. "So, this is good," he said.

"Yeah, it is," Jazmin agreed. She leaned next to him, her elbows resting on the warm stone ledge, and listened to the sound of the water rushing under the bridge, while her brain frantically tried to conjure up something interesting to say. Finally, she asked, "How is your dad?"

Tonda nodded. "He's getting better," he said. "He is still in hospital. The doctors are doing tests, but it looks like he'll pull through okay."

"That's great. Your family must've been pleased to see you again."

Tonda stared into space. "Maybe," he said obliquely. Then paused. "My mother was glad to have me there, I think. My brother is giving her a hard time right now."

"Oh? How old is he?"

Tonda eye-rolled. "Nearly fourteen." He sighed. "You know how they are at that age."

Jazmin swallowed, felt herself getting hot. "Um...yeah, I know," she agreed.

"I told her: he's only a kid, he'll grow up."

"Good advice."

Tonda turned and looked down at her. He smiled. "You decided to work for your mother's firm after all, then," he said. "I remember you said you were thinking about joining it when you left school. So how does it feel to be out in the big wide world of work?"

"Oh, um, it's...interesting," Jazmin replied. She'd forgotten about her so-called "job".

"Are they paying you a good salary?"

"Er..."

"I guess not, as you're only learning the job. So what is it they do?"

Jazmin shrugged. "They kind of check stuff out, that sort of thing," she said vaguely.

Tonda laughed. "Sounds very boring, if you don't mind me saying. You should seriously consider a career move. I'd recommend clowning. The pay's not good either, but it's never boring. How about it? You're sixteen, you're free to do whatever you want."

Jazmin pretended to smile. "Perhaps."

Tonda glanced at her. "So how long are you here in Prague?"

Jazmin shrugged. "Probably only a couple more days. Maybe less."

"We should make the most of your visit," Tonda said. "The others will arrive tomorrow afternoon, and then we'll have to start rehearsing for our next shows."

"Er...yeah," Jazmin said. This was so not going quite how she had visualized it in her head. In her head, it had been like a slushy movie: she had melted into Tonda's arms, to the sound of romantic music and under the soft, rosy glow of the setting sun. The reality was totally different. The breeze off the river was giving her goose bumps. She was finding it hard to come up with things to say, and she was beginning to feel uncomfortable with the way the conversation was going. Jazmin felt as if she was wearing a stranger's clothes and they didn't quite fit her. She made a show of looking at her watch again. "Oh, check the time! I have to get back now."

"Maybe we could meet up this evening?"

"Good idea. Why not? Tell you what, I'll text you."

Jazmin hurried back to the hotel. Unh! Mental head slap. Why hadn't she thought ahead when she'd told Tonda all that stuff about herself? Back in England, it hadn't seemed a big deal. Now, however, she could see it was going to cause problems. One little lie, she thought ruefully. Well, two little lies (or maybe three), and the whole thing was beginning to snowball. And she couldn't think of a way to unsnowball it again. She pulled a face. This was not good. Sooner or later, there was going to be thuddage.

"YOU'RE JUST IN TIME," ASSIA SAID WHEN JAZMIN ENTERED THE HOTEL ROOM. SHE BECKONED HER OVER TO THE COFFEE TABLE, WHERE THE OTHER TWO WERE GATHERED ROUND STASH'S TINY PDA screen. "There's been a development at the Roztok Institute. Havel's just sending us a c-mail."

For a brief moment, the screen remained blank. Then the image of a man appeared, fuzzily outlined, his features visible but not with any clarity. He stood behind the frosted glass entrance to the complex. They could see his mouth move, but they were unable to make out what he was saying.

"Hey, it's Mr. Fanatic," Jazmin said. She craned her neck forward to see the man's face.

"Hang on, the sound should kick in any minute," Stash said.

"...you are not welcome," the man spoke. His voice, digitally replicated, lacked any timbre and expression, making him sound slightly robotic. "Please leave. This is a polite request, not a warning." He paused, seeming to listen.

"Havel's asking him something," Suki said.

"No, we are not armed."

Another pause.

"The couple will remain here for the time being. The angel has commanded it. Please go now and leave us alone." Then the man turned round abruptly and walked away. The screen blanked.

Assia shook her head. "Not much to go on, is there? At least they're not armed. I guess that's something positive."

"Yeah, they seem pretty harmless," Suki said. "Eccentric, but harmless. So what now?"

"Havel's promised to call as soon as there are any further developments," Stash said.

"So we wait," Assia said. "Hopefully not for much longer. I can't see the police wanting to prolong this. Then we can get in and speak to Marek."

You are not welcome. Please leave. This is a polite request, not a warning.

Jazmin stood still, her eyes fixed on the tiny screen, her mind in a whirl. She had definitely heard those phrases before. Someone had said exactly the same thing to her, in the not-too-distant past. Who had said it, and where had she been at the time? Her brain did a fast rewind. Then Jazmin remembered. The strange shop. The men in the funny robes. Those were the identical words one of them had used when they chucked her out. Maybe she was playing mental hopscotch, but could there possibly be some link between the two groups?

"Mum," she said urgently, "there's something I have to tell you. And can you listen, because I think it's really important."

IAN DAWSON, ASSIA'S TWIN BROTHER, WAS SLIGHTLY SURPRISED, BUT NOT DISPLEASED TO GET AN UNEXPECTED EARLY EVENING CALL FROM HIS SISTER. SHE TENDED TO CATCH UP ON A NEED-TO-KNOW basis. The last contact he'd had with her was his call telling her Jazmin had arrived safely. Then, there had been the call from Hally. Followed by Jazmin's scribbled note saying she was leaving for Prague. Then nothing. Ian hadn't been worried. He'd presumed there hadn't been anything he needed to know for a while, and that was why he had not heard from her. So it was good to touch base once more.

Ian listened while Assia told him how beautiful Prague was in the late summertime, how it was good to see her daughter again, how grateful they both were for the way his family had looked after her. Then he in turn told her how busy and pressured it was at work, how there never seemed to be time to turn around these days, how lucky the kids were to get away on vacation – yeah, Clea was off scuba-diving in the Cayman Islands with a best friend from school. Lucky girl, eh? They agreed it was good to hear from each other, that they really needed to keep in touch more often, that it was a shame life was so hectic they couldn't find time to visit. *Ciao bro. Ciao bella Ash.*

Assia clicked the silver lid of her new communicator shut. "Sorry hon," she said. "Uncle Ian says Clea's gone away with a good friend from school."

"Did he say who?"

"Gabi Foster. Ring any bells?"

Jazmin shook her head. "I don't remember anybody called Gabi Foster," she said frowning.

"Maybe it's somebody you never knew."

"Mum, I never knew any of Clea's friends, and honestly, that was fine by me. But I did know their names. And none of them was called Gabi Foster." Jazmin looked expectantly at her mother. "You said the group comes from England, right? And that they're religious fanatics? Clea went to a group just like that. I saw her at one of their weirdy meetings. And now these people are here, and she isn't there. Hello?"

Assia pursed her lips. This was getting more and more complex. Track down an unusual archaeological find that had disappeared in mysterious circumstances. Then deal with the people who had taken it. Now the assignment was growing legs and getting more personal by the minute. "Okay, I can see what you're suggesting. But we still need more proof. Some sort of definitive ID. Do you think you'd recognize any of the men again?" she asked.

"I might. I'm sure I'd know their voices."

"Right then. Maybe we won't wait," Assia said. "I think, first thing tomorrow, we'll go back to Roztok. It seems there are some questions I'd like to ask Mr. Fanatic after all."

JAZMIN HAD ARRANGED TO MEET TONDA LATER THAT EVENING IN THE HOTEL BAR. AFTER SHE'D HAD A BIT OF TIME TO THINK MORE CLEARLY ABOUT THINGS, SHE HAD DECIDED TO GO ALONG WITH THE fictions she'd told him about herself. After all, it was only for a couple of days, she reasoned. So she'd have to vague up and stay surfacey. No big. She liked Tonda. He clearly liked her. No need to go all confessiony on him, was there?

Now she entered the hotel bar, which was decorated in a fake, upmarket-folk style with a bleached wood floor and hand-painted plates hung all round the walls.

"You look nice," Tonda said, standing up politely when she came in.

"Uh, thanks." Jazmin perched on a bar stool. She reminded herself that role-playing was part of the whole secret-agent thing. Right? So that was what she was doing here. Playing a role. In this case, herself. An older, more grown-up version.

"Can I get you a drink?" Tonda asked.

"A glass of chilled white wine, please," Jazmin said. She'd never had one, but it sounded adult and sophisticated, exactly the image she wanted to create.

Tonda ordered her a white wine, and then a beer for himself. Jazmin took tiny sips of her drink, trying to enjoy it, and listened while Tonda told her all about the theatre festival they were about to perform at, the new routines he'd come up with. She watched his face light up, becoming animated as he talked. His brown eyes shone. This is so great, she thought. I am having such a good time.

She was just mastering the technique of being able to swallow her drink without wanting to pull a face, when Stash stuck his head into the bar. "Hey, Jazmin! Suki and I are going for a late-night drive around the city," he said. "Do you guys want to come?"

Jazmin looked at Tonda. "Fancy a late-night drive?"

"Okay, that would be nice."

Stash came over to where they were sitting. He glanced at Tonda, smiling expectantly. Then he looked down at Jazmin's glass, and his expression changed. "Uh-oh. Are you drinking alcohol?"

Jazmin pushed the glass away from her across the bar. "So? It's just one drink," she said. "What's the problem?"

Stash shrugged. He ruffled her hair affectionately. "Whoa – easy, tiger," he grinned. Then he pointed to a large notice in Czech behind the bar. "The problem is that you are supposed to be over sixteen to drink in the hotel bar," he said. "Whereas you, my young friend, are only fourteen."

A large silence suddenly opened up.

"Are you coming?" Stash asked, walking towards the entrance, totally unaware of what he had just done.

"In a minute."

The silence chasmed.

"You're fourteen?"

"Um...sort of."

"What do you mean sort of?"

"Well, technically, I'm fourteen and five months. Practically fifteen, really."

"But you're actually fourteen?"

"So? It's no big deal."

"It is when you tell me you're sixteen."

"Mentally I'm sixteen, right?"

Tonda's mouth hardened into a thin, angry line. "So all

that stuff about leaving school and getting a job – you made it all up? None of it was true?"

"Well, I..."

Tonda looked at her, his dark eyes remote and unfriendly. "I think I should leave now," he said coldly. "I don't go out with kids. Especially ones that tell lies."

Jazmin hung her head, bit her lip. "Okay, I understand," she said quietly.

Jazmin felt numb. She watched Tonda stride out of the bar. He didn't once turn round and look back at her. And then, almost before she'd had time to take in what had just happened, Stash was back, the keys to the ATV dangling from his left hand. "Ready?"

Without saying a word, or making any eye contact whatsoever, Jazmin slid off the bar stool.

Stash looked round the bar. "Where's your friend?" he asked.

"He had to go," Jazmin repeated woodenly. "Sudden change of plan."

Stash stood still, looking at her curiously. Then, unexpectedly, he put an arm round her and steered her gently out into the foyer, where Suki was waiting, her leather jacket flung casually over her shoulders.

"Hey, where's the famous—" Suki began.

But Stash cut her off quickly. "Let's go, girlfriends," he said, and keeping his arm firmly round Jazmin, he led the way to the hotel car park.

Jazmin got into the back of the ATV. She kept her eyes fixed firmly on the floor and didn't say a single word the whole time they drove round Prague. I'm not going to think about this right now, she told herself. Stash and Suki carried on the heated discussion they'd been having from the moment they got into the vehicle. They appeared not to notice her silence. Good. For once, she was grateful for a bit of neglect. It gave her some time and space to pull herself together before they all got back to the hotel. Jazmin reminded herself that she'd always wanted to be a secret agent and crime fighter. And here she was, actually fulfilling her dream of a lifetime. That was what she had to try and focus on.

The bedroom Jazmin was sharing with her mum was in darkness when she returned. A silent shape in one bed indicated that her mum had decided to have an early night. Jazmin tiptoed into the room. The shape stirred, rolled over. "Hi hon. Did you have an interesting time with your friend?" her mum murmured sleepily.

Jazmin bit her lip. Oh yeah, I had an interesting time, she thought bitterly. I found out that telling lies doesn't work. I found out if you mess with people's feelings you can both get hurt.

"Yeah, it was fine, Mum," she whispered. "Sleep well."

Jazmin undressed quickly and went to have a shower. At least in the shower, she could turn the water up to full blast and nobody would know that she was crying.

THE WHITE AND GREEN POLICE JEEP SWEPT PAST THE PRESS CONTINGENT CAMPED OUTSIDE THE GATE. HAVEL SLUMPED DOWN IN THE PASSENGER SEAT, PULLED HIS HAT OVER HIS EYES AND STARED fixedly straight ahead, trying not to blink as a whole phalanx of camera flashes went off in his face like fireworks.

"I think there's more of them here today, sir," Jiří remarked.

"Really? What on earth gives you that idea?" Havel responded sarcastically.

"Well sir, yesterday there was..." Jiří's voice tailed off as he caught the edge of the look his boss was cutting him. He shut up and concentrated on his driving.

Commander Havel's mouth was set in a grim line. He'd got home very late last night to find his daughter's party in full swing and the neighbours queuing up at his door to complain. And, more seriously, there had been another murder overnight. The victim was a member of the Spiders, one of the many young criminal gangs that operated in and around the tourist spots during the holiday season. According to the victim's two buddies, they were walking back through the city centre late at night, having spent all their stolen money, when Luko had decided to nip over a convenient wall by the old cemetery to have a quick slash. Questioned later by officers at the scene, the two terrified lads could only stutter out that they'd seen a huge monster with glowing red eyes pick up Luko as if he weighed nothing at all and toss him in the air like a ball. This made the third death in almost as many days, but the first not to be directly linked to Roztok. It was enough to make Havel think that, along with everything else, he now had a serial killer on his patch. He was trying hard not to dwell on this idea, but it was one of those thoughts that had glue on it.

The jeep pulled up alongside the black ATV, which was back and parked outside the entrance to the building. Havel readjusted his hat, muttered something unrepeatable, eased himself out of his seat and went to talk to his own men. Priorities. The security people in their fancy car could wait. First, he needed to review the night's happenings with his duty officer and get a status report.

"*Dobrý den,*" STASH GREETED THE COMMANDER POLITELY, A FEW MINUTES LATER. "SO HOW ARE THINGS?"

HAVEL SHRUGGED HIS SHOULDERS. "NO CHANGE," HE SAID. "MY sergeant says it's been as quiet as the grave all night." An unfortunate, although apt choice of simile, he thought grimly.

"Is it all right for us to get out of our vehicle now?" Stash inquired, playing it by the book for all he was worth.

Havel nodded. "Go ahead. Though there's nothing to see."

"We think we may have some information on the group," Assia said.

"Yeah?" Havel grunted. "That's good." He went over to the jeep and pulled out his handheld. "We had a sighting of the man we think is the leader last night, after you'd gone," he said. "My deputy managed to get a quick shot of him. Ah, here it is."

The screen showed the head and shoulders of a youngish man, maybe mid- to late-thirties. He had long black hair tied back in a ponytail. His eyes were dark and deep set but with an intense, piercing expression in them.

Assia glanced at the man. She did not instantly recognize him, which meant he probably wasn't on the ISA most-wanted list. A good thing? She hoped so. "I'll get my daughter and see what she says."

Hearing her mother's voice calling her, Jazmin eased herself out of the ATV. She had slept badly and was feeling exhausted. But she'd resolved that she wouldn't let what had happened between herself and Tonda stop her from being a part of this. She hurried quickly across to the police jeep, and stared at the man on the police screen. And she knew who he was. *Exult*, she thought. She had been right. About everything. Assia looked into her face. "I think you should tell the commander what you told us yesterday," she said quietly.

Havel's deputy Jiří was watching the empty foyer when his chief and the security team joined him. "Nothing to report so far, sir," he said. "Are we going to continue to try and bond with them and get their trust?"

"No, we're not," Havel said shortly. "We've done it the official way and it's got us nowhere at all. Now we're going to do it my way."

CLEA WAS TIRED. SO TIRED. SHE COULD NOT REMEMBER EVER BEING THIS TIRED BEFORE IN HER WHOLE LIFE. SHE VERY BADLY WANTED TO SLEEP. TO SLEEP. TO CURL UP SOMEWHERE, anywhere, on the floor, under a bench, and close her aching eyes and drift off into a deep and peaceful sleep. But that wasn't going to happen. Gabi and the other leaders had made it quite clear to everybody from the beginning. Not much sleep was on the agenda. "We have work to do," they had told them. "We must prepare ourselves to meet Azazel, our lord. We must all search for and release the angel that lies within, so that we can be found worthy when the great day arrives."

Thus, ever since they'd arrived, the group had been preparing itself to be found worthy. Praise meetings had been held, led by one or other of the seraphim. These went on for hours on end and involve chanting and repeating words like *exult* or *worship* over and over again. Then there were study groups and lectures and talks and ministry and more praise meetings.

Even mealtimes were strictly monitored to check that no unworthiness occurred – everyone ate together in silence while the cherubim read from the writings of

Azazel. Clea had never heard these before, but Gabi had told her that they were a direct revelation from Azazel himself and had been dictated to their leader Seraph Gray during his second vision. In his first vision, Azazel had appeared in person and told the Seraph to take all of them and bring them out of the land of the nephilim, to a place of safety and security that he would show them. This place.

At least, that's what Clea thought was happening, but what with only a couple of hours' sleep, and the way that every minute of her time was being busily filled, she was beginning to lose focus. Except that you mustn't lose focus, Gabi had said, because that meant you were not trying to become worthy. And Clea really wanted to be worthy. She wanted to please Gabi and the other leaders who loved her and cared about her so much. And she really wanted to meet Azazel. Of course she did. But most of all, she wanted to sleep. Clea's eyes gradually closed, her head nodded forward. But the next minute, she was jerked awake. Gabi was shaking her by the arm. "Come on, Clea, what's the matter with you?" she exclaimed. "It's time for our next praise meeting. We'll go together, shall we?"

So Clea was hauled reluctantly to her feet and dragged along a corridor. Everything was very white in this place, she thought. All the surfaces glittered and sparkled under the high, bright lights. And it smelled funny, like chemicals. Maybe they were in heaven, if such a place existed. "Are we going to meet Azazel now?" she asked.

Gabi smiled at her and said, "Soon Clea, very soon."

And Clea wondered what time of day it was, because they had taken her watch away. And her little gold micro. And she wondered why somebody was hammering at the door, and shouting very loudly through a megaphone.

MEANWHILE, IN ANOTHER PART OF THE BUILDING, COUNT EDUARD MAREK WAS LYING TO HIS WIFE. HE WAS TELLING HER THAT OF COURSE THEY WOULD BE FINE. HE WAS CALLING HER BY THE LITTLE pet names he enjoyed using, the ones he knew she did not really like. He was reassuring her that they would soon be freed from the place and then the terrible nightmare would come to an end.

Marek was not telling her what he actually knew, which was that they would never leave this place alive. He did not share with her his knowledge that this was where it would end for both of them. That he had already made his preparations, so that when the dark angel came for them, as it had told him it would, she would not suffer as Jan suffered. Marek could not bear for that to happen. His beloved wife, his *milenka*. Crushed and torn apart by its evil hands.

No, Marek thought. This was one area at least where he could still control what happened. And some day, justice would be done to the evil thing that was not of this world. Marek had to believe this would happen, though he did not know how and he was pretty sure he would not be there to see it. He went to his office to make them both a cup of coffee, walking like an old man, shuffling along the corridor, glancing fearfully over his shoulder, his heart jumping at every new sound he heard.

OUTSIDE THE BUILDING, JUST AS HAVEL WAS BEGINNING TO RUN OUT OF VOICE – AND HOPE – THERE WAS AN UNEXPECTED DEVELOPMENT. A YOUNG, RATHER DISHEVELLED WOMAN APPEARED AT THE entrance, wearing a very cross expression on her face.

"Please stop disturbing our worship time," she snapped.

Havel put down the megaphone and indicated to Jiří that he could cease from banging on the glass. "Maybe we'll stop disturbing your worship time when you start cooperating with us," he growled. "So how about you do some talking?"

There was a pause. Then the woman's face went blank and expressionless. "We have nothing to talk about."

Assia stepped forward. "Listen, my name is Assia Dawson. I work for the ISA. We need to talk urgently to Eduard Marek. Where is he?"

The young woman barely glanced in her direction. "We do not discuss matters with nephilim. Now please go away and leave us alone."

"What is your name?" Assia asked.

"I'm not telling you."

"Is there a girl called Clea in there with you?"

"I'm not telling you."

"Is there anything you *are* going to tell us?" Havel muttered.

The woman shook her head. Havel swore in Czech. Assia gave an exclamation of annoyance.

Meanwhile Jazmin, who was hanging around on the edge of things, suddenly had an idea. She walked forward and pressed her nose to the glass. "Hey Gabi!" she called out softly, trying out the name her uncle had mentioned on the phone. Instinctively, without even thinking, the woman turned round at the sound of her name. Then, realizing what she had done, her face reddened with anger and she scurried away.

"Well done, hon," Assia said quietly under her breath. "Quick thinking."

"Yeah – nice one!" Stash said, nodding at her.

There was a brief silence, while everyone took in what had just occurred.

Then Havel observed, "Yes, as you say, nice one. But we still don't know what they're up to in there."

Suki pointed back to the ATV. "We might be able to fix that," she said. "Maybe now's the right time to get some listening devices in place."

Havel nodded in agreement. "I'm going to call in some

back-up too," he said. "I've got a feeling that we might be here for some time. Worse luck."

"Do you want to stay?" Assia whispered to Jazmin. "I can easily get someone to take you back to the hotel."

"No, I'm good," Jazmin said firmly. I've got this far, she thought. I'm not giving up now. "I think I'll walk round the building," she added. "See if there's anything interesting at the back."

ASSIA DAWSON WATCHED HER DAUGHTER STRIDING AWAY INTO THE LONG UNMOWN GRASS AND WILD FLOWERS AND WAS SUDDENLY GRATEFUL THAT AT LEAST SHE WAS HERE, WHERE SHE COULD KEEP a watchful eye upon her. And Clea? Assia tried to remain calm, to think things through logically. Okay, maybe she was going to have to acknowledge that Jazmin was right. That her niece was probably somewhere in that complex with the group.

Assia pushed herself a little further along that path. The group, whatever else it was, did not seem to be hostile. Misguided, deluded, but not dangerous. And if Clea had gone with them, it appeared to be willingly. Nobody had coerced her or bullied her into going. Why on earth she had gone, was a question Assia was not prepared to speculate about right now.

So should she tell her brother? Assia pulled a face. Of course she should. Wouldn't she want to know, in similar circumstances? But she also knew Ian inside out and guessed exactly what his immediate reaction would be: he'd be on the next plane from London. Ian had a short temper. He was volatile and not the most patient of people. And he was totally besotted with his daughter. Assia could just picture what might happen if she allowed him to come here. He'd want to organize everything. He'd go around barking out orders. He'd alienate Havel and ruin everything for them. It would be like juggling matches in a firework factory. Assia sighed. Maybe it was better not to make that call right now, she decided. At least not until there was some definite confirmation that Clea was with the group.

Satisfied that she'd reached the right decision, but not entirely happy about it, Assia walked back to rejoin the rest of her team.

THE WALL OF THE ROZTOK BUILDING WAS SMOOTH AND WHITE, LIKE THE SHELL OF AN EGG. THERE WERE NO EXITS, NO WINDOWS AT EYE-LEVEL. AN AIR VENT HIGH UP ON THE WALL HUMMED BUSILY. Crickets chirped rustily in the long grass. Jazmin leaned against the sun-warmed wall and pressed her cheek against the white brick.

You think that despair will stop you cold. But it doesn't. What it does is wrap itself up in a dark corner, allowing you to get on with things. The things that keep you going. Jazmin got out her pocket mirror and took a long look at her reflection. Her face looked different, she thought. Like somebody had crayoned over the lines rather heavily. She stood for a moment, soaking in the sun, listening to the sounds of nature all around her. Then she took a deep breath, and went back.

At the front of the building, Stash had driven the ATV right up against the wall. The antennae on the roof were busy scanning and picking up information, which was being transferred to the internal computer screen. Meanwhile, the police were also busy setting up their own listening devices.

This was more like it, Jazmin thought approvingly. At last, some proper technical stuff was happening. From the books she'd read, this was exactly how she envisaged a siege situation being handled. From the sidelines, Jazmin watched what was happening. Then she squared her shoulders and hurried forward. "Right," she said. "What can I do to help?"

LATER THAT EVENING, ASSIA AND HER TWO COLLEAGUES SAT ON THEIR HOTEL BALCONY ENJOYING THE COOL NIGHT AIR AND LOOKING OUT ACROSS THE CITY. AT NIGHT, PRAGUE WAS A MOVING FIELD of light. It was a spider's web of colour: red, white and yellow spinning across the retina of the eye. In the adjacent room, Jazmin was fast asleep, worn out by a busy afternoon's sightseeing.

"Havel's worried," Stash remarked. He had his PDA

open and was studying the screen intently. "Like he says, the group members don't want to talk, they're not asking for anybody to be freed, they haven't got any demands, and they're not making some big ethical statement. There's nothing to trade."

"It reminds me of those talking rocks in Patagonia," Suki said. "Funny isn't it, what people believe, even in the face of reality."

"Sometimes, reality is not important," Assia said. "Reality is what people *believe* is real."

"So a dead body becomes an angel."

"If you believe it, yes."

"But how on earth did they find out about it?" Suki murmured.

"These quasi-religious groups all have cyber sites and chat rooms," Assia told her. "Someone along the way probably dropped a hint on one of them."

Stash shook his head sadly. "We need to get in there and remove that body."

"If it's there," Assia reminded him. "Remember, we still have no actual proof that Marek has got the body. Nor that my niece is with that group either," she added with a sigh.

"That's another puzzler," Stash said, frowning. "From what you say, your niece is a rich girl. She's got a good home, nice parents, everything a kid could want. Why give it all up?"

Assia shrugged. "Maybe for some people, material things ultimately just aren't enough," she said thoughtfully.

"And to think I actually envied the well-off!" Stash said. "Maybe poor is really the new rich."

"Like you have a choice!" Suki teased.

Stash shrugged. Then he handed Assia the PDA. "There you go," he said. "I ran a check on the group's leader with Interfind. It's not much, but they came up with this."

Assia looked. "It certainly looks like the man the police photographed." She scrolled down past the head and shoulders shot to the brief bio.

Gray Jones, she read. Age thirty-eight. Marriage dissolved. No children. The address given was a shop called Spirit World, which was located in the high-rise complex in England where her brother lived.

Assia read on. "It says here that he used to work for a big multinational company. Reached management level. Doesn't say why he left. He hasn't ever been in any sort of trouble before though. No police record. Not even picked up a parking fine. Mr. Squeaky Clean. In fact, until now, nobody's ever heard of Mr. Gray Jones."

"Well, they're sure going to know his name after this," Stash said grimly.

"If he's inside," said Assia. "We still don't know for sure."

"So what's it all about?" Suki mused. "Some sort of power thing? The small man going up against the system?"

"Possibly. Except that this small man has got thirty-nine other people, two Czech scientists and possibly a dead body with him," Assia observed drily. "Which kind of lifts the game to a different level, doesn't it?"

Stash exhaled. "If only we knew for sure that they weren't armed, Havel's lot could blow out that front door, go in and finish the whole thing peacefully."

"If only...indeed."

"They can't stay in there for ever," Suki said, shaking her head. "Sooner or later, there has to be an ending."

Assia nodded slowly. "You're right, of course. But there are always lots of different endings, aren't there? The question is: what sort of ending will this be?"

JAZMIN LAY IN BED. SHE WAS THINKING ABOUT TONDA. DURING THE COURSE OF THE DAY SHE HAD TEXTED HIM. SEVERAL TIMES. APOLOGIZED. REMINDED HIM THAT SHE STILL HAD THE BOX containing his egg. Now there was nothing more she could do. It was up to him to make the next move. Jazmin wondered whether he'd told the rest of the clowns about her, and how they'd reacted. She had not told her mum, but she guessed that her mum knew, and understood she wasn't supposed to talk about it.

She breathed out quietly. Last night she had felt miserable to the amount of ten. Now, she felt better. She had hit a major backspace, but she wasn't going to get all Hamlety about it. And sometime in the future, she promised herself, she would make time to have a broken heart. And then she would find the strength to get over it and move on.

MEANWHILE, CLEA DAWSON HUDDLED IN THE PITCH DARK AND WRAPPED THE COARSE, GREY FIRE BLANKET ROUND HER SHOULDERS. SHE CLOSED HER EYES AND TRIED NOT TO THINK about what had happened earlier, but she couldn't stop herself. It was like the mind game she used to play with Ed when they were children. "Close your eyes," he'd say, "and don't think about tigers." And instantly, her head would be full of shadowy jungle, orange and black stripes and sinuous movement.

Clea thought instead about the supper they'd all shared that evening. It had been pasta – one of the women had cooked it in the staff kitchen. And there had been Parmesan cheese to grate on top; dry, golden dust like falling snow. She'd enjoyed eating it. But people were starting to complain. They were getting fed up with the endless confinement. They wanted to know where Azazel was. When they would see him. When he and his angels were going to destroy the nephilim.

After supper, they'd had another worship meeting, led by Seraph Gray. That was when it happened – the thing she was trying not to think about.

They had been worshipping for a long time – at least, it seemed like a long time to Clea – when all at once, Seraph Gray had stopped the chanting and announced that he had something very serious to say. Then, he had told them that someone had been seen talking to the army of nephilim who were waiting to slay them outside the building. That this person was not a true angel, but a false one. That they had a traitor in their midst. A traitor who had deceived them and tried to betray them to the enemy.

There had been a shocked silence. People had looked around, trying to identify who he meant. Then Seraph Gray had pointed directly at Gabi. "You are the traitor," he had declaimed. "You are the evildoer."

"No, it was an accident, they tricked me!" Gabi had cried.

But immediately Seraph Gray and some of the other leaders had started chanting: "Cast her out. Cast her out." And soon, everybody else was chanting too.

At this point, Gabi collapsed onto the floor, sobbing and pleading, but of course, nobody was listening to her. Then Seraph Gray gave a signal and the three archangels took hold of Gabi and dragged her, sobbing, out of the room. "Take her to Azazel," Seraph Gray shouted at the top of his voice, his face red with fury. "Let her look him in the face and deny what she has done!"

After a couple of minutes, the three archangels returned to the room and resumed their places at the front. Now there was absolute silence. Everyone was waiting to see what was going to happen. Suddenly, the silence was broken by a wretched, piercing scream.

Then Seraph Gray, his face cold and expressionless, had said calmly, "Azazel the mighty one has spoken. Praise be his name." And the chanting had resumed, just as if nothing had happened.

Nobody had seen Gabi again.

But the complaining had stopped.

Clea shivered in the darkness and tried not to think about what had happened to her friend and mentor. She didn't want to recall the pitiful image of Gabi's heels drumming helplessly on the floor as she was taken away. She didn't want to hear that scream. But most of all, she didn't want to remember that she had joined in the chanting. She had played a part in sending her friend to a lonely and terrible death.

For the first time in her life, Clea felt guilt and shame. They made uncomfortable bedfellows.

AT LEAST THERE HAD BEEN NO OVERNIGHT REPORTS OF ANYBODY BEING KILLED IN THE CITY, HAVEL THOUGHT TO HIMSELF, AS HE STOOD AND SURVEYED THE ROZTOK BUILDINGS, SHINING IN THE EARLY morning sun. Given his failure to resolve the situation here, it was one small consolation.

"Nothing to report, chief," the night officer said wearily. "Like a bloody morgue in there. What do you suppose they're up to?"

Havel shrugged. He could not envisage what was going on behind those blank, featureless walls. Yesterday, his men had drilled holes and planted listening devices. They had tried unsuccessfully on several occasions to lure another member of the group to the entrance. Now they were reduced to playing a waiting game. Sooner or later (and he really hoped it would be sooner), the weirdos behind the walls would run out of food or faith. Then they'd start negotiating. Havel reassured himself: they just had to be patient for a little while longer.

Inside the complex, in the comparative comfort of his executive office, Marek and his wife were also assessing the current situation. With slightly less optimism. They were talking about the death of the young woman last night. They hadn't known her name, but they had heard her final scream.

"Why does it kill?" the countess asked fearfully.

Marek glanced quickly towards the closed door. "Because it can," he murmured, repeating the answer the angel itself had given him, when he'd asked it the same question.

"What does it want?"

Marek shook his head. "Power and control?" he

suggested. And death, he thought grimly with a shudder. Always death. And every time it killed, it seemed to grow stronger. As if it was living off the souls of its victims. Marek knew that all this was just a warm-up. Soon the terrible angel would move outwards. The evil would start spreading like a black cancer across the city, then the country. Then wider still, unless it could be stopped.

The countess looked at him. Her husband seemed even thinner around the face, more careworn. His eyes were sunken, the skin around them baggy. But there was an inner core of strength and resolution of will that she had never before seen in him. A grim determination that he would stick it out to the bitter end, whatever the personal cost.

"I brought it back to life," he had said last night, as they held each other and tried to sleep. "It is my responsibility. I must accept my destiny. It is kismet."

The countess knew that Marek would not leave, whatever befell them. And so she stayed because she could not envisage life without him. It was as if their roles had been reversed. Now he was the strong one, and she was dependent upon him.

"What will happen?" she asked.

Marek stroked her hair, smiled reassuringly and repeated the familiar mantra. "It will be fine, *milá*," he said, soothingly. "Everything will be fine, I promise you."

Marek's thoughts returned to the early morning hours, when he had woken to the sound of someone gently knocking at the door. It had been the strangely intense man, the leader of the English group. The one who called himself Seraph Gray. Marek had left his wife sleeping peacefully upon a chair and tiptoed out into the corridor, where the man had spoken to him. At first, Marek had not understood what the man wanted. Then, when he had understood, Marek had refused. Finally, however, he had given in and gone with this strange, intense man to his lab and unlocked the door.

There, he had shown him the place where the body had lain, had also shown him the machine and explained how he had used it to revivify the decayed flesh. He had not set foot in the lab since that fateful night. He had not wanted to enter it now, but he'd had no choice. The man had told him imperiously, "Azazel commands you." And his deep-set eyes had glittered feverishly as he spoke.

It controls us all, body and soul, Marek thought sadly. *Because it can.*

ASSIA HELPED HERSELF TO CEREAL AND COFFEE FROM THE BREAKFAST BAR. SHE CARRIED THEM OVER TO THE TABLE, WHERE STASH AND SUKI WERE FINISHING THEIR PLATES OF SCRAMBLED egg and bacon, and sat down. Jazmin was with them, sipping apple juice and crumbling a bread roll on her plate.

Assia glanced quickly at her, pursed her lips, but said

nothing. We've all been there, she thought to herself, adding milk from a jug on the table to her cereal. This was one journey her daughter had to make on her own. She stirred her coffee, looking round the dining room as she did so. The other tables were full of tourists eating hearty breakfasts and planning their day's sightseeing. Assia experienced that familiar parallel-universe feeling.

"Nothing from Havel yet?" she asked.

Stash shook his head. "I'd like to get straight over there after breakfast though," he said. "If that's okay with you? I think I might have come up with something."

"Go on."

But Stash merely tapped the side of his nose with his index finger. "I need to check my idea out first," he said mysteriously. "Then I'll get back to you."

Assia scraped up the last of her cereal. Then she pushed back her chair. "Well, I'm ready," she said. "Let's go."

"YOU CANNOT BE SERIOUS!" JAZMIN EXCLAIMED.

STASH NODDED AND SMILED HAPPILY. "I GOT THE IDEA FROM YOU," HE SAID. "REMEMBER HOW YOU TOLD US WHEN YOU DID A RECCE ROUND the back of the building, that the only sound you could hear was the air vent humming? So I did a scan of the ventilation system and...bingo!" he grinned. "We have a way into the building."

"It's brilliant!" Suki exclaimed. "Well done, Jazmin. It

means you can go all over the place and nobody will know you're there."

"Whoa. Hold on," Jazmin interrupted. "Let me get the *you* bit straight. You want me to climb into an air vent and snoop around? Have I got that right?"

Assia put an arm round her shoulders. "You're the only one small enough to fit through the gap. Otherwise, one of us would do it, obviously."

"Yeah, sure. Obviously."

"You don't have to if you don't want to," Assia added.

"Oh, good. You mean I have a choice?"

"Of course."

Jazmin studied the air vent. It was about two metres up, a neat metal grid that was flush with the smooth white wall. From where she was standing, it looked tiny. Surely she'd never fit in that? And what if she got lost in the maze of tunnels and couldn't find her way back? To say nothing about the spiders! Knowing her luck, there were so bound to be spiders. Big black spiders. Scuttling about on long hairy legs. She took a deep breath. "I have to think about it."

"I understand," Assia said.

"You take as long as you want," Suki said.

"Nobody's trying to push you," Stash said.

Havel and the young officer remained silent, but their eyes pleaded with her to agree.

Jazmin walked away from them all. She went and sat on

her own on the grass and thought about what they wanted her to do. She had to admit that Suki was right; it was a brilliant idea. It made total sense. So long as you didn't factor in things like reluctance, cowardice and fear.

After a while, Stash came over and sat down next to her.

"Did I ever tell you about the time Suki and I were working off the Liberian coast trying to infiltrate a gold smuggling gang?" he asked, staring into the middle distance.

Jazmin shook her head.

"We got trapped in this disused mine. Us and two other members of the team. It was the rainy season, the water started coming in, and there was only one way out – a small, pitch-black tunnel that was only crawl height."

"Aw, don't tell me – you bravely and single-handedly rescued them all, didn't you!"

Stash smiled. "You really do read too many books. No, nothing so heroic. The problem was, Suki is terrified of enclosed spaces. They totally freak her out. But she knew if she refused to go, none of us would go. We wouldn't leave her to die alone in the dark. So she had to make a difficult personal choice – she had to set her own fear against the lives of the rest of her team."

"And you're telling me this story because...?"

Stash glanced at her swiftly, then looked away again. "I'm just pointing out that there's no *I* in team," he said quietly. "That's something we all have to learn right from the start. Otherwise, it just doesn't work." He got up. "Not that I'm putting any pressure on you, of course," he said innocently.

Jazmin covered her face with her hands. Emotional blackmail or what? Did she really have any choice after that? She went back to the group. "Okay, okay," she said. "You talked me into it. I'll do it. But I must be totally crazy."

JAZMIN HAD OFTEN IMAGINED HERSELF LEAPING INTO ACTION AS A FEARLESS CRIME FIGHTER. IF ASKED TO PROVIDE ACCOMPANYING WARDROBE NOTES, SHE'D PROBABLY HAVE COME UP WITH A SEXY, black figure-skimming outfit, low-cut, with a double pink stripe down each side. Footwear might be ankle boots – black leather would be nice, with possibly a small heel. The whole outfit completed by a black leather belt (hand-stitched) with loops for her gun, cuffs and assorted gadgetry. Hair in high ponytail, held in place by something glittery. Make-up subdued, but enhancing.

Funny how reality, which so often let her down, had done it again.

Jazmin stood at the foot of the ladder, watching Stash remove the grid from the vent. Suki had equipped her from the field kit in the ATV, which was why she was wearing a skintight lightweight diving suit in a colour that could best be described as squashed slug. The material had a slimy viscous feel to it, which she'd been told would help her move easily along the tunnel. It had a close-fitting hood, which she'd been advised to pull up as soon as she entered the vent. The outfit had all the sex appeal of a road accident. It was so majorly not how she'd imagined it.

Jazmin carried breathing equipment, a clip-on mike and earpiece so that she could communicate, a tiny searchlight on a headband and Suki's minute digital camera. Somewhere on her person was a micro tag that would enable the others to monitor her progress and tell her where to go next. She was technologically enhanced in all areas, but she still hadn't been allowed to carry a gun.

Sadly, no gun seemed to be the story of her life.

Stash shinned down the ladder. "All yours, girlfriend," he said, stepping aside and helping her onto the first rung. "Now remember—"

"Follow the instructions, and stay in contact at all times," Jazmin repeated robotically.

"You are so great, you know that?" Stash grinned.

Yeah. That's me, Jazmin thought. Great but gullible. She began to climb the ladder.

"Good luck, hon," Assia called from below. "I'm really proud of you."

"Yeah, you're really brave, Jazmin," Suki added.

Jazmin went a bit further. Then she looked down. The ground seemed a long way away. She swallowed. Then suddenly she saw the white clown in her mind. He was looking at her, just as he used to when they were all waiting to start a performance. The white clown smiled at her, circled his thumb and first finger. "It's show time," he said. Jazmin nodded. She climbed to the top of the ladder, pulled the hood up and dived head first into the open air vent.

FEAR AND CURIOSITY ARE NEIGHBOURING BRAIN CELLS. WHICH WAS JUST AS WELL, JAZMIN THOUGHT, AS SHE INCHED HER WAY ALONG THE NARROW AIR VENT, PAUSING OCCASIONALLY TO LISTEN FOR sounds of people on the other side of the dividing wall. Thinking about them was certainly taking her mind off herself. She wondered what the strange group was up to. Also, what her invisible progress through the building sounded like to them. She grinned. Maybe they thought she was a rat.

The tunnel was just wide enough for Jazmin to crawl on her hands and knees. There were cables and pipes running all along the ceiling. It smelled cool, yet slightly musty and she could feel the fresh air moving around her. To her great relief, it was also quite clean. Just a fine layer of dust on the floor. She tried to crawl carefully, so as not to stir it up too much.

"Jazmin?" Stash's voice sounded in her ear.

"Yes, I can hear you."

"Have you checked your breathing apparatus?"

"Of course I have," Jazmin lied. She checked her breathing apparatus.

"Have you switched the camera on?"

Jazmin pressed the tiny button on the top of Suki's camera.

"Great. We've got you on the monitor too. Keep going until you reach a kind of junction. Then the tunnel will split two ways."

Jazmin moved slowly forward. "I've reached it," she murmured.

"Good girl. You're now directly above the inner corridor. Can you hear anything yet?"

Jazmin paused. "Nope." Not a sound.

"Not to worry. Attach one of the bugs to the wall. Done that? Okay, now take the right-hand fork and keep going to the end."

Jazmin did as Stash instructed. She moved along the tunnel, noticing how the semi-darkness began to become lighter as she went. "I'm coming up to a grille or something on the left-hand side," she told Stash. Then, "Hey, I can see into a room."

"Is there anybody there?"

Jazmin pressed her nose to the metal grille. "No. It looks like it's a staffroom. I can see chairs and coffee tables. And there are lots of blankets and sleeping bags on the floor," she said. She slid her arm down her side and extracted one of the tiny, black listening devices from a flap pocket in the suit. She wedged it between two of the metal cross struts.

"Good, Jazmin, that's great," Stash said. "Can you keep going? The tunnel will bend sharply in a while, but you should be able to get round."

Jazmin crawled on and on, placing bugs on the walls at regular intervals. The light had begun to fade gently as she moved away from the room and the faint humming noise was starting to get louder and louder. Finally, she reached the bend in the tunnel. It was blocked.

"I can't go any further," she said. She held the earpiece away from her. "Can you hear that sound?"

There was a pause at the other end. Then the sound of faint swearing.

"Damn!" Stash said. "I suspected this might happen, but I kind of hoped it wouldn't. Okay, I think you've probably reached the filtration unit that separates the two buildings. Right, plan B. Go back to the fork in the tunnel and we'll try the other way."

Jazmin began to retreat slowly along the narrow tunnel. This was much harder. She had to crawl backwards, and her knees and shoulders were beginning to hurt. Also her mouth was getting dry and she was trying not to think about wanting the loo. "Keep going," she muttered encouragingly, trying to envisage herself as Jaz Dawson, super-skinny secret agent and crime fighter. Currently saving the world by crawling backwards along a tunnel. Eventually, she reached the metal grille once more and paused to get her breath back and cool down a bit.

Jazmin peered into the messy room, trying to pick out something that she could recognize as belonging to her cousin. She took in a couple of deep breaths, then peeled back the uncomfortable hood, which was making her ears go into meltdown. She bent down to wipe her sweaty forehead on her arm. And as she did so, somebody entered the room.

WHEN YOU'RE PART OF AN ISOLATED GROUP OF PEOPLE, ON AN ISLAND FOR EXAMPLE, OR A SHIP, OR EVEN IN A LOCKED BUILDING, YOU BEGIN TO LOSE YOUR INDIVIDUALITY. IT DISSOLVES, BECOMING partially replaced by a sense of unity. Unconsciously, at any given moment, you develop the ability to place everybody in the small universe you inhabit. From their footsteps, their breathing, the rhythms of work and sleep, a familiar pattern emerges. You know where they are. Just as they know where you are.

So Clea Dawson was aware that the rest of the group was in the worship room. She could hear the faint rhythmic sounds of their voices raised in praise of Azazel. There were a couple of angels in the kitchen preparing lunch. She also sensed the silence radiating from the rest of the building. Clea had slipped out of the meeting and returned to the sleeping quarters to get a migraine tablet. She had not had an attack for weeks. Now, precipitated by stress and exhaustion from lack of sleep and insufficient fresh air, she was starting to get the early-warning symptoms.

Flashes of red and yellow light were shooting behind Clea's left eye. Soon, she would begin feeling dizzy, then nauseous. Then the heavy, hammering bright-edged pain would hit. At this point, Clea always locked herself in her room, pulled down the shades and curled up in bed to sleep it off. She was not sure what she would do here. Everything was different now Gabi had died. Gabi had been her friend and guide. She had relied upon her totally. Now she felt scared and lonely, and for the first time, she was beginning to think the unthinkable: that this had all been a terrible mistake and she wanted to go home.

And then, just to add to her torment, the air vent suddenly started speaking to her.

IT DID NOT SURPRISE JAZMIN TO SEE CLEA ENTERING THE ROOM. THERE HAD BEEN SO MANY COINCIDENCES, SO MUCH SYNCHRONISM ALREADY THAT SHE WOULD HAVE BEEN SURPRISED HAD IT NOT been Clea. But she was shocked to see the state her cousin was in. This was not the confident, in-your-face, bandbox fresh Clea she remembered. Instead, her cousin looked pale and grubby and thoroughly miserable. Jazmin leaned forward, pressing her face right up against the metal grid.

"Clea," she called quietly.

At first, Clea seemed not to realize where the voice was

coming from. She checked all around the room, trying to locate it. She seemed unusually nervous, as if she was scared of something.

"Up here," Jazmin said. "The air vent."

Clea glanced up at the gridded opening high on the wall. Her eyes widened in terror. "Are you Azazel?" she whispered fearfully.

"Who?" Jazmin queried. "Listen, it's me, Jazmin."

There was a brief pause while Clea's mind tried to realign itself to reality. "What are you doing in there?" she asked finally.

How long have we got? Jazmin thought grimly. "Never mind that. Listen, are you all right?" she asked.

Clea's pretty face crumpled. "He killed Gabi," she gulped.

"Who?"

"Azazel."

"Who is Azazel?"

Clea looked horrified. "Azazel is the mighty one."

Oh, for freak's sake, Jazmin thought despairingly, get a grip on reality down there. "Look, there is no Azazel," she told Clea firmly. "Azazel doesn't exist, right? He is just some old dead body that was dug up in Antarctica by a bunch of scientists."

Clea stared straight ahead, her eyes huge and dark-rimmed with exhaustion and the fast-approaching migraine. "Then who killed Gabi?" she asked.

"Somebody got killed?" Jazmin exclaimed, finally taking on board what her cousin was telling her.

"She was talking to the nephilim," Clea spoke woodenly as if repeating a learned lesson. "We had to cast her out. She was a traitor. She was not worthy."

Omigod, Jazmin thought. They've done brainwashy stuff to her.

Suddenly, Clea's expression changed. She went chalk white. Even her lips lost their colour. A look of absolute terror crossed her face. "I can't talk to you any more," she gasped. "What if Azazel finds out?"

"Clea, wait – you must listen to me," Jazmin called urgently, but Clea shook her head. She put her hands firmly over her ears and scurried out of the room.

Outside in the corridor, Clea Dawson leaned against a wall. She felt sick and dizzy. She was also very, very scared. Suppose somebody had noticed her sneak out of the meeting and had told Seraph Gray? They would cast her out, just like they did Gabi. She would be sent to Azazel. She would have to look him in the face and confess what she had done. Clea's heart pounded so loudly, she was sure everyone could hear it. The sounds of worship swirled all around her, stabbing at her like sharp spears.

Suddenly, hot acidy liquid flooded Clea's throat. She leaned over and threw up on the floor. Then she straightened up, took a couple of deep breaths to steady herself. She stared down in disgust. There was vomit all over her pretty shoes. Stepping out of them, Clea stumbled barefoot down the corridor, deliberately taking herself away from the loud chanting noise that was hurting her head. Her head was splitting. She felt absolutely terrible. All she wanted to do now was find a dark, quiet solitary place in which she could curl up and die.

JAZMIN WAITED A FEW SECONDS TO SEE IF HER COUSIN WAS COMING BACK. THEN SHE RESUMED HER SLOW, PAINSTAKING CRAWL ALONG THE NARROW AIR VENT TOWARDS THE OPENING. She decided she'd better report back on this at once. It was difficult to reach her mike now she'd taken the hood off. Also, she desperately needed a break to stretch her cramped limbs before attempting the second part of her mission. She reached the opening of the air vent and shouted down for someone to come and get her.

"What happened?" Assia exclaimed, when Jazmin finally reached ground level once more.

"Yeah, you suddenly went out of contact. We were worried," Suki added.

"I took the hood thing off," Jazmin admitted. "It got too hot. But I..."

"Uh-uh. That wasn't a good idea, girlfriend," Stash said sternly. "I know it's uncomfortable, but it's essential that you stay in touch with us at all times, for your own safety.

What would have happened if something'd gone wrong in there?"

Gee, thanks for doing all that work, Jazmin. It was really good of you. We are so grateful. What a hero you are, Jazmin thought to herself. She pulled a face at Stash. Then turned to her mum. "Can I have a drink, please?" she asked, blanking the other two. Assia handed her a cold can. Jazmin took a long slurp, then wiped her mouth on the back of her hand. "So do you want to know what happened?" she said, glancing from Stash to Suki to her mum and back again. "Or shall I just shut up and let you go on ripping my head off?"

THE NEWS THAT AT LEAST ONE OF THE GROUP INSIDE THE ROZTOK INSTITUTE MIGHT HAVE BEEN KILLED, PRODUCED AN INSTANT FLURRY OF ACTIVITY. SUDDENLY, THINGS BEGAN TO GET SERIOUS. HAVEL ordered up his armed-response unit to go on standby. It was decided to abort the second part of Jazmin's bugging attempt and she was asked to go off site. There was a sudden and perceptible change in the atmosphere. Everything was ratcheted up a notch. The tension strings began to tighten.

From deep within the complex, Gray Jones, self-proclaimed leader of the Angels (now renamed The Followers of Azazel), was well aware of what was taking place outside the walls. He remained calm and unsurprised.

It was just as Azazel had revealed to him in the writings: "Many will come against me; the armies of the nephilim will gather outside the walls and plot evil deeds. They will shoot fiery darts and try to overthrow my kingdom."

In Seraph Gray's mentally enclosed, intense world, the fires of fanaticism flamed brightly. Let them gather, he brooded darkly. Let them plot. They come not against mere mortals. Powers and principalities, thrones and dominions stand in their way.

The nephilim were obviously getting ready to attack. It was time to call upon the old man again. Everything must be prepared and ready for them. The Seraph's dark eyes glowed feverishly. They were entering the last times. The apotheosis of everything he had worked for. And it would be exactly as Azazel had predicted: "They may fight, but they will not prevail. They may seek, but they will not find."

JAZMIN DAWSON STOOD UNDER THE SHOWER, LETTING THE WARM WATER WASH AWAY ALL THE ACCUMULATED GUNK. SHE HAD GOT REALLY FILTHY PLANTING THOSE BUGGING DEVICES. SHE'D ALSO somehow managed to catch her elbow on a protruding nail and rip a big hole in the sleeve of Suki's suit. Suki had been very nice about it, but Jazmin was feeling annoyed with herself. Jaz Dawson, spy girl and detecting diva, would never have ripped her own, or anybody else's clothing. It was so klutzy. Still, she'd done something positive, she'd contributed. Now the team could listen in to everything that went on in the staffroom and in the inner two corridors.

Jazmin stepped out of the shower and wrapped herself in one of the hotel's fluffy, white bath towels. She had got rid of the external stuff all right, but there was still stuff inside her head that she couldn't get rid of quite so easily. She sighed. However hard she tried, she just could not seem to free her mind of her cousin Clea's absolutely terrified expression as she had hurried from the room.

Tonight, they were all going out to a nice restaurant in Josefov. They would sit round a table covered with a spotless, white linen tablecloth and laid with silver cutlery and fine Bohemian crystal glasses. They would be served beautifully cooked food, drink sparkling wine – well, the others would.

And yet Jazmin knew the whole time, she would be haunted by Clea's face and the thought that she would not be enjoying her meal tonight. How much longer could this siege continue? she thought. And what was it going to take to finally bring it to an end?

ASSIA DAWSON LAY IN BED WATCHING THE NIGHT SKY THROUGH A CRACK IN THE DRAPES. THERE WAS SECURITY AND A COMFORTING SILENCE ABOUT A NIGHT SKY, SHE DECIDED. THE STARS LOOKED AS

if they'd been there a long time. Assia could hear Jazmin's gentle breathing from the next bed. Her daughter. Whom she loved to bits, even if they didn't always see eye to eye. Her daughter, who was safe and here with her. Assia knew that she could not delay calling Ian for ever. She had to contact her brother soon, and tell him where his daughter was and what had happened to her.

Assia pursed her lips. Technically, she knew that she ought to have called him as soon as Clea had been identified. But she had taken a calculated risk and had held back because Havel had indicated that he and his team were going to try to enter the building in the early morning, before the group was fully awake. The ISA team fully intended to be there when this happened. The success of *their* mission depended upon finding the body and transferring it to a proper government-funded research establishment. An interview with Eduard Marek would also have to be arranged.

So, if everything went according to plan, Assia hoped to be able to call her London office in the morning with the news that this assignment had ended successfully. Followed by another call to her brother Ian to tell him that his beloved daughter was safe and well. Which was infinitely preferable to telling him that she wasn't. She checked the time. It was 11.30 p.m. Another seven hours, and it should all be over.

COUNT EDUARD MAREK MADE HIS WAY IN THE DARK FROM THE ADMINISTRATIVE BLOCK WHERE HIS WIFE WAS PEACEFULLY SLEEPING, TO THE MAIN BUILDING OF THE ROZTOK INSTITUTE. He waited patiently inside the insulated metal cube that separated the two areas, as he and his grubby and unwashed clothing were scrupulously decontaminated by the high-powered air jets. The irony of this procedure did not escape him. There was stuff inside his head that no high-tech cleaning procedures could ever reach.

Released and physically cleansed, Marek entered the main building. Passing through the canteen area, he saw to his surprise that the plates and glasses from the evening meal had been left on the tables. Nobody had bothered to collect them and take them to the kitchen. That was unusual. Normally, the group was scrupulous about keeping the place absolutely spotless. And there was nobody around. It was completely deserted. This gave him a funny feeling, as if he was walking on the deck of the *Mary Celeste*. Marek paused to listen. Everything was very still and silent. Even the noise of the air conditioning seemed unnaturally muted. Or was it just the night and his mind playing tricks on him?

Marek left the canteen and headed for the core of the building. This was where his lab was located and where everybody had gone to spend the night. Since the conversation with Seraph Gray, when Marek had revealed that it was there he had brought to life the demonic presence now stalking the city, his laboratory had been declared a sacred place, a kind of holy of holies, an inner sanctum where only Seraph Gray entered to commune with Azazel. Marek shuddered. He could barely begin to imagine what the strange Englishman and the evil angel found to talk about.

Earlier that evening, however, Seraph Gray had informed Marek that the entire group would join him in the inner room for the first time. And that it would happen tonight. Gray had talked a lot of weird rubbish that Marek did not understand. About an army waiting outside to attack them, and how Azazel had ordered his followers to gather together to be strengthened and prepared for the forthcoming battle. When dawn broke, Seraph Gray had told him excitedly, Azazel had promised that they would all be like him, mighty and invincible, and the army at the gates would not prevail against them.

Now, fearful and curious, Marek approached the lab. He wanted to see for himself what bizarre ritual the group was going through. He reached the heavy sliding door. And stopped in amazement. The red warning light was flashing. But that could only mean one thing – the nanoparticulator was switched on and working. Marek froze. His heart stood still. After that terrible night, he had spent time deliberately disconnecting the power supply, dismantling the outlet valves so that never again could anybody ever attempt to use the machine.

And now? And now? How had this happened?

Marek tried to open the door. It was locked. He hammered on it and shouted. No one responded. What were they doing in there? None of the group possessed the proper breathing equipment! They were not wearing protective clothing! Without these things, they were all in terrible danger! A pulse began to beat in Marek's brain. He had to find protective clothing, breathing apparatus. He had to warn them before it was too late.

OUTSIDE THE ROZTOK INSTITUTE, HAVEL'S MEN CONTINUED TO KEEP UP THEIR WATCHING AND LISTENING BRIEF. BUT NOTHING SEEMED TO BE HAPPENING. THEY'D LISTENED WHILE THE GROUP HAD EATEN their silent evening meal. Soon after that, they had distinctly heard a man's voice announcing that there was to be a special praise and worship meeting which would take place in the inner room. Since then, they hadn't heard a thing.

It was past midnight. Everything was peaceful and still. Somewhere in the dark wood, a hunting owl called. A solitary car roared past in the distance. Small animals rustled in the undergrowth. Night sounds patterning the silence. The men hunkered down in their mobile unit, counting the hours as they slowly dragged by. Another three, and the first streaks of light would appear over the eastern horizon. That was what they were all subconsciously waiting for. Daylight.

Because there was something weird about this place. It was creepy. They all felt it. And they were experienced, hard-bitten cops. Havel's elite. Normally nothing scared them; they'd seen it all. Of course, nobody was admitting that they were scared now. But it was very noticeable that not a single man had set foot outside the mobile unit all night. Now they sat in uneasy silence, watching and listening, and waiting for dawn.

MAREK WONDERED WHETHER OTHER PEOPLE EVER THOUGHT ABOUT DEATH, AS HE DID. NOWADAYS, HE FOUND HIMSELF THINKING ABOUT IT CONSTANTLY. HE ENVISAGED DEATH RATHER LIKE DIVING INTO A deep, clear pool. Cool waters closing silkily over his head. A cessation of struggle. He longed so much to surrender himself to its gentle embrace. Death, when it arrived, would come as a welcome friend.

But this was not the death he visualized.

The followers of Azazel, dressed in their ceremonial white robes, lay on the floor. They appeared to be resting, but they were not asleep. They lay very still, but they were not at peace. Over in one corner, the machine whirred and hummed like a giant beehive. Its tentacular valves waved gently in the air. By Marek's reckoning, the nanoparticulator must have been spewing out billions of necrotizing microparticles for many hours. While they slept, the group had been breathing them in, absorbing them through their skin cells.

Marek was all too well aware of the effects of this wholesale and totally unregulated absorption. Once inside the bodies, the nanoscopic particles would have attached themselves to every cell, every tissue, every organ. Then they would begin the process of breaking down and destroying, which, if not superseded by the rejuvenation process, would inevitably result in rapid death from necrosis. Basically, the body would be eaten away. He glanced around and shuddered. He could see that the terrible process was already happening.

Wearing his breathing apparatus, Marek crossed the lab, picking his way gingerly round the fast disintegrating bodies. He turned off the machine. Then he picked up one of the steel chairs and, raising it high above his head, brought it down upon the nanoparticulator with as much force as he could. Over and over again he struck at it. Only when the machine was reduced to twisted and shattered pieces, did he cease and stagger back, dizzy and gasping for breath. Marek had invented this machine. It had taken him years of work and effort. Once, it had been a source of pride. Now, his greatest scientific achievement lay in ruins all around him.

Suddenly, a shout of triumphant laughter pealed around the room. Shocked, Marek spun round and saw the demon angel near the glass pod. Its beautiful face radiated evil joy. Its fiery eyes shot red sparks of glee. Marek remembered

Seraph Gray saying that Azazel himself had told the followers they would find strength and solace in this place. But, of course, the angel had lied. It had deceived them. They had been lured here for a very different purpose. Azazel had destroyed them, as it destroyed everyone who came into contact with it. Marek shrank back into a corner, covering his eyes as the angel rejoiced and gloated over the bodies of the worshippers. Then, sick with terror, he crawled away.

COUNTESS MARKOVA OPENED HER EYES. LIGHT WAS FILTERING DOWN INTO THE ROOM THROUGH THE FROSTED CEILING PANELS OVERHEAD. SHE CHECKED THE TIME; IT WAS 5.45 A.M. BUT WHERE was her husband? The countess scrambled stiffly to her feet and set out in search of him.

As she prowled the empty corridors looking for Marek, the countess remembered how excited her husband had been when he'd first heard on the scientific grapevine about the discovery of the body. How they'd planned and schemed together to get hold of it and bring it here. And when the body had finally arrived, how it had been like Christmas – her husband had been so happy, like a child with a new plaything. But then the magic had gone wrong; instead of him playing with the toy, the toy was now playing with him. And Christmas had turned overnight into Hallowe'en.

The countess approached the insulated metal cube that separated the two sections of the building. Now she recalled how she had brought Marek the sample of hair, the DNA of which exactly matched that of the body. If she had known then what she knew now, she would have burned it, lied to him. Anything to prevent him from carrying out his terrible experiment.

And then Marek himself appeared through the metal door, and it seemed to her that he looked even paler, the lines of fatigue etched even deeper than before. Yet as soon as he caught sight of her, he made an effort and straightened his bent shoulders. His face broke into a pale, wintery smile.

"Ah, there you are, *milá*," he said, exactly as if she had been the one missing. Marek took her by the arm. "Let us walk together," he said.

"Where have you been?" the countess inquired as, arm in arm, they made their way back to the office.

Marek did not answer at once. Then he gave a deep sigh that seemed to come from the bottom of his soul. "I was just dealing with something," he said, choosing his words with care. They reached the office door and Marek stood aside to let his wife enter first.

The countess watched as her husband went straight to his desk, where he picked up one of the framed photos that stood on top and handed it across to her. The picture showed the countess and the count, standing on the steps at the front of the house. They both looked very much younger. The count was clasping a huge fish in both arms.

"The Christmas carp," the countess said, her eyes lighting up. "I remember. You caught it in the lake."

She took the photograph and stood under one of the light panels, studying it intently. "It all seems such a long time ago," she murmured forlornly, shaking her head in disbelief.

Marek dipped his hand back into the drawer. Then he came and glanced over her shoulder at the picture. "You know, you are still a very beautiful woman, *milenka*," he said softly.

The countess smiled. Foolish man, she thought. Nevertheless, she was pleased by his compliment. Marek looked at the back of his wife's head, and for the first time in what seemed like for ever, his arm did not shake as he raised the gun, and brought the muzzle close to the spot where the skull and spine joined. His hand was absolutely steady as he pulled the trigger, then placed the barrel swiftly against his right temple and pulled again.

The cracks of the two shots reverberated through the early morning silence, like stones dropped into a still pool. They were picked up immediately by the monitoring team outside the building.

"I think I just heard gunfire, chief!" one of the officers shouted.

Havel's mouth set in a grim line. "Get that door down," he ordered. "We're going in now!"

JAZMIN DAWSON FOUND HERSELF FACED WITH A DILEMMA. IT WAS QUITE POSSIBLE THAT SHE HAD BEEN TOLD TO STAY WHERE SHE WAS. IN FACT, IF SHE THOUGHT ABOUT IT VERY HARD, SHE probably could remember both her mum and Stash yelling something along those lines as they leaped out of the ATV and raced towards the building. On the other hand, maybe in all the excitement and confusion, she might not have heard them properly.

Time to apply a little creative misunderstanding, Jazmin thought to herself. She slid out of the rear of the vehicle and ran after them.

ASSIA DAWSON AND HER TEAM SPRINTED ALONG THE EMPTY OUTER CORRIDOR. THEY WERE NOT FOLLOWING THE SAME ROUTE AS HAVEL'S MEN. INSTEAD, THEY WERE HEADING FOR THE SECOND BUILDING, the one where Marek and his wife were believed to be located. Please let them be safe, Assia prayed. Let them be alive. They reached the interconnecting metal cube. It was closed. Stash took a running leap and kicked the door open. Assia and Suki stood back while he did the same with the door on the other side.

"Let's split up," Assia suggested.

"Check," Suki said. "I'll do the rooms along here." She pulled out her gun, opened the door to the first room and stuck her head round cautiously.

Assia and Stash headed deeper into the maze of corridors, shouting Marek's name. They were answered by silence.

Suddenly, Stash's pager bleeped. "Back this way," he yelled.

Assia ran after him, until eventually they came across Suki standing in a doorway, her face grave. "I've found them," she said. "But it's not good news, I'm afraid."

JAZMIN PAUSED ON THE THRESHOLD. THE BUILDING SEEMED TO BE SWARMING WITH BIG BURLY POLICE OFFICERS IN FULL BODY ARMOUR, CARRYING RIOT SHIELDS AND GUNS. SHE FOLLOWED them, trying to be a short poppy. Sometimes there were advantages to being small, she thought. It was slightly easier to be inconspicuous, although a badge, some sort of uniform and a utility belt stuffed with impressive equipment would also have helped her to blend in. Fortunately, everyone was so busy rushing around that nobody was paying her any attention.

Jazmin went straight to where she thought the sleeping room was located to see if Clea was there. When she arrived, she saw the room was empty, apart from Havel's men, who were lifting blankets and shouting at each other in Czech. She glanced up at the air vent. It seemed strange to think that she had actually been crawling up there only a short time ago. And Clea had stood down here. They had talked. And now she was standing in practically the same spot as her cousin. But where was Clea?

ASSIA LOOKED DOWN AT THE SHATTERED, BLOODY REMAINS OF COUNT EDUARD MAREK AND HIS WIFE. "DAMN," SHE SWORE SOFTLY. "DAMN, DAMN."

"It looks like he shot her first, then turned the gun on himself," Suki said. She pointed to the small, powerful handgun lying next to Marek's lifeless body. "That's interesting. Where would a scientist get hold of a weapon like that?"

Assia pulled a face. "It's mine," she said. "They took it off me when they went through my things." She ran her hands through her hair and groaned. "Oh, no – what a mess! Oh, hell! Even if we locate the body now, we'll never know how Marek got hold of it or what he was intending to do."

Stash stepped back into the corridor. "I'll go find Havel and tell him," he said quietly. "He needs to know what's happened."

Silently, Assia and Suki followed him.

I failed, Assia thought bitterly. I wasn't on top of this at all. I should have pulled rank, overridden the police, and insisted we went in sooner. I should have secured a confession. Now Marek will take his secret with him to the grave.

MEANWHILE, JAZMIN HAD MADE AN INTERESTING DISCOVERY. SHE HAD FOUND CLEA'S TINY, HIGH-HEELED JEWEL-ENCRUSTED SHOES IN THE CORRIDOR. EVEN THOUGH THEY WERE SPLATTERED WITH dried vomit, she recognized them instantly. Nobody else would wear such ditzy, unsuitable shoes in a place like this. Ewww, she thought, poking them gently with the toe of her shoe. Gross!

Jazmin knew from reading crime fiction that she must never move or disturb anything found in the initial stages of an investigation. It might be evidence. It was a cardinal rule: nothing at the scene of a crime must on any account ever be tampered with. She wondered whether she ought to draw a line round the shoes, in case they turned out to be vital clues. She was just searching her pockets for something to draw with when one of Havel's men stopped by her. He pointed at the shoes.

"They belong to my cousin, Clea," Jazmin said. "She's one of the group."

Without a word, the man picked up the shoes and began to walk quickly away with them.

"Hey," Jazmin exclaimed indignantly, scuttling after him. "Hey, you can't do that. You're removing important evidence!"

HAVEL HAD ARRIVED IN MAREK'S OFFICE AND WAS STARING DOWN AT THE BODIES IN GRIM SILENCE. "YOU'RE ABSOLUTELY SURE IT'S MAREK AND HIS WIFE?" HE ASKED AT LAST.

"Quite sure," Assia said quietly. "I can make a formal identification if you want."

Havel grunted an assent. He turned to his deputy, who was leaning against the wall. He was white-faced and sucking in air. "For God's sake, Jiří, get a grip. Haven't you ever seen someone with their brains blown out before?" Havel said drily. He took a roll of crime tape out of his pocket. "If you don't mind," he said to Assia, gesturing towards the open door, "I'm going to have to ask you to leave. I need to seal things off here and secure the site until the guys from forensics arrive."

Reluctantly, Assia led the way out of Marek's office. She would really have preferred to search the room thoroughly, but she realized she had no choice. She was on Havel's territory. And he was doing it by the book. The ISA wouldn't be allowed in to investigate until the forensics people had cleared up. Havel ran a length of tape across the door. "Well, that's two accounted for," he said laconically. "But we still haven't found the others yet, and I don't mind telling you, I'm beginning to get a very bad feeling about this."

COMMANDER HAVEL MARCHED BRISKLY BACK TO THE MAIN BUILDING. THE THREE ISA AGENTS FOLLOWED HIM, EXCHANGING PERPLEXED GLANCES BEHIND HIS BACK.

"Er, what did you mean when you said that you hadn't found the others yet?" Stash inquired cautiously.

Havel continued walking. "My men have searched the building. Every room. Every corridor." He shrugged his shoulders, gave them a palms-up. "Nobody."

"But I don't understand..." Suki frowned. "How can you *not* find forty people?"

"Search me," Havel growled. "I had men on duty all night. You couldn't sneak a gnat's eyebrow past them. But somehow, don't ask me how, these fanatics have all magically vanished into thin air."

They rounded a corner and came face to face with an officer carrying a pair of shoes at arm's length. He was being chased by a cross-faced Jazmin.

"Now what?" Havel barked crossly. The officer launched into an explanation in Czech while Jazmin stood at his elbow, eyeballing him.

"I thought we asked you to stay in the ATV." Assia frowned.

"Did you? I didn't hear you say that," Jazmin responded, deliberately not looking round.

"What's the problem?" Stash asked.

"I found Clea's shoes. That stupid policeman took them," Jazmin told him, glaring up at the officer.

Assia covered her face with her hands. "Clea," she groaned. "Omigod, I can't believe it. I'd forgotten about her."

Jazmin stared at her mum. For the first time, she noticed the expression on her face. Then the sadness hovering in Suki's eyes. The grim set of Stash's mouth.

"Something's happened, hasn't it?" she said.

Assia glanced away. "Marek and his wife are dead," she said flatly.

"Oh, no," Jazmin breathed. She realized at once the significance of this tragic event. Her mind leaped ahead. No Mareks, no questions. No questions, no proof. No proof, no case to answer. It was the ultimate agent's nightmare. No wonder her mum and the other two looked unhappy.

"Um...right, so I'll go and sit in the jeep, yeah?" she said, anxious not to add to their problems.

Her mum nodded. "I think that would be a good idea."

"That way, we'll know where you are when we find your cousin," Suki said encouragingly. "She may be very scared. You're the only one of us whom she actually knows well."

As she spoke, Havel finished talking with the officer. He turned to face them, his expression grim and determined. "Right," he said. "I am now going to conduct a systematic search of the premises and grounds. I am going to find out what has happened to these people, even if I have to take the whole place apart, brick by brick."

CLEA DAWSON AWOKE AND OPENED HER EYES CAUTIOUSLY. OH, YES. SHE FELT SO MUCH BETTER. THE MIGRAINE HAD LIFTED, AND FOR THE FIRST TIME IN DAYS, SHE HAD HAD A REALLY LONG, undisturbed sleep. She was so glad she'd not returned to the meeting, but had gone to find somewhere to rest and be alone instead. And she had found here. It had been a good place. She'd felt safe, less afraid. She lay back, her head resting on the folded dishcloths she'd turned into a pillow. The light coming from under the utility-cupboard door indicated that it was daytime once more.

Clea unwrapped herself from the roller-towel she'd been using as a blanket, sat up, then got to her feet. Time to have a wash and grab something to eat before morning worship. She pushed open the door and went to find the female staff cloakroom, where she quickly splashed her face with a trickle of lukewarm water.

Gone were the days when she could begin her day by luxuriating under a steaming-hot power shower in her beautiful en-suite, she mused ruefully, then rebuked herself for the thought. It was not worthy, she told herself sternly. She was here now. She had to be found worthy of appearing before Azazel instead. Clea ran her fingers through her untidy hair and set out to find some food, and then the rest of the group.

STASH MCGREGOR WAS STANDING IN THE DOORWAY OF MAREK'S LABORATORY, TRYING TO FIT TOGETHER A PUZZLE THAT APPEARED TO CONSIST OF PIECES FROM AT LEAST THREE SEPARATE JIGSAWS. What was going down here? There was no pattern. It didn't make sense. Outside the complex, Havel's men were doing a line search of the grounds. Meanwhile, Assia and Suki were checking every conceivable storage area for the body.

Stash went on asking himself questions he could not answer. Where had the weird religious people gone? Why had they smashed up a very complicated piece of machinery and wrecked a computer terminal before they left? And what were the heaps of strange, grainy, grey-white powder that covered the floor of the lab?

Stash was just bending down to examine one of the coarse, gritty piles more closely when he became aware of a familiar small figure with a wild mane of dark curly hair, standing in the doorway and blocking the light.

"Hey, girlfriend," he chided gently, without bothering to look up. "I thought we agreed you'd go back to the ATV."

There was a pause. The figure did not move, did not respond. Stash looked up sharply. Then he sat back on his heels, his eyes widening. He slowly folded his arms. "Uh-huh," he said, very quietly. "So who are you?"

"My name is Clea Dawson," Clea said stiffly, her eyes widening into a look of total amazement. "Who are you?"

JAZMIN STALKED OVER TO THE HOTEL ROOM MINI-BAR AND POURED ANOTHER FRUIT JUICE INTO A FRESH GLASS. SHE TOOK IT BACK TO THE SOFA.

"Thank you, Jazmin," Clea murmured faintly. She reached out a pale, limp hand from under the flowered duvet.

"Do you want anything else?"

Clea looked up at her, big blue eyes filling with tears, like saucers in the rain. "Can you stay with me?" she whispered pathetically. "I don't want to be on my own."

Jazmin grimaced. "Sure," she said.

She perched uncomfortably on the edge of one of the sofa arms as Clea sipped some of the juice, then handed back the glass and smiled shakily. "Thank you so much, Jazmin," she whispered again. She sighed, sank back under the duvet and closed her eyes. A single lucent pearl of a teardrop forced itself out from under her eyelid and rolled slowly down her pallid cheek.

Jazmin clicked her teeth and eye-rolled. All this supportiveness was hard work, she thought gloomily. Plus, it was about as much fun as sticking pins into her eyes. She glanced down at Clea and sighed. Okay, so nobody doubted that her cousin had been through a bad time. That had been obvious from the moment Suki and Assia had brought her out to the ATV, where they'd wrapped her in a blanket and given her a hot drink.

Clea had looked dazed and very frightened. She'd kept

mechanically repeating, "I must find the others," and refusing point blank to believe that the group was no longer there.

It was only when Commander Havel returned from his ground search to announce gruffly that he and his men had found nothing, that Clea seemed to finally accept that the group had gone. Whereupon she had broken down and cried her eyes out.

Finding Clea coincided with the arrival of the forensics team. Assia therefore decided to take her back to the hotel and begin the gentle process of reintroducing her to the real world. Havel said that he would come over and see her after he'd instructed the forensics team. And given some sort of press statement to the vultures at the gates. So Clea Dawson was driven to the hotel, where she enjoyed the luxury of her first long, hot shower for days. Followed by a good vegetarian lunch. Which, yeah, she probably deserved, Jazmin admitted grudgingly, after what she'd been through. But that was as far as her sympathy went.

Jazmin's feelings towards her cousin Clea had not changed. Clea had bossed her around, treated her like a stupid kid and generally made her feel as welcome as an attack of zits. It was kind of hard to feel sympathy for her. Instead, Jazmin found herself desperately wanting somebody to say, just once, that her cousin Clea had been a stupid, selfish cow who'd lied to her friends, deceived her parents and was actually damn lucky to be here right now.

But of course, nobody did. Exactly the opposite. Everybody went out of their way to praise Clea up, to make her feel special. Nobody appeared to see things from Jazmin's perspective. It just seemed that whatever she did, her cousin Clea always landed on her pretty little feet and always came up smelling of roses. It was so unfair!

"Aww, I thought you said your cousin was nasty," Suki had remarked, after she'd helped Clea to unpack her few belongings and settle in. "She's just the sweetest, nicest girl."

Jazmin had mentally stuck two fingers down her throat, and refrained from answering.

Her mum was no better. "You're doing so well. We're all really proud of you," she kept telling Clea every five minutes, patting her shoulder encouragingly while kitty-cute Clea lapped up all the attention like cream, smiling bravely, and murmuring, "Thank you, Aunty Assia."

The final indignity, as far as Jazmin was concerned, came when Stash had remarked innocently, "You know what, you two girls look so alike, you could be sisters."

This last comment had made Jazmin suck in her breath sharply. "No, we couldn't," she'd said stiffly, feeling both offended and threatened by the idea. Then she had got to her feet, announcing, "I'm going out for a walk, okay?"

But of course, she wasn't allowed to go out for a walk.

Nonono. The very idea! How selfish was she? Because Clea needed her. Clea had Been Through a Terrible Experience. Clea mustn't be left on her own. And so, in a role-reversal, the irony of which did not escape her, Jazmin had been tasked with looking after her cousin Clea. Which, translated, meant hanging around in a stuffy hotel room all afternoon, waiting on Clea hand and foot.

Jazmin sighed, dragged her fingers through her untidy hair. There was a noise in her head. Things conflicted.

Over the last few hours, Jazmin Dawson had learned a lot about herself. She had somehow managed to reconnect with her inner toddler and she really wasn't enjoying it. She didn't like feeling mean and jealous. She didn't like being a horrible person. And being cooped up here with her cousin was only stirring up all this emotional mess and making her feel ten times worse.

MEANWHILE, DOWNSTAIRS IN THE HOTEL BAR, ASSIA DAWSON AND HER TEAM WERE SITTING AT A QUIET TABLE IN THE CORNER, REVIEWING THE DAY'S EVENTS WHILE THEY WAITED FOR Commander Havel to arrive.

Assia picked up her glass of beer, took a reflective sip, set it down again. She sighed, and stared blankly, her eyes unfocused. Stash and Suki exchanged a meaningful glance over the top of her head.

"So..." Stash began.

"Good news and not so good news, huh?" Suki said.

"Mmm." Assia transferred her moody gaze down into her glass.

"It's good that we found Clea, isn't it?" Suki remarked encouragingly.

Assia nodded. "Yes, it's certainly an enormous relief," she agreed. And it was true, she thought to herself. She had been dreading making that call to her brother. "But we still haven't found the body, have we?" she went on. "Nor is there any sign of all those other hostages." Assia pursed her lips. "I really want to search Marek's office," she said, her eyes narrowing. "There has to be some clue what he was up to."

"There was an industrial incinerator out back," Suki reminded her.

"I know. But I'm trying not to go there quite yet. Not until we've explored all other options. We mustn't jump to conclusions. We can't afford to get this wrong. If we put out a statement saying the body has been destroyed, and then it turns up in some obscure corner of the Roztok complex, we'll get every rogue scientific institute and quasi-religious group in the world chasing after it again and the whole thing will recycle itself."

Stash sipped his beer. "The good old science and religion schtick strikes again," he remarked thoughtfully. "Nothing ever changes, does it? Always been the cause of major argument and trouble."

"You mean because science is logical, but religion is irrational," Assia said. "Science proves something exists by observation and experimentation. Religion relies on faith and feelings."

"Something like that."

"But maybe they have things in common," Assia pursued. "Maybe they aren't as mutually exclusive as we've always thought. After all, both rely on a certain level of belief – that leap in the dark, when you don't know for certain, but you very much hope something, or someone, will work for you."

Stash looked at her. "Go on."

"Consider Marek and Jones: the scientist and the religionist. Superficially, two very different people, but at the same time, very similar. Single-minded, fanatical, totally committed to what they believe in. The sort of closed-off individuals who build walls rather than windows. Who retreat from reality into some strange world of their own creation. And in the end, it's turned out pretty well the same for both of them, hasn't it?"

"Uh-huh. I guess," Stash conceded.

As he spoke, Commander Havel entered the bar and looked around expectantly.

Stash raised a hand. "Over here."

Havel crossed the room. He pulled up a stool and lowered himself down onto it wearily.

"You have some news for us?" Assia asked.

"Yeah – you could say that," Havel said, pulling a face. "It's not looking good, I'm afraid."

MEANWHILE UPSTAIRS IN THE HOTEL SUITE, CLEA DAWSON FINALLY FELL ASLEEP, TEMPORARILY RELIEVING JAZMIN OF HER NURSING DUTIES. SHE GOT UP FROM THE SOFA, STRODE OVER TO THE window and peered out across the city. The sky was draining of colour and street lights were coming on one by one. The ancient city was slowly gearing itself up for evening. A cool breeze filtered temptingly through the net curtains.

Jazmin suddenly realized how badly she wanted to get out into the fresh air. She was getting cabin fever shut up here all afternoon with Clea. She glanced quickly across at her cousin; she was clearly sound asleep. Surely Clea could be left alone for a bit? Surely Jazmin was entitled to a bit of free time – on her own? She scribbled a brief note on a pad of hotel paper – Gone 4 walk 2 bridge – and left it by Clea's sleeping form. Then she quietly tiptoed out of the room.

Jazmin rode her beloved elevator to the ground floor. She crossed the lobby and peeped into the bar. Her mum and the other two agents were sitting round a table in one corner, deep in conversation with the grumpy police officer. Good. That meant they were much too busy to care about what she was up to. Jazmin pushed the hotel's heavy, revolving glass door and slipped out into the greying dusk of the August evening.

"FORENSICS HAVE BEEN AND GONE," HAVEL SAID, SHIFTING HIS BULK TO A MORE COMFORTABLE POSITION ON THE SPINDLY BAR STOOL. HE PAUSED. "INTERESTING..." HE ADDED, LOOKING SLYLY around at each one of them and nodding his head slowly and significantly.

The three agents waited, sensing instinctively that Havel was not a man to be hurried. He liked to take his time, do things his way.

"I asked them about that strange dust in Marek's lab," Havel continued. "Know what they think it is? Skin. Tiny shreds of skin, mixed in with cotton fibres. Apparently, there are thirty-nine little piles of skin. And no bodies anywhere." He glanced at Assia. "See what I mean about not good news?"

Stash whistled between his teeth.

"What do they think happened?" Suki asked.

"Forensics reckon it was some sort of accident. You remember the machine, the one that was smashed up? It's called a..." Havel took a folded piece of paper out of his breast pocket and glanced down at it. "...It's a nanoparticulator. Produces billions of tiny...things...that eat up cells and stuff. One of the forensics people had seen one in action in a hospital. Marek pioneered them for use in surgery and cancer treatment. Designed the prototype. Forensics think there must have been some sort of massive computer malfunction. Machine turns itself on, lab fills up with little microscopic flesh-eating things. By the time somebody wakes up and realizes what's going on, it's too late. Everybody's dead, if you see what I mean." Havel smiled grimly. "Not a particularly nice way to go, I wouldn't think. Being eaten alive by something you can't even see."

"Ewww. You don't think Marek could have done it?" Suki asked, shuddering.

"The revenge of the mad scientist?" Havel said drily. "It's possible. Who knows?" He sighed heavily, then eased himself off the barstool with a grunt. "Anyway, we'll probably never know what really happened, will we? Now, if you don't mind, I'd like to talk to the girl. I have to get this case done and dusted quickly. You heard about the murders in the city? I got a couple of city high-ups leaning heavily on me at the moment. They don't want us to lose our reputation as a safe place to visit." Havel laughed mirthlessly. "Mustn't miss out on all that lovely tourist revenue, must we?" he said, glancing quickly from Assia to Suki. "Right then, if one of you ladies would like to come with me?"

Assia rose. "I'll come," she said instantly.

Commander Havel strode quickly ahead, glancing down at his watch. The city high-ups weren't the only ones leaning on him right now, he thought ruefully. He had promised his wife faithfully that he would be home in time for a family dinner tonight. The in-laws were coming round to eat. After the fiasco over his daughter's party, he didn't dare break his word for a second time.

Assia turned to Stash and Suki. "I'll send Jazmin down. Keep her with you, will you? I don't want her wandering off by herself. Particularly not if what Havel says is true and there's some sort of killer loose in the city."

ASSIA DAWSON'S DEPARTURE FROM THE BAR COINCIDED WITH TONDA'S ARRIVAL OUTSIDE THE HOTEL. HE ENTERED, APPROACHED THE RECEPTION AREA, AND WAS TOLD BY THE GIRL BEHIND THE DESK that the English group were drinking in the bar.

Stash and Suki both got to their feet as Tonda came towards them, recognizing him instantly. They beckoned him over, pulled out a chair for him, sat him down, introduced themselves. Then Stash went to buy him a drink.

"Well, it's good to finally meet you," Suki said encouragingly.

Tonda gave her a half smile. He looked awkward and clearly felt ill at ease in their company. Stash put a glass of beer down in front of him. Suki shot him a warning glance over the top of Tonda's head and shook her head quickly.

"So Tonda, how's it going?" Stash inquired innocently.

Tonda looked around the bar. "Is Jazmin here?" he asked. "I really came to see her. She has something of mine I need to collect."

"She's upstairs with her cousin," Suki told him. "She should be down any minute."

They sat and waited.

"So...you and Jazmin..." Stash said, trying to break the silence.

The silence returned. They waited some more.

"Look, I don't know what's keeping her," Suki said eventually. "I'll just nip up and tell her you're here, shall I?"

Suki disappeared. Tonda buried his nose in his drink. Stash took the hint. He listened to the jolly background music. He picked up a beer mat and turned it around between his thumb and fingers, pretending to count the corners. Eventually Suki returned.

"Guess what? Remember Assia telling her to stay in the hotel and take care of her cousin? Well, she's left her on her own and gone for a walk."

"Uh-oh!" Stash said. "That's our Jazmin!"

"Do you know where she has gone?" Tonda asked.

"She's heading for the Charles Bridge," Suki told him.

Tonda drained his glass, stood up. "I think I'll go and find her," he said. "I have some important things I should say. Thanks for the drink."

Stash and Suki watched Tonda make his way between the tables. They could almost see the misery encircling him like a miasma. Stash shook his head and expelled air. "That is one unhappy guy."

Suki touched his shoulder lightly. "Maybe we should follow? At a discreet distance, of course. Just in case we're needed?"

Stash nodded in agreement. They picked up their jackets and swiftly left the hotel.

THE CHARLES BRIDGE ONCE CARRIED KINGS ACROSS THE RIVER TO BE CROWNED OR BURIED IN THE CASTLE ON THE HILL. CRIMINALS WERE DECAPITATED ON THE BRIDGE OR HUNG FROM IT. IT IS AN ancient, magical, mysterious place and never more so than in the late afternoon, when the crowds begin to thin out, and the dying light of day touches it for the last time before it sinks into the western sky, leaving night to settle its dark wings over the city.

Jazmin Dawson stood at the centre of the bridge. She leaned her arms on the stone parapet and gazed thoughtfully down into the dark, swirling water. She was not thinking about the bridge's long history. She was thinking about Tonda, about how he might be feeling right now. She was wondering whether she would ever see him again. And if she did, what she could say to him; what she wanted to say to him.

A grey mist was beginning to rise from the river. Jazmin remembered reading somewhere that mist was the steam from two fighting dragons, one water, one fire. The mist swirled across the bridge, flowing upwards, forming pools of grey shadow. It was accompanied by a chill breeze that made the hairs on her arms stand up, and ruffled the long robe of the statue that she hadn't noticed a moment ago.

Puzzled, Jazmin glanced up. The last rays of sun slanting through the low, grey clouds touched with gold the statue's beautifully chiselled face and its long, curling hair, and then lit up its evil eyes with a fiery red glow.

THERE ARE LIMITS TO THE DIMENSION OF FEAR. UNTIL ONE MEETS THE UNKNOWN. THEN TERROR HAS NO BOUNDARIES, NO WALLS TO KEEP IT CONTAINED. SO IT WAS THAT, ONCE AGAIN, JAZMIN Dawson stared up into the cold eyes of the angel and sensed that she was in the presence of something so terrible that it was beyond anything she had ever encountered before. She felt herself paralysed, unable to run away. Unable even to open her mouth in a scream of pure fear. Jazmin stood motionless, waiting for death to come. The angel did not utter a word. Its eyes held hers, probing the black water in her bones, the icy depths of her terror. Slowly, it bent down towards her, reaching out its hands to grasp her by the throat.

And then all at once, Jazmin heard strange music in the

distance. Discordant, twangy music. It sounded just as if someone was running a small stick up and down the strings of a very large harp. Out of the corner of her eye, she also became aware of two figures walking steadily towards her through the mist. At first, she assumed they must be tourists. Then she thought they might be Czech police, but as they got nearer she noticed that they weren't wearing police uniforms and also that their feet didn't seem to be touching the ground.

Air rippled away from the two beings, as if they were stepping into pools of shallow water. Bright light burned from their bodies like dry ice, and their faces were calm and radiantly beautiful. The angel's eyes burned with fury when he saw them, and his lips drew back from his teeth in a snarl of hatred.

The two beings came on, walking side by side, their steps exactly matching until they were almost level with the centre of the bridge. Then they halted and Jazmin heard them speak, their voices ringing out together in unison, strong and clear.

"O Azazel, fallen cherub, ensign bearer to Lucifer the Dark Lord," they chanted. "Do you know who we are?"

The evil angel on the parapet writhed and struggled, as if each word was a blow striking at him. "I know who you are," he hissed.

"Then you also know the One who sent us," the radiant beings continued. "And in His great name we command you: resume your true shape, and return to the place to which you were sent, and in which you were destined to dwell, before the world began."

What happened next took place so quickly that Jazmin found it hard to recall it afterwards. She remembered suddenly hearing shouts, the sound of running feet on the bridge, Tonda's voice somewhere far off in the mist calling her name and yelling something in Czech. Then one of the figures calmly drew a great circle in the air and, immediately, the sky opened up and she saw a long black tunnel stretching away into infinity, flames belching from its mouth. The two figures pointed and said:

"There is your way, fallen spirit. It is time to join your fiendish lord and live with him in fire and chains for evermore." Having spoken these words, they both instantly vanished.

At once, Jazmin saw the angel begin to change shape. His face blackened and twisted. Dark scales began to sprout and cover his skin, and a massive pair of leathery, bat-like wings grew and unfurled from his shoulders, beating the air furiously as the fiery tunnel started to pull him inexorably towards its entrance.

And then, Tonda was there. He leaped onto the parapet, trying to shield her from the frantically beating wings. But as he stretched out his arms to balance and steady himself, as she had seen him do so many times, when performing some acrobatic trick, one huge black wing hit him square across the shoulders. The force of it lifted Tonda off his feet and knocked him over the side of the bridge. It happened so fast that there was nothing the white clown could do to save himself. There was a loud splash. Then, with a terrible ear-splitting scream, the apostate angel leaped into the circling vortex of fire and was swallowed up in its flames.

Jazmin remained where she was. Frozen. Her hands were locked onto the stone parapet of the bridge. A split-second later, Stash and Suki ran up and grabbed her by the shoulders. "What happened?" Stash cried. "We heard a splash."

Jazmin stared straight ahead. Her face was expressionless. "Tonda fell off the bridge," she said, in a voice that seemed to come from a very long way away.

Stash and Suki exchanged a glance across the top of her head. "Okay," Stash said. "Right. Okay. I'll go back and get help. Don't worry. He'll be all right. They'll find him." He turned and sprinted off towards the Bridge Tower. Suki stripped off her jacket and wrapped it around Jazmin's shoulders. "Come on," she said. "Let's get you back to the hotel, shall we?"

Still Jazmin didn't move or show the slightest sign that she had heard. Suki put an arm round her and gently tried to pull her away from the parapet. "Jazmin? Hey, can you hear me – it's time to go now."

Jazmin still didn't answer. Instead, she stared down at

her hands rigidly gripping onto the stonework. "Can you help me?" she whispered faintly. "I can't seem to let go."

IAN DAWSON ACTED IMMEDIATELY, AND SOMEWHAT PREDICTABLY, THE MOMENT HE RECEIVED THE CALL FROM HIS SISTER TELLING HIM THE ASTONISHING NEWS ABOUT HIS BELOVED DAUGHTER. HE chartered a private plane and flew to Prague to bring her straight back to England. To his great surprise, however, Clea initially got quite upset at the suggestion. She told him that she wanted to stay and be with her aunt and help look after her cousin Jazmin, who was suffering from shock.

Quite understandably, of course, her father would not allow her to do that. She was the one who needed to be taken care of after her terrifying ordeal. This was so typical of Clea, he told his sister privately. His beautiful, unselfish daughter. Always thinking of others, always putting their needs before her own. So Clea's feelings and wishes were overruled and she was flown out of the country – back home to the safety of her beautiful apartment in the city in the sky.

DURING ALL THIS TIME, JAZMIN DAWSON LAY IN HER HOTEL BED, SEDATED AND RECOVERING FROM *HER* TERRIFYING ORDEAL. HER MOTHER, STASH AND SUKI TOOK TURNS WATCHING AT HER BEDSIDE. When she finally awoke, there was only one question on her mind. Sadly and gently, the adults broke it to her that Tonda's body had not yet been recovered from the water. The police had declared the white clown missing, presumed drowned.

ASSIA DAWSON WAITED UNTIL HER DAUGHTER WAS FEELING BETTER AND WAS BACK ON HER FEET AGAIN, BEFORE BEGINNING HER SEARCH OF THE ROZTOK COMPLEX. INITIALLY, SHE FELT THAT ALL her worst fears would be confirmed. Havel's forensic team had gone right through the site with a fine-tooth comb. They had been thorough and painstaking, removing everything they thought might be helpful to the police investigation. After they'd finished, there was not much left for the ISA to investigate.

So it seemed to Assia on her return to Roztok, as she stood with her colleagues and her daughter in Marek's silent office. She wondered whether she would ever find the proof she needed that the scientist had stolen the body. And what had happened to it afterwards.

Jazmin stared around the room, its walls and floor no longer bearing witness to the terrible things that had taken place there. "It's all so clean," she observed quietly. She walked across to Marek's desk, now cleared of its clutter by the police and stood behind it, surveying the room, trying to think herself into the scientist's anguished, tortured mind.

"The police and forensics have done a good job. Sadly." Assia sighed. She was trying not to consider the possibility that her investigation was going to nose dive for lack of evidence. But everything had pointed to the body being brought here, she thought desperately. Her sources in Paris, the way Marek and his wife had tried to keep her drugged and a prisoner as soon as they realized who she was. The arrival of the strange cult. There had to be proof somewhere, she decided, her expression narrowing as she looked around. There had to be something they'd missed.

Jazmin cut a sympathetic glance at her mum, feeling her frustration. If this was a crime novel, she reflected, they would have reached the point where the brilliant detective has an Aha Moment. But, of course, this wasn't a crime novel.

Stash did a palms-up. "So, where do we start?"

"Maybe you could go back to the lab and pick up where you left off," Assia suggested. "Suki and I will begin in here."

"And me?" Jazmin inquired.

Assia expelled air. "Listen hon, can you rustle up some tea for everyone?" she asked.

"Now?" Jazmin replied, her face falling. She was rather hoping she'd be allowed to search Marek's desk. Everybody knew that desks were a major source of good cluage. You always found important evidence. Usually in a secret drawer that you stumbled upon by accident.

Assia nodded. "Please. I could really use a cup of tea. And I'm sure Stash and Suki would appreciate something as well."

"Okay. Tea coming up." Jazmin trailed out of the office. After all she'd contributed, and all she'd been through, she still ended up making the drinks, she mused resignedly, pulling a face as she went into the tiny kitchen that adjoined the office, and switched on the kettle. How depressing was that? Although, as Stash would probably be the first to tell her, there was definitely a *T* in "team"!

Jazmin searched through the kitchen cupboards until she discovered mugs and tea bags and sugar. The kitchen was immaculate, the surfaces wiped down and shiny clean. She also observed an equally spotless white labsuit hanging behind the door. Small size. She wondered idly whether it might have belonged to Marek's wife. While she waited for the water to boil, Jazmin's eyes were drawn irresistibly back to the labsuit. She found herself contemplating it with interest. She noticed that it had two deep pockets. People put things in pockets, she thought to herself. She slipped her hand into one of the pockets and pulled out a small handheld. Aha, she thought. She flipped up the lid, and pressed the start button.

Instantly, the screen lit up. Jazmin stared at the words forming. They looked like the notes of an experiment. 12.15 (she read) Nanoparticulator assembly line on and working at full capacity. She read on.

Sometime later, Jazmin Dawson appeared in the office doorway carrying three mugs of lukewarm tea and a small handheld containing some very important evidence.

THAT EVENING, WHILE HER MOTHER AND HER TWO COLLEAGUES WERE BUSY REVIEWING THE DAY'S EVENTS AND TRYING TO DECIDE WHAT WAS FACT AND WHAT WAS FANTASY, JAZMIN TOOK A CAB across town to the theatre where she knew the festival was taking place. Earlier, she'd seen the young police officer and given him a full account of what had happened on the bridge. Now, there were other people she had to see and speak to, and something very important that she had to arrange.

AND SO IT WAS THAT ON A RAINY AFTERNOON, NEARLY A WEEK AFTER TONDA HAD FALLEN FROM THE CHARLES BRIDGE, THE CITIZENS OF PRAGUE WERE SURPRISED TO SEE A LITTLE BAND OF clowns – and a small dog – making their way in solemn procession through the narrow streets of the Staré Mĕsto. Each clown carried a musical instrument, and as they walked, they played slow, sad music. A large crowd accompanied them, curious to see what was going on. It was remarked upon by many of the crowd that, although every clown was dressed in a bright, colourful costume, each one was also wearing a black armband.

The crowd followed the clowns as far as the centre of the Charles Bridge. Once there, the procession came to a halt. The music ceased. The clowns doffed their hats and bowed their heads. Then each clown in turn stepped forward and dropped a single white rose into the murky waters of the Vltava. There was a moment's complete silence, after which the band of clowns made its way quietly back across the bridge and vanished into the maze of tiny side streets. Whereupon the crowd, realizing that the show was over, also dispersed – the whole, peculiar event already a minor incident in their lives.

But one single clown remained behind, long after all the rest had gone. A small, sad-faced little clown, wearing a yellow costume and a pineapple-coloured wig. It leaned on the stone parapet in the gently falling rain, and stared thoughtfully down into the darkly swirling water.

MEANWHILE, THE OWNER OF THE MIMOSA, AN UPMARKET FLOATING RESTAURANT MOORED DOWNRIVER OF THE CITY CENTRE, SAT BEHIND THE BAR AND WATCHED HIS NEWEST MEMBER OF STAFF with a sense of quiet satisfaction. He had never had to deal with a stowaway before, he thought, let alone one who seemed to be suffering from some sort of memory loss. The lad had been discovered one morning, fast asleep under a tarpaulin, by a member of the crew. From what the owner could make out, he appeared to have fallen into the river upstream, and had been swept along in the current until he had somehow managed to grab hold of one of the boat's gantries. The poor boy had been soaked and confused, with a massive bruise on his forehead.

Naturally, the restaurant owner had tried to find out the strange boy's name and where he came from, but to no avail. He had no papers on him, and every question was answered by a mute shake of the head. After a while, the owner had simply given up, deciding that the boy must be one of the many foreign guest workers who flocked to the city every summer looking for employment. So he had shrugged his shoulders and given the lad a good meal. Then, being a shrewd businessman, he had offered him a job. After all, this was the height of the tourist season and a busy restaurant could always use an extra pair of hands.

And he had made the right decision, the owner reflected to himself. Damn right he had. For, even though he seemed unable to speak, the lad had learned how to wait on tables in a flash. To see him now, making his nimble way across the gently rocking restaurant floor, balancing three full dinner plates on each arm, well, it was almost as if he'd been doing it all his life!

THE DAY AFTER THE FUNERAL PROCESSION HAD TAKEN PLACE, AND AFTER MUCH CAREFUL THOUGHT AND CONSULTATION WITH HER COLLEAGUES, AGENT ASSIA DAWSON SENT HER FINAL REPORT BACK

to the head of the ISA in London, detailing her findings at the Roztok Institute. The report stated only that the body, discovered in the Antarctic ice by the three government research scientists, had been stolen on the instructions of the scientist Eduard Marek. That it had been taken to and stored at Roztok for experimental purposes, but had been ultimately destroyed in the course of these experiments.

The instant it was received, the report was "leaked" to several scientific journals. It was also placed upon certain strategic cyber sites. Whereupon many in the worldwide scientific community breathed a great sigh of relief, as the bitter controversy between science and religion was allowed to quietly shuffle off into the mists of obscurity once again. As soon as she had sent her report, Agent Dawson and her daughter packed their things and were driven to the airport in the ATV. There, they said goodbye to Stash McGregor and Suki Smith. Then, their mission accomplished, Assia and Jazmin flew out of Prague and returned home to England.

THE END

(well, almost...)

EPILOGUE

The public inquiry into the Roztok tragedy, together with the inquiry into what the local media dubbed *The Beast of Prague*, opened in the October of that year. The ISA was invited to participate, but declined to do so. However, the court was able to hear evidence from Commander Havel of the municipal police, several experts in forensics and nanotechnology, as well as former staff from Roztok.

As part of the inquiry, a witness statement was also read out from the English girl, Clea Dawson. The presiding judge praised the plucky teenager in her absence, for her bravery and courage in escaping from the Roztok Institute.

After many weeks, a report was finally issued. It declared that the mysterious disappearance of thirty-nine members of the quasi-religious cult known as the Angels was caused by a computer malfunction. An unfortunate systems error had led to the accidental release of billions of necrotizing nanoparticles into the atmosphere. This horrific event was cited as a possible contributory factor to the suicides of the chief scientist Eduard Marek and his wife Valentina.

The conclusion was also reached that, since there had been no more horrific killings in the city since the events of August 18th, the so-called Beast was probably amongst those who had perished so tragically at Roztok.

It was decided, however, not to present the witness statement of the second English girl, Jazmin Dawson, to the court of inquiry. This statement was taken down as part of the police investigation into a fatal accident involving the circus student Tonda Palach. But, as the judge remarked after reading it, the statement seemed so preposterous and irrational that it was perfectly obvious that the teenager must have made the whole thing up as she went along.

ABOUT THE AUTHOR

Carol Hedges is the successful author of seven books for children and teenagers. Her writing has received much critical acclaim and her novel, *Jigsaw*, was shortlisted for the Angus Book Award and longlisted for the Carnegie Medal.

Carol has one grown-up daughter and lives in Hertfordshire with her husband, two cats and a lot of fish.

Don't miss Spy Girl's next mission

Out of the Shadows

Jazmin Dawson is a kick-ass gorgeous crime fighter, single-handedly saving the world from evil...in her dreams! In reality, Jazmin is an ordinary schoolgirl whose biggest battle is fighting her way to the cookie counter.

But when her secret agent mum needs help with a vital assignment, Jazmin is ready to ditch her homework and plunge into a world of espionage and crime fighting. Her mission is to befriend a crucial witness in an international case of identity theft. But when the witness vanishes Jazmin finds herself at the heart of a deadly game. She must find this man before it is too late...